the perfect veil

(a jessie hunt psychological suspense—book 17)

blake pierce

Blake Pierce

Blake Pierce is the USA Today bestselling author of the RILEY PAGE mystery series, which includes seventeen books. Blake Pierce is also the author of the MACKENZIE WHITE mystery series, comprising fourteen books; of the AVERY BLACK mystery series, comprising six books; of the KERI LOCKE mystery series, comprising five books; of the MAKING OF RILEY PAIGE mystery series, comprising six books; of the KATE WISE mystery series, comprising seven books; of the CHLOE FINE psychological suspense mystery, comprising six books; of the JESSE HUNT psychological suspense thriller series, comprising nineteen books; of the AU PAIR psychological suspense thriller series, comprising three books; of the ZOE PRIME mystery series, comprising six books; of the ADELE SHARP mystery series, comprising thirteen books, of the EUROPEAN VOYAGE cozy mystery series, comprising four books; of the new LAURA FROST FBI suspense thriller, comprising six books (and counting); of the new ELLA DARK FBI suspense thriller, comprising nine books (and counting); of the A YEAR IN EUROPE cozy mystery series, comprising nine books, of the AVA GOLD mystery series, comprising six books (and counting); and of the RACHEL GIFT mystery series, comprising six books (and counting).

An avid reader and lifelong fan of the mystery and thriller genres, Blake loves to hear from you, so please feel free to visit www.blakepierceauthor.com to learn more and stay in touch.

BOOKS BY BLAKE PIERCE

RACHEL GIFT MYSTERY SERIES
HER LAST WISH (Book #1)
HER LAST CHANCE (Book #2)
HER LAST HOPE (Book #3)
HER LAST FEAR (Book #4)
HER LAST CHOICE (Book #5)
HER LAST BREATH (Book #6)

AVA GOLD MYSTERY SERIES
CITY OF PREY (Book #1)
CITY OF FEAR (Book #2)
CITY OF BONES (Book #3)
CITY OF GHOSTS (Book #4)
CITY OF DEATH (Book #5)
CITY OF VICE (Book #6)

A YEAR IN EUROPE
A MURDER IN PARIS (Book #1)
DEATH IN FLORENCE (Book #2)
VENGEANCE IN VIENNA (Book #3)
A FATALITY IN SPAIN (Book #4)

ELLA DARK FBI SUSPENSE THRILLER
GIRL, ALONE (Book #1)
GIRL, TAKEN (Book #2)
GIRL, HUNTED (Book #3)
GIRL, SILENCED (Book #4)
GIRL, VANISHED (Book 5)
GIRL ERASED (Book #6)
GIRL, FORSAKEN (Book #7)
GIRL, TRAPPED (Book #8)
GIRL, EXPENDABLE (Book #9)

LAURA FROST FBI SUSPENSE THRILLER
ALREADY GONE (Book #1)
ALREADY SEEN (Book #2)

ALREADY TRAPPED (Book #3)
ALREADY MISSING (Book #4)
ALREADY DEAD (Book #5)
ALREADY TAKEN (Book #6)

EUROPEAN VOYAGE COZY MYSTERY SERIES
MURDER (AND BAKLAVA) (Book #1)
DEATH (AND APPLE STRUDEL) (Book #2)
CRIME (AND LAGER) (Book #3)
MISFORTUNE (AND GOUDA) (Book #4)
CALAMITY (AND A DANISH) (Book #5)
MAYHEM (AND HERRING) (Book #6)

ADELE SHARP MYSTERY SERIES
LEFT TO DIE (Book #1)
LEFT TO RUN (Book #2)
LEFT TO HIDE (Book #3)
LEFT TO KILL (Book #4)
LEFT TO MURDER (Book #5)
LEFT TO ENVY (Book #6)
LEFT TO LAPSE (Book #7)
LEFT TO VANISH (Book #8)
LEFT TO HUNT (Book #9)
LEFT TO FEAR (Book #10)
LEFT TO PREY (Book #11)
LEFT TO LURE (Book #12)
LEFT TO CRAVE (Book #13)

THE AU PAIR SERIES
ALMOST GONE (Book#1)
ALMOST LOST (Book #2)
ALMOST DEAD (Book #3)

ZOE PRIME MYSTERY SERIES
FACE OF DEATH (Book#1)
FACE OF MURDER (Book #2)
FACE OF FEAR (Book #3)
FACE OF MADNESS (Book #4)
FACE OF FURY (Book #5)
FACE OF DARKNESS (Book #6)

WATCHING (Book #1)
WAITING (Book #2)
LURING (Book #3)
TAKING (Book #4)
STALKING (Book #5)
KILLING (Book #6)

RILEY PAIGE MYSTERY SERIES
ONCE GONE (Book #1)
ONCE TAKEN (Book #2)
ONCE CRAVED (Book #3)
ONCE LURED (Book #4)
ONCE HUNTED (Book #5)
ONCE PINED (Book #6)
ONCE FORSAKEN (Book #7)
ONCE COLD (Book #8)
ONCE STALKED (Book #9)
ONCE LOST (Book #10)
ONCE BURIED (Book #11)
ONCE BOUND (Book #12)
ONCE TRAPPED (Book #13)
ONCE DORMANT (Book #14)
ONCE SHUNNED (Book #15)
ONCE MISSED (Book #16)
ONCE CHOSEN (Book #17)

MACKENZIE WHITE MYSTERY SERIES
BEFORE HE KILLS (Book #1)
BEFORE HE SEES (Book #2)
BEFORE HE COVETS (Book #3)
BEFORE HE TAKES (Book #4)
BEFORE HE NEEDS (Book #5)
BEFORE HE FEELS (Book #6)
BEFORE HE SINS (Book #7)
BEFORE HE HUNTS (Book #8)
BEFORE HE PREYS (Book #9)
BEFORE HE LONGS (Book #10)
BEFORE HE LAPSES (Book #11)
BEFORE HE ENVIES (Book #12)
BEFORE HE STALKS (Book #13)

BEFORE HE HARMS (Book #14)

PROLOGUE

Beatrice knocked, just to be safe. And then she knocked again.

She'd been burned too often. More times than she could count, despite the absence of "do not disturb" placards on the outside of hotel room doors, she'd opened them to discover private activities going on inside. That usually led to yelling, and sometimes to complaints. So Beatrice had a system.

She knocked loudly and called out, "Housekeeping!" If there was no response after ten seconds, she knocked a second time. After ten more seconds, she did a final knock, with one more announcement of who she was. Then she used her key card to open the door a crack and made her presence known one final time before actually entering the room.

That's the procedure she used before entering suite 1002 of the Buckingham Sunset Hotel in West Hollywood at 8:02 in the morning. And it seemed to work fine. She propped open the door, and walked in to survey the room before determining what needed to be done.

Suite 1002 was one of six suites on the tenth floor, all of which typically required twice the cleaning time of a regular room. She moved past the small entryway into the main sitting room of the suite, hoping the mess wouldn't be too time-consuming.

She sensed something was off right away. At first she couldn't place it. But after a few seconds she realized what it was. The large table lamp by the window overlooking the Sunset Strip was missing. She walked over to the adjoining couch to see if it had fallen behind it. That's when she saw her.

The woman was lying face up on the carpet. Her eyes were closed and she appeared to be passed out. She was beautiful, with long black hair and dark skin. Beatrice guessed that she might be of Hispanic or Middle Eastern heritage. She was wearing a tight, black mini dress that looked like something one might wear out for a night on the Strip. The lamp was on the carpet beside the woman's head and for a second Beatrice thought maybe she'd drunkenly knocked it over when she collapsed. But then she noticed the blood. It was pooled under the back of woman's head, glowing slightly in the morning light.

Beatrice froze for a moment, unsure what to do. She could hear her own blood pumping loudly in her ears and her wheezing breaths told her that her asthma was kicking in. Oddly, she had no inclination to scream. Should she try to help the woman? Should she call the police?

In the end, she did the only thing she knew wouldn't cost her the job she so desperately needed to keep. After taking a puff of her inhaler, she called the Housekeeping line and asked to speak to the manager on duty.

CHAPTER ONE

It was already a crazy morning.

Jessie had gotten up early to run five miles, part of her revamped fitness routine, now that she wasn't in hiding from a serial killer. By the time she got back home, her fiancé, Ryan Hernandez, had done his workout, showered and gotten dressed. Her half-sister, Hannah Dorsey, was still in sweats, but at least she was up and moving around the kitchen.

"Don't forget, we have to be out the door in twenty minutes," Jessie told her as she started for the bedroom to prep for her own shower.

"You're kidding, right?" Hannah asked in disbelief.

"About what?"

"I told you this last night," her sister said, exasperated. "It's a teacher in-service day. I don't have school. Why do you think I'm moving around so leisurely?"

"Oh right. Sorry. I forgot," she admitted. "With everything going on this week, I'm all turned around. Say, as long as you're in leisure mode, do you think you could make me one of your famous pesto egg breakfast sandwiches to go? Otherwise, I'll never make it to the station on time."

"What will you do for me?" Hannah asked, only half-joking.

"Well, here's my offer: Kat is coming by to return an old textbook I lent her on Behavioral Criminology and if you make my sandwich, I *might* not ask her to stick around and watch you for the day. How's that for an even trade?"

Hannah rolled her eyes almost completely out of her head.

"First of all, you two middle-aged women and your shared textbooks are shockingly lame."

"You know I'm thirty—," Jessie said, but Hannah wasn't done.

"And secondly, we need to have a real talk about how *quid pro quo* works. I will make your sandwich but I expect that it will engender some goodwill that will pay off in unexpected ways down the line."

"Thank you," Jessie said, deciding to leave it there and head for the shower.

All things considered, it was a decent interaction, of which there had been surprisingly many recently. Of course, it was all relative.

Everything short of shooting and killing an unarmed, handcuffed man to death counted as "decent" these days.

Admittedly the man that Hannah had shot went by the title of the Night Hunter and was a notorious serial killer who had stalked their whole family. But that didn't change the troubling fact that when Hannah killed him, he was no longer a threat.

That's why she'd been seeing Dr. Janice Lemmon regularly for the two and half weeks since the incident, though she had yet to admit to the psychiatrist what happened that night. Despite that fairly large omission, Hannah seemed to be making progress in therapy. And in most other ways, she was thriving.

As Jessie reminded herself while getting in the shower, there had been no additional acting out—that is, not putting herself in danger for the thrill of it. She was doing well in school, so well in fact that Jessie wondered if she ought to reconsider Hannah's plan to go to culinary school in the fall. At this rate, despite all the traumas she'd suffered and school time she'd missed, she was on target to graduate with honors and could probably get into most public schools in the state.

In addition, Hannah still planned to go to the mountain town of Wildpines this summer. That's where she, Jessie, and Ryan had hidden out from the Night Hunter for a few nights. While there, she'd learned that a local private school, the Wildpines Arts Conservatory, had a culinary arts program. Conveniently, a cute boy named Chris that she'd met in town would also be in the Conservatory's summer program.

Jessie got out of the shower and dressed quickly in her standard work attire: comfortable but professional shirt, along with pants that looked nice but that she could run in. She tied her brown sneakers, which could pass for loafers, and grabbed a jacket to protect against the early February bite.

She gave herself a once-over in the bathroom mirror and declared herself satisfied. Those early morning workouts were paying dividends. She looked healthy and refreshed. Her shoulder-length brown hair had lost its former limpness and her green eyes were bright and clear, with none of the typical exhausted bleariness. Standing straight rather than slouching, she looked even taller than her five-foot-ten-inches.

When Jessie came out of the bedroom, there was a pesto egg sandwich and a to-go cup of coffee waiting for her on the breakfast table. Ryan was seated in his chair, sipping a coffee. Hannah was munching on a breakfast bar by the sink.

Jessie's best friend, Katherine "Kat" Gentry was in another chair at the table, nibbling at a banana. Her work clothes—she was a private

4

detective— were even more casual than Jessie's. She wore jeans, a casual shirt and a brown leather jacket. Her dirty blonde hair was in a loose ponytail.

"Thanks for the sandwich, Hannah," Jessie said.

"Earn it," her sister muttered dramatically under her breath.

"Kat says she's got news," Ryan said, diverting Jessie's attention.

"Oh yeah?"

"I left your textbook in the living room," Kat said. "Thanks for letting me borrow it, though it was pretty dry stuff."

"That's your news?" Jessie asked, "That Behavioral Criminology textbooks are boring? What else have you got for me? That the sun is burn-y?"

"I'm getting to it, Jessie Hurts—er, Hunt," she said, feigning bruised feelings. "Before I share my news, how are things going on the teaching front? Does the UCLA student body still adore you?"

"I actually had my first seminar since the whole Night Hunter thing," Jessie said, unable to hide her excitement. "It was the best-attended one so far, although I have a sneaking suspicion that was a result of that very same Night Hunter thing. I thought I saw some students checking me for visible scars."

"Silly kids," Kat chuckled, "Don't they know all the really impressive scars are on the inside? What about the other big event? How are things going on the wedding front? Choose a date yet? Got a venue? Picked out a pastor? Where's the reception? Most importantly, who are your bridesmaids?"

"Ugh, my blood pressure just went up listening to you," Jessie said.

"We're taking it slow," Ryan added. "Right now, we're in the 'tell our co-workers about it' stage. That's been interesting enough."

"Yeah," Jessie said. "Callum Reid already told me that he wants to give me away. He says now that he's off the force he needs something to focus on."

Jessie didn't mention the other reason the recently retired detective was probably offering: all her other father figures had been murdered.

"We figure we'll linger in the joy of engagement-hood for a little while before getting into the stressful stuff," Ryan said, interrupting her thoughts. "Remember, I've been to this wedding rodeo once before and the planning part was definitely *not* my favorite."

"See," Jessie said. "That's why he's the guy for me. We're simpatico on this. Enjoy now. Stress later."

She flashed back to the proposal: up in the snowy mountain town of Wildpines, just after finally stopping the Night Hunter, with Ryan

5

down on one knee in the snow, a small black ring box in his hand on a gorgeous, sunny morning. He really was the guy for her.

"I'm glad to hear no crucial decisions are imminent," Kat said, pulling her back into the present, "because I wouldn't be able to help with any of them."

"Why not?" Hannah asked, expressing interest in the conversation for the first time.

"That's the news I wanted to tell you about. I'm going to be out of town for a bit."

"Why?" Hannah asked.

"For how long?" Jessie added.

"Whoa," Kat said, taken aback, "it's nice to be wanted but settle down. I'm just going up to Lake Arrowhead."

"To see your boyfriend?" Hannah teased.

Kat's long distance boyfriend, Mitch Connor, was a sheriff's deputy up in the mountain town of Lake Arrowhead, about two hours northeast of Los Angeles. They'd met when she assisted Jessie on a case last year and visited the town while following a lead. He helped her out; they hit it off and had been going back and forth to see each other every few weeks for months now.

"That's part of it," Kat said evenly, not taking the bait, "but I've also got a case. Mitch said some guy he knows who runs a ski resort in Big Bear thinks his wife is cheating on him and wants her tailed by someone who's good but not local. Mitch said he had the perfect candidate."

"So you've basically found a way to get a free ski vacation out of this," Ryan observed.

"I don't ski," Kat said coquettishly. "So I guess Mitch and I will have to find other ways to keep busy when I'm not on a stakeout."

"Oh my God," Hannah said, pressing her hands to her ears as she hurriedly left the room, "You realize I'm still technically a child, right? Why am I being subjected to this? I'll be in my room until either you all leave or my therapy appointment, whichever comes first."

She dashed across the room, red-faced. As Jessie watched her go, she wished she could embrace the 'technically a child' assertion. It might be true, but her half-sister, just months from turning eighteen, had long since left childhood behind.

Apart from all the traumas she'd recently suffered, physically, no one would mistake her for a kid. She was barely an inch shorter than Jessie. They shared the same green eyes. And with her long, skinny frame, her medium length blonde hair, and her attitude, she sometimes looked closer to thirty than to twenty. At certain angles they could be mistaken for fraternal twins, though Jessie would never say that out loud. The three adults waited until Hannah slammed closed the door to her room to continue.

"I should keep you around all the time," Jessie said. "That way I can deploy you whenever her sarcasm levels get too high."

"Happy to be of assistance," Kat told her, starting for the front door, "but not until after I conquer the sin in the snow. That's what I'm calling this case."

"I'm very happy for you," Jessie said. "I hope it's all you're dreaming of and more. Let me know when you're headed back to town and we can discuss your hot tub adventures."

"Now you're going to make *me* run out of the room," Ryan threatened, though he was smiling.

They ignored him.

"Hey," Kat remembered, "any updates on our unstable, incarcerated friend who shall not be named? Has she tried to get in touch with you again? Did you agree to write that letter for her?"

Jessie shook her head, not wanting to think about the Andy Robinson situation. After all, this was a woman who had tricked her into trusting her—even befriending her—during an investigation, then tried to poison her when Jessie discovered that she was the killer all along.

"I've been putting it off," she said. "I know that she was helpful on the Night Hunter case, and that she says she can provide good info on other cases, but the idea of writing a letter in favor of transferring someone who tried to kill me to a nicer prison just rubs me the wrong way."

"I don't blame you," Kat said. "That woman is bad news, no matter how much help she offers. Be careful, okay?"

Jessie gave her friend a hug.

"I will," she promised. "You have fun up there in the mountains with your boy toy. And stay safe."

"You too, lady," Kat replied. "With a teenage hormone monster in one room, a tough guy fiancé in the other, students to teach, endless killers to catch, and an incarcerated, obsessed sociopath trying to wheedle her way back into your life, you've got a full plate. And now you won't have me watching your back, so keep your head on a swivel."

"Always," Jessie said.

As if on cue, just as she closed and locked the door behind Kat, Ryan's phone buzzed.

"What is it?" she asked warily.

"It's Captain Decker," he said, looking at his text. "He wants us at the station. He says he needs to talk to both of us."

"What happened?"

"He didn't say," Ryan told her. "Just that it's *not* about a case."

CHAPTER TWO

Even though their boss said their meeting didn't involve a case, they moved quickly.

Less than twenty minutes after getting the call, they passed through the bullpen of the downtown Los Angeles Central Station on their way to Captain Roy Decker's office. It was surprisingly quiet considering that it was already after 8 a.m.

The rest of LAPD's Homicide Special Section team was already at their dedicated section. Each of them looked up but no one said anything. Detective Karen Bray gave them a little smile. Detective Jim Nettles half-nodded. The newest detective, Susannah Valentine, gave Jessie a hard, less than friendly stare. She pretended not to notice, not wanting to give Valentine the satisfaction.

Because of a string of recent successes, including stopping the Night Hunter and solving the murder of a beloved social media star—both of which Jessie had been central to making happen—Homicide Special Section had gone from being on life support within the department to getting press accolades and an infusion of financial and human resources. Valentine, who Jessie found to be arrogant to a fault, was the first resource in the latter camp.

Another detective was supposed to be hired within the next month but, so far, Decker hadn't found the perfect candidate. It was understandable. Homicide Special Section, or HSS for short, was one of LAPD's most elite units, handling high profile cases, many with intense media scrutiny, often involving multiple victims and serial killers. It deserved a top investigator and there were dozens of applicants for the remaining position.

They reached Decker's door, which was slightly ajar, and Ryan raised his hand to knock when Jessie stopped him, grabbing his arm.

"What?" he asked, startled.

"I just wanted to get a good look at you," she said, smiling. "We were moving so fast earlier that I didn't get my usual morning moment to appreciate what a dish you are."

Detective Ryan Hernandez blushed. Jessie loved that she could still cause that reaction in a man who made other women's heads turn when he walked by. With his short, jet black hair, his kind, brown eyes, and his broad-shouldered six-foot frame, he was hard not to notice.

He still wasn't quite back to his "pre-stabbing and multiple week coma" muscled, 200-pound physique, but he was getting close. His rehab workout regime was even more arduous than Jessie's routine and it was paying dividends. Another six weeks at the same intensity and he'd be back to full strength, and a full three months before even the most optimistic doctors thought possible.

"Are you done?" he asked, embarrassed. "Can I knock now?"

"Are you sure I can't get you to do a little butt wiggle before we go in?"

He pretended to scowl as he knocked on Decker's door.

"Come in," the captain called out.

They stepped into the office, which was furnished with an old desk, an old rolling chair behind it, two old metal chairs across from it, and an extremely old sofa along the back wall. The sofa looked like it had been purchased at a 1970s garage sale and not cleaned since. Jessie took a seat in one of the metal chairs. Ryan took the other.

Decker was standing, studying a file that he held about five inches in front of his face. He still looked as weathered and worn out as usual, way more than a sixty-one year old man should be. He was slouched with his chest caving in on itself. His face was still a mass of wrinkles, and his few clumps of gray hair shot out wildly. His eyes were as piercing as ever. But something about him was different than usual. And then, in a flash, she realized what it was: Captain Roy Decker almost looked happy. It was so rare that it was actually cause for concern.

"Everything okay, Captain?" Ryan asked, when Decker still hadn't spoken or looked up after half a minute.

"To be honest, I'm not sure," he said, finally placing the file on the desk and sitting down. "I've been reviewing department policy on romantic relationships between professional partners."

Jessie felt the tension rise in her chest, not out of nervousness so much as out of annoyance.

"What does it say in there about congratulating folks on getting engaged, Captain?" she asked. "Because I noticed you haven't done that yet."

Decker's wrinkled features briefly softened.

"You're right. I'm sorry about that. I move straight from hearing the news to judging the news. Congratulations. I'm very happy for you."

"Thank you," she said.

"Thanks, Captain," Ryan joined in.

"And now back to the judging," Decker said, the wrinkles returning.

"What's the problem, sir?" Ryan asked. "Jessie's not formally my partner. She's not even a detective or an LAPD employee. She's a criminal profiler who consults for the department on a case by case basis. She's worked more cases with Detectives Bray and Reid than with me lately."

"Come on, Hernandez," Decker scoffed, "we all know that was because you were out of commission for most of the last seven months after the whole 'stabbing and coma' situation. If you'd been available, you two would have been working together."

"So what?" Jessie protested. "Like Ryan said, I'm not a detective. I'm a consultant. The standard rules aren't applicable."

"I'm not so sure," Decker countered. "And just as important, public perception matters. There are a lot more eyes on us now, jealous folks looking for us to fail. They'll use any excuse to make us look bad to the media and get our funding redirected to their departments."

"That won't work," Ryan said. "The press loves Jessie."

"Right now it does," Decker agreed, "but remember it wasn't all that long ago that her ex-husband tried to frame her to make it look like she was racist, anti-police, and a drug addict all at the same time. Don't you recall the crowds protesting outside this station? Hell, after she took down Sergeant Hank Costabile—that corrupt bastard—there are still some cops in the Valley Division she'd be wise not to run into in a dark alley."

"What's your point, Captain?" Jessie demanded.

"My point is that we need to make sure this isn't a potential conflict of interest and that's not a decision I can make alone. And we have to think about what this says to the other members of the unit."

"What?" she asked incredulously. "Do you think Susannah Valentine is going to make a play for Jim Nettles? The guy's a decade older than her, is married with three kids, and can't button his dress shirts properly."

"There aren't just detectives in this unit, Hunt," Decker reminded her.

"Are you talking about Jamil Winslow?" Ryan laughed, referring to their brilliant head of research. "The kid's twenty-four and could get knocked over by a strong gust of wind. I'm not sure he's ever even

11

been on a date. If she hit on him, he'd probably pass out then and there."

"Not the point," Decker said, clearly growing impatient. "I don't want any complaints or bad press. And that means I need the all clear on this from the human resources review board before I'm willing to pair you two up on any more cases. That's how it has to be for now."

Jessie was about to object. Maybe she hadn't been clear that this was a consulting gig and that she was only willing to do it on terms she found acceptable. But before she could say anything, Ryan touched her hand. She looked over to see him giving her what could best be described as a "don't poke the bear" look. She closed her mouth and nodded. After all, this wasn't just a gig for him. He was a full-time LAPD employee and he could only push so hard.

"Was that all, Captain?" he asked, starting to stand up.

"Actually, I'd like to speak to Hunt privately for a moment."

Jessie and Ryan exchanged a look of trepidation before she responded.

"Sure."

"Please close the door on your way out, Hernandez," Decker said.

Once they were alone, Decker fixed his eagle eyes on Jessie.

"I'd like you to consider coming back to HSS full-time," he said bluntly.

"What?" she asked, stunned that he would make such a request after what he'd just told them.

"I'm going to be straight with you," he said. "I know Garland Moses was your mentor. He was a good friend of mine too. His murder has left a big hole in both our lives. But it has also left a professional hole in the department. He was the best criminal profiler the LAPD had for the last two decades. You're the only one who has even come close to him. But you only show up when I call you, desperate for your help on a major case."

"Garland was a consultant too," Jessie noted.

"Technically, yes," Decker acknowledged. "But he showed up here every day. He had an office. We had a special arrangement with him but he was *available*. And with him gone and you off educating future generations, when it comes to profilers, we're often left with what I'll generously call the 'B' team. It's not sustainable."

"I'm sorry to hear that, Captain," Jessie said sincerely. "But I enjoy educating those future generations. I had my first seminar in weeks yesterday and being in that lecture hall, I realized how much I'd missed it. Those kids hung on my every word."

"They sound more like groupies than students," he pointed out.

"Some of them probably are, which I don't love," she admitted. "But still, I feel like I'm making a difference."

"You make a real difference here too, Hunt, every time you solve a murder, every time you give a family some measure of closure."

"That matters to me too, Captain, but I'm just not sure I'm willing to open myself up to that darkness every day, especially with a kid in the house."

She recalled the constant sense of dread that came from dealing with worst that humanity had to offer each day. She remembered how it weighed on her and cast a shadow over her home life. Most important, she couldn't forget how her daily work often put those she loved at risk. On more than one occasion, Hannah had become a target because of what her sister did for a living.

"A kid—doesn't Hannah graduate in a few months?" Decker asked, knowing full well that she did.

"Yes," she conceded. "But I still need to be there for her. Besides, I'm also not sure how interested I would be if I can't work with Ryan. We make a good team. You know that."

"Just think about it," he said as his phone rang. "In the meantime, I'll let you get out there so you can discuss wedding reception centerpieces and whatnot."

"Thanks, Captain," she said, rolling her eyes as she got up.

"Go ahead," he said to the person on the line.

As she walked to the door, she could hear the urgency in his voice as he asked questions. She wasn't surprised when, before she stepped out, he called out to her.

"Hold on a second there, Hunt—I think I may have a case for you."

CHAPTER THREE

"Who do you want?" he asked her after he'd finished up his call.

"What do you mean?" Jessie said.

"Your fiancé is off limits for now," Decker told her. "So you can work this case with Bray, Nettles, or Valentine. Who do you prefer?"

"Why me?' she asked. "Why don't you assign the case to Ryan?"

"Because he's here every day and I'm not sure about the next time I'll get you. You've made it clear that with your class schedule, your availability is limited. But you're here now so I'm taking advantage. So who's it going to be? Maybe break in the newbie?"

Jessie looked out at the bullpen where Ryan was chatting with the other detectives. Susannah Valentine tossed her thick, lustrous, black hair back as she laughed at something funny he said.

"Can you give me the basics?" she asked. "That might help me decide who would be the best fit."

"I don't know a ton yet. The victim's name is Addison Rutherford, twenty-four years old. She's a model, influencer, and aspiring actress. She was just found bludgeoned to death in a suite at the Buckingham Sunset Hotel in West Hollywood."

Jessie knew immediately who the right person to work the case was and she wouldn't have to fudge it. Karen Bray had worked at the Hollywood station for years before joining HSS and knew adjoining West Hollywood well, along with the entertainment industry milieu.

Jim Nettles had been a downtown beat cop for fifteen years before getting his detective shield. If this was a case involving gangs or political corruption, he'd be the perfect choice. Susannah Valentine had also worked downtown patrol for half a decade, and then joined the Santa Barbara detective bureau for two years, before coming back to L.A. last month. Jessie figured that if the case involved flirting with surfers, she would be the ideal selection. But for a show business case, Karen was the pick. So it was only with a mild amount of self-satisfied petulance that she gave her answer.

"This sound like it's right up Detective Bray's alley," she told him.

"Then grab her and head out," Decker said.

*

Navigating the Sunset Strip on a Friday morning was a challenge. As they inched west on Sunset Boulevard toward the Buckingham Hotel, which was actually just off the Strip on San Vicente Boulevard, Jessie was glad that Karen had agreed to drive.

"You still have all your industry contacts?" Jessie asked Karen.

"Some," Karen said. "I guess we'll find out if they're enough. Is that why we're working this case together?"

"Karen, you insult me. We're working this case together because I missed our time together solving the murders of over-the-hill actresses, busting pedophile billionaires, and learning what breakfast food your son would accidentally spill on your top."

Karen looked down at her shirt apprehensively.

"I'm just talking generally," Jessie added quickly. "I don't see any stains this morning."

"He's getting much better," Karen pointed out. "My dry cleaning bill can attest to that. So you just wanted the pleasure of my company?"

Jessie relented.

"Well, I'll admit that in addition to your expertise in the industry and your charm, my choices were limited. Because of our engagement, Decker's not letting me work with Ryan until he gets the okay from HR. And my other options were Nettles, who doesn't have the most delicate touch, or Valentine, who I worry might bail on the investigation to start her own modeling career."

"That seems a bit harsh," Karen said. ""She's a little abrasive, but she's pretty good at what she does. I think she's just trying too hard."

Jessie shrugged.

"Maybe," she replied. "That's what Callum Reid told me too before he retired. He asked me to give her a chance. But I get the sense that if I fell asleep in the break room, she might slit my throat and keep walking."

"Wow," Karen said as she passed the famous Book Soup bookstore and the infamous Viper Room nightclub, "I guess it's true what they say about good profilers."

"What do they say?" Jessie wondered.

"That it's a fine line between genius and paranoia."

She pulled off Sunset Boulevard onto Larrabee Street and then into the hotel valet entrance. There were several police cars, an ambulance, a forensics truck, and a coroner's van off to the left. Karen found a spot next to them and they got out.

Just as Jessie opened her door, a gust of bitterly cold wind slammed into them. She hurriedly zipped up her coat. It was still in the mid-forties and the high temperature wasn't supposed to climb much above fifty today. So much for sunny L.A.

Jessie watched impatiently as the detective tucked in her button-down shirt, adjusted her slacks, and checked the professional ponytail that secured her dirty blonde hair before finally putting on her own jacket. In her late thirties, Karen Bray was the picture of self-effacing professionalism. Petite and polite, she tended to blend in, which made it easy to underestimate her. Jessie knew that to be a mistake.

They made their way to the main entrance automatic doors, where an officer was waiting. After they showed their IDs, he directed them to the bank of elevators that led to the tenth floor. After having seen so many, Jessie typically didn't blink at the ostentatious opulence of hotels like this. The outside of the Buckingham was actually fairly restrained, with painted tans and grays and curlicue stonework finishes. The inside was a different matter.

But she was almost blinded by the glimmering glass of the dozens of chandeliers as she walked into the entrance hall. All the walls were mirrored, which made the place look bigger but also somehow like a circus funhouse. The furniture in the expansive lobby was comprised of lavender couches, pink loveseats, and sky blue easy chairs.

Both bars, on either side of the lobby, were open, even though it wasn't yet 9 a.m. One of them continued the dreamy, pastel energy of the lobby with its look, while the other one went for more of a brooding vibe, with gray, black onyx, and ivory dominating the décor.

They reached the elevators, where a second officer checked their IDs and sent them to the tenth floor. Once they arrived, a third officer did another check before pointing them to the proper suite door, 1002, where one final duty officer gave them the once over before letting them enter.

"Who's in charge?" Bray asked him.

"Sergeant Ziegler," he said, pointing to a thickset woman in her mid-forties standing in front of a couch near the window. "She's been waiting for you."

As they walked over, Jessie took in the suite. It was impressive, certainly not the sort of place an "aspiring" actress could afford on her own. Either both her modeling and influencing careers were going extremely well, or she had a benefactor.

A separate door led to the bedroom, which she couldn't see much of from where she stood. But the living room was expansive, with floor to ceiling windows, an oak dining table, a sitting area with the large sofa where Sergeant Ziegler now stood, a wet bar, and a balcony that looked out over the Strip and the Hollywood Hills.

Jessie couldn't see where the victim was, but considering that multiple forensics and coroner's office personnel were on the other side of the sofa, one of them taking photos, she could guess. They approached Sergeant Ziegler, who looked like she could handle herself.

As tall as Jessie but with an extra forty pounds, she had a bit of a paunch but also broad shoulders that suggested she worked out in order to keep arrests manageable. Her brown hair was cut short enough that it wouldn't get in the way during a chase or an altercation.

"Sergeant Ziegler?" Karen said, "I'm Detective Karen Bray out of HSS over at Central Station. This is our profiler, Jessie Hun—."

"I'm familiar," Ziegler cut her off, her voice raspy. Jessie prepared herself for a snarky quip about being a media darling. "You do good work, Hunt. Call me Rhonda."

Relief flowed through her.

"Nice to meet you, Rhonda. Please, call me Jessie. What have we got here?"

Rhonda sighed.

"What we've got is a damn shame. Victim is Addison Rutherford, twenty-four. She'd been staying here since Wednesday, was scheduled to check out on Sunday. Preliminary time of death is last night between 9 p.m. and midnight. She was found by the housekeeper this morning around 8 a.m., after which she called her manager. He called the hotel manager. He called us. We called you."

"What made you think it was right for our unit?" Jessie asked.

"It was funny, actually. One of the younger officers recognized her, said she's all over TikTok and Instagram. Apparently she's a model and one of those social media influencers. We remembered that you solved the murder of that big-time influencer a little while back and thought this was right up your alley."

"Got it," Jessie said. "Shall we take a look at the body?"

Ziegler looked at the collection of folks scurrying around behind the couch.

"You guys almost done?" she asked them.

"Give us a second and we'll make room," said a tall, skinny guy with blond hair who looked to be pulling fingerprints.

"Are you finding a lot of those?" Karen asked him.

"Almost too many to keep track of," he said. "I don't know if that means she had a lot of visitors or that they just don't clean this place up

17

as well as you'd expect for somewhere so fancy. The interesting thing is that there is one item that has been wiped entirely clean of prints."

"What's that?" Karen asked.

"The table lamp that we're almost certain is the murder weapon," he said pointing at something just out of sight on the ground.

Jessie and Karen moved over and saw the lamp lying bagged on the carpet. It had a cream circular cover over the bulb and a silver base that looked heavy. To the naked eye, it was pristine—no smudges and certainly no blood.

"We'll check for DNA," the guy said. "Unless the killer wiped it down with bleach, we should find some evidence of blood. The indentation in her skull matches the base perfectly."

He nodded to his right. Jessie and Karen stepped in that direction to find Addison Rutherford lying on the carpet. She wore a black mini dress, and even in death, it suited her. She looked to be about five-foot-four, with a curvy but still athletic physique. She wasn't wearing shoes.

She had long black hair and skin that was somehow still dark despite the ghostly imprint of death. Her lips were full and her features were delicate in an almost sculpted way. She didn't appear to be wearing any makeup. She was breathtakingly beautiful.

Her eyes were closed. Because she was lying on her back, the wound to her skull wasn't visible. Were it not for the red stain underneath her head, she looked like might be asleep.

Jessie sighed silently to herself. Another young life snuffed out before it had really gotten started. It was seeing exactly this sort of thing that made her skeptical that a full-time return to HSS would be good for her mental health.

"We didn't want to bag her until you got to take a look," Rhonda Ziegler said quietly.

"I think it's okay now, don't you, Jessie?" Karen asked.

Jessie was about to agree when she noticed something on Rutherford's chest, just at the edge of where the mini dress top stopped. It was a black speck of some kind.

"What's that?" she asked pointing at it.

Everyone looked closer.

"Is that a fly?" Ziegler asked.

The forensic tech closest to Rutherford bent down. She looked up at Jessie and held up her gloved hand.

"Should I?" she asked.

Jessie nodded. The tech carefully pulled back the top of the dress. On the woman's left breast, just above her areola, was a word tattooed in tiny black scripted letters. Only it wasn't a word Jessie had ever heard before.

It read: *twil*.

CHAPTER FOUR

"What does 'twil' mean?" Rhonda Ziegler asked.

Jessie shook her head.

"I have no idea."

"Can you get photos of that too?" Karen asked the tech with the camera.

While they took the remaining photos and bagged the body, Jessie, Karen, and Rhonda moved over to the dining table.

"Is there anything else we should know about?" Karen asked. "Any video footage? Witness statements?"

"I have people reaching out to the staff right now. Give me a minute and I'll have them check in."

They left her alone to make her calls, stepping into the bedroom to see if there was anything worthwhile there. The bed was still made, which didn't shock Jessie. If Rutherford was murdered last evening, she likely wouldn't ever have made it to the bedroom. It did at least suggest that her activities in the room hadn't been amorous.

Jessie poked her head in the bathroom, which offered nothing suggestive. There were hygiene and hair care products on the counter, along with some makeup and a package of disinfectant wipes. Nothing seemed unusual.

"Hey, check this out," Karen said from the bedroom.

Jessie looked over to see her holding up a book from the bedside table.

"What's that?"

Before the detective could reply, Rhonda Ziegler poked her head in.

"I've got updates for you," she said, "Lots of them."

They returned to the living room, where two new officers were standing by the front door, along with a hotel staffer in a lavender vest.

"Frye, Greggs, come on over. Mr. Almeida, if you could just wait there for a moment, please."

Frye, a terrified, pimply-faced officer in his mid-twenties with curly, red hair, and Greggs, a thirty-something black officer who looked like he'd been on duty all night, joined them.

"Tell them what you learned, Frye," Rhonda instructed.

"Yes, Sergeant," he said, his voice squeaky with nerves. "I checked the hotel surveillance system. Everything looks fine up until 10:15 p.m., when the feed cuts out to this floor and elevator number three."

"How long was it out of commission?" Jessie asked.

"Exactly one hour, until 11:15," Frye replied. His face had turned a shade of bright pink.

"Well that's suspicious," Karen said.

"It could be," Frye muttered under his breath.

"Could be?" Jessie repeated. "What do you mean?"

Frye's face was now suddenly more red than pink.

"I just mean that, yes—of course, it's quite a coincidence that the cameras went out during the window of death for the victim. But it could be a legitimate coincidence too. According to the guy on duty in the control room, these cameras go down pretty often. He says that it happens at least a couple of times a week, maybe more. And when it does, it takes a full hour for the individual cameras to reboot. That doesn't mean someone didn't do it on purpose. But he says the system's so old that it would be impossible to tell."

"Okay," Jessie said. "Can we have them collect footage from the other elevator cameras and the lobby footage for that window of time? Maybe something will pop."

"Yes ma'am. They're transferring it for us now."

"Thank you, Frye," Rhonda said, before turning to the other officer. "What about you, Greggs?"

"Yes, Sergeant," he said, stepping forward slightly. "When we were up here earlier, Frye mentioned that he recognized the victim from some of her online videos. It got me thinking that someone who posted so much might have given some insight about her situation leading up to the moment of her death. So I started looking around for her phone but couldn't find it anywhere, which struck me as odd. What social media star is ever without her phone?"

"Good point," Jessie mused.

"Thanks," he said. "So I checked with the front desk and got the number she used when checking in. I have it and thought I'd dial it while I was up here, in case it's somewhere out of sight."

"That's not a bad idea," Rhonda said, "Any objections?"

No one had any so Greggs dialed the number and put the call on speaker. They all heard it ring six times but there was no corresponding sound anywhere in the suite. The call went to voicemail and Addison Rutherford's calm, sunny voice filled the room.

You've reached Addison. I'm not available right now. Share your truth and I'll respond in kind. Wishing you potential unlocked. Talk soon.

The message ended with a beep. Greggs hung up.

"What the hell was that?" he said.

Jessie glanced over at Karen and the look in her partner's eyes suggested she knew but wasn't comfortable saying anything with so many people around.

"More importantly, where's her phone?" Rhonda asked.

"We'll have our tech guy get on it right away," Jessie said. "If anyone can locate it, it's him. Maybe we'll get lucky and find it in the killer's car. Can I get that number, Greggs?"

He gave it to her as Rhonda motioned for Mr. Almeida to come over. Calling him "Mister" was generous. Jessie doubted he was much older than Hannah.

"My understanding is that you have information to share, sir," Rhonda said.

"I already told that guy everything," he said uneasily, pointing at Greggs.

"Mr. Almeida gave me a formal statement earlier," Greggs explained before to turning to the kid, "Eli, just tell the folks what you told me, okay?"

Eli seemed to calm down a little at the sound of his first name. After gulping hard, he nodded.

"Yeah, okay. So, like I told him, I'm an overnight bellboy. Last night, around 11 p.m., I was taking up some bags for a couple that had a late arrival. They're staying on this floor, down the hall. I delivered the bags to them and when I was coming out of their room, I saw some dude walking to the elevators from the direction of this suite. He was walking real fast. He hit the elevator button a bunch of times, like he couldn't wait for it to come. When the elevator came, I called out to him, asking him to hold it for me, but he didn't. By the time I got to it, the doors had closed. I thought it was a jerk move, you know? I figured that if I saw him in the lobby I'd say so. But he was gone by the time I got down."

"Can you describe the guy?" Jessie asked.

"Yeah, kind of," Eli said. "First of all, he was old."

"Like, how old?" Jessie pressed.

"Pretty old—older than her," he said pointing at Sergeant Rhonda Ziegler. "Like maybe fifty? No offense lady."

"None taken," Rhonda replied, her tone world-weary.

"Anything else?" Jessie asked.

"Yeah, he had on blue jeans. He was in pretty good shape for an old guy, no fat on him. I couldn't see his face because he was pretty far away and he had on a baseball cap."

"Then how do you know he was old?" Karen asked.

"Because his skin was kind of leathery around the eyes and his hair—I could see it in the back. It was dark but had a lot of gray in it too."

"You're sure about that?" Jessie demanded.

"Yeah, it's not like *I'm* old. My vision's fine."

"Okay, Eli," Karen said, "Sergeant Ziegler's going to hook you up with a sketch artist, okay?"

"I guess," he said, "as long as it doesn't affect my job."

"You'll be fine," Karen assured him before turning to Jessie. "Can I talk to you in the other room for a second?"

Jessie nodded and followed her into the bedroom. Once inside, Karen closed the door behind them.

"I know you've been dying to tell me something for a while now," Jessie said. "What is it?"

Karen walked back over to the nightstand and picked up the book she'd been holding earlier.

"Have you ever heard of this?" she asked.

"What is it?"

"It's *The Purifying Power of Potential: A New Creed for a New Era* by Sterling Shepherd. He's a self-styled personal improvement guru who runs an outfit called the Eleventh Realm."

"I've heard of them," Jessie said. "That's the cult that operates over near Beachwood Canyon, right?"

"Shepherd wouldn't call it a cult," Karen said. "He'd describe it as a resource to unlock unlimited human potential."

"That sounds a lot like what Addison Rutherford said in her outgoing voicemail," Jessie noted.

"Exactly," Karen said. "Between that line and this book, I think there's a decent chance she's an Adherent of the Eleventh Realm. And if she is, things just got a lot more complicated for us."

23

CHAPTER FIVE

Livia Bucco wasn't used to being patient.

Being "a" patient? Yes, that she was used to, she thought, chuckling at the wordplay. She'd spent most of her adult life in and out of mental institutions. But being *patient*? That was something different entirely.

Of course, lots of things were different now that she had the Principles to work from. She had to admit that, at first, she'd been skeptical that they would work. It was only a week ago that she'd been discharged from the Female Forensic In-Patient Psychiatric Unit at the Twin Towers Correctional Facility in downtown L.A.

When she first stepped out that front door, she was so scared that she was literally shaking in her tattered boots. But then she remembered what her good friend, Andrea "Andy" Robinson, had told her: When you feel like you're getting into trouble, just follow the Principles, especially the Primary Principle; and lastly, always remember that your mind is your strongest tool. It can take you anywhere if you let it.

That's what she'd done in the days since. When she had trouble getting admitted to the halfway house, she stayed patient, followed the Principles, and used her mind. Now she had a room and a bed. When the manager at the grocery store balked after looking at her application to be a bagger there, she applied the Principles and managed to get hired on a probationary basis. She even got a library card and a membership to the local YWCA, where she'd started swimming.

That's where she was now, doing laps in the pool, wearing a bathing suit she'd picked up at a nearby Salvation Army store. She longed to visit Andy at Twin Towers to update her on her progress, but had promised that she wouldn't. That was part of the deal. She had to show that she could stand on her own two feet. If she did that, Andy said that she'd know it, no matter where she was.

When she was done with her laps, Livia got out the water, toweled off, and headed for the locker room and the showers. Andy had told her it was important to shower regularly. People wouldn't let you get close to them if you had strong body odor and Livia was making an effort to get closer to people. Besides, the place was so empty at this hour that she could shower without getting gawked at.

She stopped briefly to stare at herself in the mirror. Andy had advised her against doing that too often. She said that true beauty radiated from the inside out and that judging yourself too much on what was on the outside reinforced a bad self-image.

Livia knew she was right. Even now, as she looked at her body, she felt the familiar revulsion bubble up in her chest. She was well over six feet tall. Her stomach was big and her chest was small. Even with the showers, her skin was red and blotchy. She knew part of that was due to all those years on the street, as well as the drinking and the drugs. But she also had something that the clinic nurse had called Rosacea. It was one of the many reasons she got picked on as a kid. Because of that and her size, she got the nickname The Red Hulk, which stuck until she dropped out in 10th grade.

The self-loathing threatened to overwhelm her. Livia closed her eyes and pictured Andy Robinson standing in front of her, and began to quietly recite the Principles they'd discussed so many times in the psych unit chapel. As she did, she felt her breathing slow and a sense of calm return.

"You okay, Liv?"

Livia opened her eyes to see Kaylee McNulty walking by, wrapped in a towel, heading for the showers.

"Hi, yeah," she replied quickly. "Just doing a little locker room meditation."

"I should try that," Kaylee chuckled. "Any way to reduce the stress, right?"

"Right," Livia agreed, watching her go.

Kaylee was a sweetheart. A student at Southwestern Law School just across the 110 freeway, she volunteered at the Y a couple of days a week. She was the one who'd helped review Livia's job application for the grocery store before she turned it in.

She was also incredibly petite and cute. Livia guessed she was a full foot taller than the girl. With her tiny body and effervescent disposition, Livia imagined that Kaylee was what a real life pixie cheerleader might look like.

The thought made her smile. She now felt like she once again had full control over herself. She recalled the Principles. She repeated the mantra that Andy had taught her: *Your mind is your strongest tool. It can take you anywhere if you let it.* Suddenly she had complete clarity. She knew exactly where her mind needed to take her.

With a sense of tranquility she'd never experienced before, Livia returned to her locker and undressed. Then she grabbed her towel, along with the machete hidden in her gym bag, and headed for the showers, where she could hear Kaylee softly humming to herself.

CHAPTER SIX

"Nothing?" Jessie repeated incredulously.

"Nothing," Jamil said again, clearly embarrassed that he didn't have better news.

"How is that possible?" she asked, as she and Karen leaned over his monitor in the research department.

She didn't mean to sound so testy. It was just that they'd been back at the station for an hour now and so far, every lead that they thought they had was drying up. Jamil Winslow, HSS's head of research, had been tasked with finding the location of Addison Rutherford's phone, which was usually child's play for him. Both Jessie and Karen were stunned that he hadn't cracked it by now.

Jamil didn't look too offended. Jessie had noticed that since he'd been named head researcher for the unit, something had changed. He was still polite and hard-working to a fault. But he was more relaxed. She knew that he was going to the gym regularly to add some muscle to his scrawny frame, which seemed to give him confidence. But most importantly, he didn't take every critical comment personally anymore.

"It was there in the hotel until 11:06 p.m. and then the signal completely died," he told them. "It's hard to know what happened. Just removing the SIM card in a populated area like that with other phones and Wi-Fi and cell towers everywhere probably wouldn't be enough to lose it entirely. Neither would just smashing it to bits. If the killer took her phone, they managed to disable it quickly and effectively, which suggests they knew what they were doing."

"What about checking her call and text logs?" Karen wondered.

"I'm working on getting authorization," Jamil said. "But once I do, it'll likely take a few more hours after that to get the data from the phone company."

"Okay," Jessie said, managing to rediscover some semblance of self-possession after her brief, crotchety slip, "Still no luck on the hotel camera footage?"

"There's lots of footage. That place was hopping," Jamil told her. "The problem is the quality and angle of the cameras in the elevators and the lobby. First of all, it's all black and white and grainy. I think this system is from last century. Plus, the cameras are positioned so high up that it makes facial recognition virtually impossible. I counted at least eight guys in baseball caps and jeans in that window of time but I couldn't accurately tell you their ages within two decades. By contrast, the camera angles on the actual floors with the suites are pretty decent. If the camera for the 10th floor had been working, we might have something to work with."

"So we've got nothing," Karen grumbled.

"From a tech perspective, it's not looking good," Jamil said apologetically. "But if you bring me some suspects, I can always check their location statuses and see if any of them match. Otherwise, I'm out of ideas for now."

Jessie sighed.

"I guess it's back to you and me and some old-fashioned human investigating," she said to Karen. "You want to fill me in some more on this ER situation?"

"Sure, let's talk in the courtyard," Karen said.

Jessie followed her out to the interior courtyard in the center of the rectangular Central Station building. Back in the Buckingham hotel suite, "ER" was the coded term that Karen suggested they use when referencing the Eleventh Realm. She said that the group was surprisingly powerful, having infiltrated a number of industries in Los Angeles, and that it would be advisable to discuss the group cryptically and in private whenever possible.

But before the discussion got any further, they had been inundated with requests from other officers on the scene, as well as forensics and coroner's office personnel. This would be the first opportunity they'd had to discuss the group confidentially since then.

They walked across the grass to the center of the courtyard, where there was one bench completely shaded by a large tree. Though they were protected from the worst of the wind, it was still chilly and as they sat down, Jessie zipped up her jacket. Karen looked around to make sure no one was nearby before speaking.

"Did you get a chance to do any research on the group?" she asked.

"A little bit, in between calls with all the different units," Jessie answered. "Most of it was stuff I already knew: charismatic guy starts a self-help group, gets devoted acolytes who pay big bucks for his wisdom, people who get disenchanted and leave are maligned by those who stick around. Is that about right?"

"That's a solid Cliffs Notes version," Karen said. "But it's more complicated than that. Working at Hollywood Station for so many years, I got to see the inner workings of the group up close. What you said is true. To many in the general public, the Eleventh Realm comes across as a group interested in self-actualization. They have seminars and retreats, all of which are incredibly expensive, by the way. And through those events, Sterling Shepherd has accumulated a cadre of influential supporters. Many are in the entertainment industry. Some are in politics and finance. But he also has rank and file supporters, a number of which are in law enforcement."

Karen said that last line in a barely audible whisper.

"It sounds a lot like some other organizations in town that I could name," Jessie noted.

"In many ways, it is. They're incredibly secretive, which is what worries me most. If Addison Rutherford was an Adherent and her death was tied to the group, it's going to be like pulling teeth to get anything out of them."

"So you think she's one of them because she had that book, *The Purifying Power of Potential*?" Jessie asked.

"That's only partly why," Karen explained. "First of all, she didn't just *have* the book. I flipped through it. It was highlighted with hand-written notes on almost every page. She *studied* that book. For Adherents, it's like the Bible. They refer to it reverently as *P3*. And then there was her voicemail. Did you hear her wish callers 'potential unlocked?'"

"Yeah—what does that mean?"

"It's part of Shepherd's philosophy about 'unlocking Adherents' full potential.' That's what they're called by the way—Adherents, not members. There's a lot more to unpack but that's the headline— unlocking full potential. And then there's the part where she said that callers should share their truth and that she'd respond in kind."

"Right," Jessie recalled. "What was that all about?"

"That's standard Realm-speak," Karen said. "Adherents, no matter whether they're brand new or long-time veterans, are supposed to regularly participate in something called 'Truth Sessions,' or 'TS' for short, which is basically a euphemism for confession."

"Like Catholicism?"

"Only on the surface," Karen said, dropping her voice to a whisper as an officer passed by on the way to a far corner of the courtyard for a smoke break. "I'm a Presbyterian these days, but to the best of my knowledge, Catholic priests don't have two people in the same confessional at the same time, facilitating both of them trading admission of sins while the whole thing is recorded."

"What?" Jessie asked, flabbergasted.

"Yeah, it's a thing. The facilitators are called Truth Catalysts or 'TCs.' Everything in TEROTH has an acronym or an abbreviation."

"You're losing me here," Jessie said, holding up her hands. "I thought 'ER' was the shorthand for the group. What's TEROTH?"

Karen laughed as if her young son had asked some ridiculous question like 'are clouds alive?' Jessie was getting the strong sense that her partner's knowledge about this group came from more than just professional experience.

"'ER' isn't a term they use," Karen clarified. "It could be confused too easily with the hospital. That's why I'm comfortable using it with you. No one who overhears us will make the association. TEROTH isn't something widely used in the outside world. It stands for The Eleventh Realm of Truth and Harmony. It's how Adherents refer to the group among themselves. It's kind of like an inside joke; only it's no laughing matter."

"I guess I don't get the joke."

"There's no reason you should," Karen told her. "For them, the 'E' is silent, so it becomes TROTH, which sounds a lot like 'truth.' Pretty lame, right? Anyway, the point is, through these Truth Sessions, the Realm's leadership gathers all kinds of personal information on their Adherents, which can be used as blackmail fodder against them if they ever try to leave. That means it's going to be incredibly hard to pry any information out of people close to Addison, who will likely fear repercussions."

"What about her?" Jessie asked. "What might they have done to her if she had tried to leave?"

"That depends on who you believe," Karen said. "According to reps for the Realm, they have no issues with former Adherents who leave. They merely defend their good name when attacked by what they call the Disavowed, or DVs for short, because, of course that's what they'd be called."

"I think I'm getting the hang of this," Jessie said.

"It's not as clever as they think it is, right?" Karen said, before continuing. "Anyway, the 'Disavowed' tell a very different story. There are allegations of harassment, threats, even physical violence. And while the Realm consistently denies those accusations, they're pretty open about their use of what they call Rightful Targeting."

"Another glossary term?" Jessie asked.

"You wouldn't believe," Karen quipped. "This one asserts the right to come back hard at anyone who makes what they consider false claims against them. That might include picketing outside a DV's home or business, calling their boss to make disparaging comments about them, often using information gleaned from a TS, that is, a Truth Session. They've set up entire websites and Facebook pages devoted to demonizing people who left. And it can get worse."

"Worse how?" Jessie pressed.

"If they have friends or family in the Realm, those Adherents are prohibited from communicating with the Disavowed other than to make pre-scripted pleas to return to the fold. They can't directly respond to any comments or questions from the DV and they have to make their plea to return in the presence of a Proctor, who is basically a Realm-sanctioned security officer."

"That seems pretty restrictive," Jessie said.

"That's not all. Adherents in good standing can't have any physical contact with the DV either. Then, once the plea is formally made, the person being coaxed to return is considered Provisionally Disavowed. If, after eleven days, the Disavowed hasn't returned to the Realm, made an offering, and engaged in a comprehensive solo Truth Session with just a TC present, the Disavowal becomes permanent."

"What does that mean?" Jessie asked.

"It means that communication with all Adherents in good standing is irrevocably cut off. No meeting for coffee. No calls on birthdays. No e-mails. No letters. No waving from across the street. No asking someone else to pass along a friendly word. If communication of any kind is uncovered then the Adherent who communicated or willingly received the communication is also Disavowed, only in their case, without any provisional period."

Jessie shook her head in disbelief.

"I'll admit that all sounds pretty bad," she acknowledged, "but it seems like these Disavowed people can at least start over fresh when they leave. Remember, after I was framed by my ex-husband, cops thought I was disloyal and the public thought I was a racist. I had people outside this very station, picketing me personally. I was hanged in effigy. That really sucked, but I dealt with it."

"I remember," Karen said. "I saw that on the news. But remember, you still had Ryan and Hannah and Kat and a support system here at the station. Most of these people are so wrapped up in the Realm that it defines their entire life. To them, getting cut off from it is almost like being tossed out of a space station. You still have your spacesuit on so technically you can survive for a while. But everything you've depended on is gone and the rest of the people on the planet below seem so far away. It can be terrifying. That's why so few leave, even if they've become disenchanted."

Jessie hesitated briefly, unsure if she should say what was in her head. But in the end, she decided that to navigate this case together, they couldn't have any secrets.

"But you left," she said.

CHAPTER SEVEN

Karen's shoulders slumped.

She looked around furtively again, making sure that the cop on his smoke break, flipping through his phone, hadn't perked up.

"Is it that obvious?" she asked softly.

Jessie smiled sympathetically.

"I'm sorry but no amount of casework would get a detective to that spacesuit analogy. That's based on personal experience," she said. "You want to tell me what happened?"

"Do we even have time for this?" Karen asked.

"If we're going to go up against these folks, I should probably have the whole picture. I don't want to get blindsided by something you revealed in a Truth Session, excuse me—a TS— ten years ago."

"Okay, but it was actually longer ago than that, closer to twenty years now," Karen said. "I was a freshman at Occidental College up in Eagle Rock. I had just moved here from Toledo, Ohio. I went to an all-girls school back there, led a very sheltered life. I never even went on a real date in high school."

"Oh, Karen," Jessie groaned.

"Believe me, I know," she said. "All of a sudden I was in La La Land. One of my dorm mates had a car. On weekends, we would all pile in and she'd take us to Hollywood. On one of those trips, I met a cute boy in a club who seemed interested in me. His name was Derek Burke. He was an actor, a little older, in his early twenties. We exchanged numbers, went on a few dates—movies, picnics in the parks. By the time he invited me to join him on a Personal Potential Realm Retreat with this group he was part of, I was smitten. The event was up the coast near San Luis Obispo. It was over a long holiday weekend and I viewed it as a chance to go on a romantic getaway with the guy I was falling in love with. I figured there was no better way to lose my virginity."

Jessie couldn't look her in the eye as she asked her next question.

"What happened?"

Karen half-giggled.

"I *did* lose my virginity, which was pretty awesome, despite everything that happened later. We did some standard retreat stuff—

trust falls, rock climbing with harnesses, that kind of thing. We also had a lot of small group discussions, often on the beach, by fire pits, late at night. I had a few seemingly legitimate personal breakthroughs in those discussions. Truth be told, if it had ended there, the event would have been a success, something I looked back on with fondness."

"But it didn't end there," Jessie prompted.

"No. There was also the sleep deprivation, which I didn't even notice at first. There were just so many interesting conversations to be had. And there was the food deprivation."

"They didn't feed you?" Jessie asked, aghast.

"No, they fed us. But it was always in individual portions, which were slightly smaller than you needed to stay at full strength. And when you asked if you could have more, they seemed disappointed in you. They'd talk about providing enough sustenance for a healthy person and if I needed more, perhaps I should ask myself if I was working towards achieving better health. They pointed to this bony, haggard looking girl named Inara and said that she consumed fewer than a thousand calories a day but still ran marathons and was on the Council of Harmony and Potential, or COHP, which was the leadership team. I have no idea if the marathon stuff was true. Looking back, it seems ridiculous. But in that moment, she became my physical aspiration. I wanted to look like her, to be her."

"Jesus," Jessie muttered. Her own youth had been an endless series of traumas but even she had never been brainwashed into wishing herself to be a walking skeleton.

"And all that was before Sterling Shepherd arrived at the retreat," Karen said. "Up until that point everyone had been talking about his arrival as if it was the second coming. They all referred to him as 'The Shepherd.'"

Another officer, a young guy from Narcotics, came outside and wandered over near them. He leaned against the large tree, only feet from them, seemingly oblivious to their presence. Jessie had no reason to suspect he was an Eleventh Realm spy but she wasn't surprised and didn't object when Karen motioned for them to move over to the far, unoccupied corner of the courtyard.

"Sorry for the paranoia," she said when they got there. "I've just been burned too many times not to be cautious."

"I understand," Jessie said, at least trying to. "You were talking about Sterling Shepherd arriving at the retreat."

Right," she said, picking up where she had left off. "He showed up at the beach on that Saturday afternoon and people freaked out. They didn't just treat him as some sort of guru. He was almost like a god to them. But I didn't get it. He was about thirty but he was dressed in a Pixies t-shirt, cut-off jeans shorts, and flip flops. He had shaggy brown hair and a few days' worth of stubble. He didn't look like the prophet for a new generation or the leader of some movement to me. He looked like a stoner or a surfer or both."

"But...," Jessie said, certain there was one.

"But then he started talking," Karen replied. "He was magnetic but in this really casual way. He told everyone to call him Shep, which no one did. He talked about the degradation of society being a reflection of the degradation of the soul. He explained that we were trapped by a conventional social order that prevented us from achieving our full potential. He preached that sacrifice and love were two sides of the same coin and that we could only achieve enlightenment and find real truth through spiritual and, sometimes, even physical pain. It was a sermon and it went on for over two hours. A few people fainted, were dragged off along the sand to get some water, then crawled back to hear more. I felt like a door to a whole new world had been unlocked for me."

"A world where you have to sacrifice to prove your love and endure pain to learn the truth?" Jessie asked skeptically.

Karen gave her a bittersweet smile.

"Those are the questions I should have been asking but didn't."

"But you eventually did or you wouldn't be sitting here," Jessie noted.

"I might not have been if not for one thing," Karen told her.

"What?"

"They overplayed their hand with me, though I didn't know it at the time," she said. "But later, it turned out that what they thought was their greatest advantage ended up being what set me free."

"I have to hear about this," Jessie insisted.

"Okay, so on the last day, Sunday, a few hours before Derek and I were set come back to L.A., he said I had been selected for a special honor. It turned out that I was going to have a TS—."

"A Truth Session?" Jessie reconfirmed.

"Right," Karen said. "Derek was my partner, and the special honor was that our TC—our Truth Catalyst—was Sterling Shepherd himself."

"Impressive," Jessie said mockingly.

"It was actually hugely intimidating. Remember, I'd never been a part of any of this or ever had a TS before. So they started in with the questions. Tell us about your most embarrassing moment from childhood. Share the biggest lie you ever told. Reveal your most shameful moment. The problem was that I didn't have much to offer. Derek was talking about stealing money from his little sister's piggy bank and robbing liquor stores and pressuring an old girlfriend to get an abortion. But I had led a pretty boring, 'good girl' life. I couldn't think of much at all. I mean, I was telling them about running out of biology crying when we had to dissect a fetal pig."

"I suspect that didn't cut it for them," Jessie mused.

"Not even close. But they kept pushing. So I gave them other stuff that I was embarrassed about but hardly seemed worthy."

"But it wasn't enough," Jessie guessed.

"Nope," Karen said. "And they kept pushing and I was so tired and so hungry and I just wanted go home at that point so I made something up."

"What did you say?"

"I came up with a variation on Derek's piggy bank story," Karen told her. "I figured they were looking for something illegal, no matter how minor. So I said I stole some of my little brother's paper route money and used it to buy makeup at the mall."

"Not true though?"

"I don't even have a little brother. I'm an only child. And my parents didn't allow me to wear makeup unless I bought it with one of them present. But it got me out of there."

"So you quit when you got back?" Jessie asked.

"I wish I could say that I did. Once I had a little distance from the retreat, the TS faded. What stuck with me was Sterling Shepherd's charisma and, frankly, the constant buzz I had going from regular sex with Derek. After the first semester, I moved out of the dorm and into his apartment. I stopped hanging out with my school friends and spent all my time with Realmers."

"So why did you decide to leave?" Jessie asked. "What happened?"

"Spring Break happened."

"I'm sorry," Jessie said, trying not to laugh. "What?"

Karen smiled patiently.

"It's okay. I deserve it," she said, leaning in closer even though there was no way either cop in the courtyard could hear her. "About midway through the second semester, some of my school friends came to me and said they were really worried about me, that I might flunk out. To their credit, they never said they thought the Realm was a bad influence. I think they knew that would only push me away. They asked me to go to Palm Springs with them for Spring Break, just to get

36

a little distance and some perspective. They framed it as a chance to reboot, to refresh. And they said that a week away from me would make Derek want me even more."

"I'm guessing the folks at the Eleventh Realm weren't enthused?" Jessie speculated.

"Not at all," Karen corroborated. "Derek didn't understand why I wanted to be apart from him. Inara, the bony marathon girl, told me that my school friends wanted to immerse me in a 'fetid pool of commercialism.' I still remember that phrase. I felt bad about it but I went anyway. I was just so exhausted and beaten down that the idea of getting away from everything and lying by a pool reading a book or taking a nap in my hotel room sounded like heaven."

"How was it?"

"Great and terrible at the same time," she said. "I constantly felt guilty. Shepherd had preached that sleeping more than six hours in a night was wasting precious time that could be used to unlock our potential. That first night I slept almost twelve hours and probably could have gone longer. I berated myself for that."

"Oh, Karen," Jessie whispered.

"It gets worse. Every time I went to the buffet at our hotel, I was ashamed if my plate was full. One of my friends was appalled when she saw that all I had for breakfast one morning was two slices of cantaloupe, two slices of honeydew and two slices of watermelon. She marched me back to our hotel room and pulled out a pair of shorts that she'd lent me one time, soon after we got to school in the fall. Back then we were the same size. She had me try them on in the room. I buttoned them up and they immediately fell down around my ankles. It was a real eye opener. I'm not a big person but I checked and found that I'd gone from 127 pounds to 98 pounds in six months. I was as skeletal as Inara. That was when the light started to come on."

Karen went silent as the officer who had been leaning against the tree in the middle of the courtyard stood up straight and stretched his arms up to the sky. He turned and started in their direction. For a second it looked like he might headed directly for them. But he merely picked up a candy wrapper on the ground a few feet from them, tossed it in the trash can, and returned inside.

"Now you've got *me* paranoid," Jessie said.

"Good," Karen told her.

"So give me the happy ending, Detective Bray. How did you go from bony cult acolyte to pride of the LAPD?"

"Here's the short version. After Spring Break I went back and told Derek I wasn't comfortable with some of the ways the Realm operated. I was moving back into the dorms. I was going to eat normal meals and sleep normal hours. I wasn't paying for any seminars that didn't interest me and I wasn't doing any more Truth Sessions. You can imagine his reaction."

"He brought in the higher ups?" Jessie guessed.

"He did. They started with Inara, who they thought I was tight with. She tried to guilt me into staying more active. Even Shepherd made a push. He already knew what I would eventually figure out: that once an Adherent pulled away, it was hard to get them back. They needed to be kept in constant thrall. At the time I didn't understand why he spent so much time on little old me. But in retrospect, it made sense. I was their only Adherent at Occidental College. I was the gateway to a pool of 2,000 impressionable young people. If I bailed, it would be hard to rev that up again organically."

"But their pressure campaign didn't work?"

"Nope," Karen said. "So that's when they brought out the big guns. Remember how I said that Shepherd was the TC at my first TS back at the retreat and that they unknowingly overplayed their hand?"

"Yeah."

"This was when that came back to bite them. They started to threaten me. Inara told me that if I left, they'd have to tell my parents about how I stole my brother's paper route money. I remember being stunned for a second before laughing in her face. Of course, the threat held no weight. My parents would only be confused by the allegation. But more significantly, it was all so petty. They were trying to intimidate me with the best piece of intel they had, no matter how lame. In that moment, I realized that they probably had a lot better stuff on people—stuff that might actually work. I remembered Derek's admission about robbing that liquor store. What had other people confessed to on tape? I walked out of the Heartbeat Hub—that's what they call their Hollywood headquarters—that day and never went back."

"And that was the end of it?" Jessie asked, sure that it wasn't.

"Not even close," Karen assured her. "I was an early victim of Rightful Targeting. No one picketed me but they did other stuff—called constantly, had me followed everywhere, even tried to manufacture a traffic accident so that they could sue me. And I got off comparatively easy."

"What do you mean by that?"

38

"That's what I want to impress upon you with this whole story, Jessie," Karen said, leaning in close and staring at her unblinkingly. "These people are dangerous."

"You mean, you think they might have killed Addison Rutherford if she tried to leave?"

Karen's eyes clouded over.

"Possibly," she said. "I wouldn't put it past them. But to be honest, based on her outgoing voice message and that dog-eared copy of Shepherd's book, I'm inclined to think she died a true believer. And if she *wasn't* trying to leave, it doesn't give them much motive. Still, even though I have my doubts, we have to follow that lead, which is why I'm more worried for us."

"Why?"

"Think about it. I was nobody back in college and they harassed me relentlessly. Imagine what they'd do now if they found out we were investigating them in relation to a murder. They have a whole unit, kind of their own Homicide Special Section devoted to Rightful Targeting of DVs. It's called the Department of Restricted Activities, or DRA, and there have been rumors for years that they do a lot more than just picket people."

"Like what?" Jessie asked, slightly embarrassed that she didn't already know all about this.

"There are countless documented cases—some of which I handled—of disappearances of Adherents who were rumored to be leaving. DVs who have spoken out against the Realm have met with suspicious suicides or strange, deadly accidents. I've never been able to close a single case involving allegations about the Eleventh Realm and I'm pretty damn good at my job. That alone should give you pause. We could be in real danger here."

Jessie slouched against the courtyard wall. The magnitude of their task was starting to sink in.

"So if nobody will talk to us for fear of being Rightfully Targeted," she said, "how are we ever going to learn about Addison—her routines, her contacts, and why she was in that hotel?"

Karen stared off into the distance for a moment. When she returned her attention to Jessie, it was clear that she had an idea.

"I don't know about specifics about her day-to-day life, but I might have a thought on how we can learn a little more about how Addison fit into the organizational structure of the Realm, which is a start at least."

"I'll take a start," Jessie said. "What did you have in mind?"

Before Karen could reply, Jamil shoved the courtyard door open. He was breathing heavily. It was clear that he'd been running.

"What is it?" Jessie asked.

"I've got something," he said excitedly. "Addison Rutherford had a boyfriend. And he was at her hotel last night."

CHAPTER EIGHT

Ryan regretted having that extra cup of coffee.

As he stood at the edge of the shower stall at the downtown YWCA, looking at the hacked-up body of the young woman, he felt his stomach churn uncomfortably. He'd seen hundreds of dead bodied, some mangled worse than this. But the combination of factors at play in this case was particularly unsettling. He looked over at his partner for the day, Susannah Valentine, and could tell that she was equally troubled.

"So," he said, turning away from what remained of Kaylee McNulty to focus on the officer in charge, an older black sergeant named Moss, "you're saying she volunteered here two to three times a week. What was she doing in the locker room?"

"Apparently she was also a member," Moss told him. "The program director said she swam most days either before or after she did a volunteering session."

"What kind of work did she do?" Valentine asked.

"Mostly legal services," Sergeant Moss said. "She was in her second year over at Southwestern Law School. But the director said she'd help out anywhere she was needed: employment services, youth recreation. Apparently she was a delight to have around."

"Wonderful," Ryan said heavily, glancing back at Kaylee. "When is Forensics getting here?"

"I requested them a half-hour ago, Detective. Maybe a follow-up from you would expedite things. This girl shouldn't have to stay like this much longer, if you ask me."

Ryan didn't disagree. Kaylee McNulty deserved better. While most of her body was on the floor of the shower stall, her feet had slid against the side wall, creating tension and preventing her upper torso from completely collapsing. As a result, her left arm and shoulder were pressed against the tiled shower wall and her neck was bent at an awkward angle.

Her blue, vacant eyes were still open and her wet, stringy blonde hair had fallen down to partially cover her face, but not enough to hide her beauty. From where Ryan stood, he could see six large slices, likely made with a large knife along the lines of a machete. None were above the neck. Two were to the chest and they continued down the body from there. One blow, to the back of her right forearm, had cut all the way through to the bone. That was almost certainly the arm Kaylee had raised in futile self-defense.

"And there are no cameras?" he asked Moss, tearing his eyes away from the girl again.

"Certainly not in here. There's one in the main lobby and one outside the main entrance. We're checking the footage on those now. But those are the only working cameras. All the others are fakes for deterrence. And there are multiple other entrances and exits to the facility. Unless whoever did this was dumb enough to enter and leave through the front door, we're not going to have footage of them."

"What about sign-in sheets?" Valentine asked. "Or witnesses?"

"There is a sign-in sheet at the front desk but they don't enforce it. The pool only has a lifeguard during child lessons and free play so we don't know if there was anyone around when she was swimming. And according to the recreation director, this area is pretty quiet on Fridays until after lunch. It's possible that the victim and the assailant were the only ones in here at the time. Considering the ferocity of the attack and how loud it probably was, I'd say it's likely they were alone."

"I tend to agree," Ryan said. "Even if there *was* someone else in here at some point, the killer would have surely waited until they were alone to do this. It's a long shot but we should have the entire locker room fingerprinted, and especially the area right around this shower stall. Maybe the killer gripped the side for leverage."

"As soon as Forensics arrives, Detective, I'll make them aware," Moss said, his eyebrows raised expectantly.

Ryan nodded.

"I'll make the call," he said before turning to Valentine. "While I light a fire under Forensics, can you start to pull up a list of family and friends? Maybe Jamil Winslow can help out with that. After we notify the next of kin, I'm thinking we should talk to some of her law school friends. It's possible she mentioned someone who threatened her. Or maybe someone she did legal work for here wasn't happy with how it turned out."

"I'll get on it, Ryan," Valentine said. "Don't worry, we'll catch this bastard."

He nodded hopefully. While he appreciated Valentine's optimism, he wasn't sure he shared it. This was the kind of case that gave him an unpleasantly familiar feeling. It was the kind that, if it wasn't solved in the first few hours, it likely never would be. He stepped outside and called Forensics. Once he got the supervisor, he tore him a new one.

"You guys are literally a mile and half away from here," he growled. "There's a dead twenty-three-year-old good Samaritan lying naked and chopped up in a shower stall. The officer in charge called you a half-hour ago. It's 9:53 a.m. right now. If there's not a complete unit here in ten minutes, I'm going to make life very ugly for you. Get your ass in gear. Now!"

He hung up without waiting for a reply. After allowing himself a moment to regroup, he texted Jessie. Decker had assigned him and Valentine the case so quickly that he hadn't had a chance to say goodbye before they left or even let her know his status.

He filled her in on the situation and concluded: *Not many leads so far. Valentine is looking into close contacts. Hoping we get lucky with Forensics. Could be a late one for us. Will keep you posted. Love you.*

He had just hit send when Valentine came outside.

"Jamil's pulling up contacts as we speak," she said. "I thought we could head over to the law school in the interim, see what we can turn up on our own."

"Sounds good," Ryan said. "We'll go as soon as the Forensics unit gets here. I want them to see the steam coming off my head when they arrive."

Valentine smiled.

"Whatever gets the job done," she said.

Ryan was glad to see the newcomer got it. So far, she'd been a halfway decent partner. He hoped it stayed that way.

CHAPTER NINE

"His name is Josh Sawyer."

Jamil had just punched up footage of Addison's boyfriend walking into the hotel at 9:36 p.m. That was thirty-nine minutes before the cameras went down at 10:15 but well within the 9 p.m. to midnight estimated window of death.

"How did you find out about this guy?" Jessie asked.

"I was able to access Rutherford's e-mail," Jamil explained. "Apparently this Sawyer guy isn't a fan of texting. He says, in an e-mail, that it ties him down too much. He always feels beholden to the little black rectangle. Frankly, I get where he's coming from. Anyway, he likes to go old school, which to him means e-mail. That's how I found his message to her saying he'd be at the Buckingham at 9 p.m. Of course, after all that, he showed up over a half-hour late."

"He's wearing jeans," Karen noted, studying the screen.

"But no baseball cap," Jessie pointed out. "And he looks a lot younger than fifty."

"Are we sure we trust eighteen-year-old bellboy Eli Almeida as an accurate judge of people's ages?" Karen asked.

"No," Jessie conceded. "But Sawyer looks closer to thirty to me."

"Twenty-eight actually," Jamil said.

"What do we know about him?" Karen asked as Jamil let the footage play, showing the guy enter an elevator. He switched to another camera that tracked Sawyer traveling to the tenth floor.

"He's an aspiring musician," Jamil said. "He's the guitarist for a rock band called Loaded for Bare, as in naked. I guess it's supposed to be clever. They play semi-regular sets, mostly around Hollywood and Los Feliz. But his day job is working in a warehouse at an office supply place on Santa Monica Boulevard."

The elevator doors opened and Jamil switched to a different camera, which showed Josh Sawyer approaching suite 1002. Once he entered, the screen went dark.

"He's in there for fifteen minutes," Jamil said. "I'll skip ahead."

Jessie thought back to the untouched bed in Addison's suite. Fifteen minutes was obviously long enough for the couple to have gotten romantic, but it seemed less and less likely that it was that kind of visit.

The next clip showed him exiting the room. As he walked away, he didn't look exactly relaxed, but he also didn't look overly stressed.

"You never know," Jessie said, "but he certainly doesn't carry himself like someone who just bashed his girlfriend in the head with a lamp."

"Plus" Jamil added, "he walks out the front door of the hotel at 9:54 and we know that her cell phone was still pinging there well after he left. Remember, it didn't go dark until 11:06."

"That doesn't eliminate him as a suspect," Karen countered. "Maybe this visit was to scout the hotel, the points of entry and exit. We don't know that he didn't come back later in a baseball cap to finish the job."

"Fair point," Jessie conceded. "I guess the best way to find out is to talk to the guy. Let's head out. Jamil, can you shoot us the address for his work please?"

"You got it," he said, already typing it into his phone.

They checked in with Decker to let him know their plan, and then headed down to the garage, where Karen volunteered to drive. Jessie was just getting into the passenger seat when her phone buzzed. It was a text from Ryan. As she read it, her heart sank.

"What's up?" Karen asked.

"Oh, it's just Ryan," she replied, trying to keep her tone even. "He and Valentine caught an ugly case—female law student butchered in a YWCA shower stall. No good leads yet. He was just warning me that it could be a long night for them."

She didn't mention that, independent of the awful nature of the crime, something far pettier was eating at her. She realized that, had she not been so averse to working with Susannah Valentine when Captain Decker allowed her to pick her partner this morning, Ryan wouldn't be spending "a late one," as he called it, with her.

It's not like she thought that her fiancé would start flirting with the woman over crime scene photos of a dead girl. That was ridiculous. But just the idea of Susannah Valentine laughing at his mildest quips and tossing her hair around extravagantly as she batted her eyes at him was quietly infuriating.

"What's wrong?" Karen asked, snapping her out of it.

"Nothing," Jessie told her. "Let's go."

*

Josh Sawyer's apartment was a dump.

As Jessie and Karen tiptoed up the rickety outdoor stairwell that led to his second floor unit, Jessie was on high alert.

They already had reason to be suspicious. When they went to Office Pros earlier, the warehouse manager said that he hadn't shown up today, hadn't even called in sick. So the next stop was this place, a grimy two-level apartment complex, just three blocks from the famed Hollywood Forever Cemetery, and classily named Corpse Court. It looked it too. The front gate was missing entirely. Pieces of metal siding dangled precariously from the exterior and paint was peeling back from the outside walls to form curled, snail-like designs. The cracks on the first floor courtyard pavement were wide enough to get a shoe stuck in.

Once on the second floor, they approached Sawyer's unit, 207. They hadn't even reached the door when they could hear loud voices, not quite yelling, but definitely animated. Karen released her holster lock and Jessie followed suit. Karen was about to knock when Jessie held up her hand. There was something odd—heightened— about the argument going on inside. After another moment, she understood why.

"It's the TV," she whispered.

Karen nodded in recognition, pointed to the adjoining window, which appeared to be partially open, and moved in that direction. Jessie waited while she peeked inside.

"I can't see anyone," Karen said when she returned. "I'm going to knock. But with him missing work, the television on, and the window open in this neighborhood, we may be talking exigent circumstances if he doesn't answer."

Jessie tended to agree. If Sawyer had left his place like this, that likely meant either something had happened to him or he was in a condition where he didn't care what happened to him. Karen knocked loudly.

"Mr. Sawyer, this is Detective Karen Bray with the Los Angeles Police Department. Can you please open the door?"

After ten seconds of silence, she knocked again and repeated the request but still got no response. She turned the knob. It was locked.

"I'm going in through the window," Karen said. "Hold tight."

Jessie watched anxiously as Karen shimmied through the small opening. She kept her hand on her weapon, ready to grab it if necessary. After a painfully long half minute she heard the front door unlock. Karen opened it, looking unscathed.

"He's not here," she said.

Jessie stepped inside. It was immediately clear that, even amidst the mess, someone had packed and left in a hurry. A small suitcase rested on the couch, along with some clothes and toiletries. From what was there, Jessie gathered that Sawyer had decided he didn't need the extra items or the suitcase.

"You check the bedroom yet?" she asked.

"Just a cursory search to make sure he wasn't hiding in there or the bathroom."

"I'm going to look around," Jessie said, heading back.

The bedroom wasn't much use in terms of clues. It looked like a tornado had torn through it. But the bathroom offered some hints. She found a razor, cologne, and some over-the- counter medications. But there was no sign of a comb, toothbrush, toothpaste, or prescription meds. It looked he'd taken the essentials and bailed.

When she turned around, Karen was standing in the bathroom doorway with an expectant look on her face.

"You thinking what I'm thinking?" the detective asked.

"If you're thinking that Josh Sawyer left this place fast, with no intention of ever coming back, then yes I am. I'm also thinking we don't have much time to find him."

"We better get started then," Karen replied.

CHAPTER TEN

Even though she was staring at her own shoes, Hannah could feel Dr. Lemmon's eyes on her. Despite the older woman's tiny frame, coke bottle glasses, and woefully outdated perm comprised of tight little blonde ringlets, she could be an intimidating presence.

The two of them had been dancing around the same issue for the last ten minutes and unlike all their prior sessions, the therapist didn't seem willing to let it go this time. She was insistent on learning more about what happened that night two and half weeks ago: the night when the Night Hunter broke into their cabin and held her, Jessie, and Ryan at gunpoint before they created a distraction and Hannah shot him in self-defense.

That was the official story, the one that made it into the police report. But of course that wasn't the whole story, and it was clear that Lemmon sensed that she was holding something back about what occurred that night, even if she wasn't clear on exactly what had *really* happened. But what was Hannah supposed to say? We managed to outwit a serial killer in his seventies who'd murdered hundreds of people for decades, then my sister and her cop boyfriend subdued and handcuffed him, after which, to their shock and dismay, I shot him while he was unarmed and no longer a threat?

That didn't seem like the kind of admission that could be easily worked through with a prescription and some hand puppet theater. Hannah knew that Jessie wanted her to tell Lemmon the truth herself— that it would be more…therapeutic if she was the one to reveal what really happened. But admitting that she'd shot the man when he couldn't hurt them anymore would inevitably lead to other admissions.

Technically, she could argue that the Night Hunter (who'd suggested that they call him Wally while he was still in control) was a potential danger to them even then. He could theoretically have gotten out of prison or manipulated a guard or a soon-to-be-released inmate into doing his dirty work. But that wasn't the real reason she'd shot him. She shot him because she wanted to.

And if she acknowledged to Dr. Lemmon that she shot him for reasons other than self-defense, then she'd eventually have to concede the real reason. And when Dr. Lemmon asked *why* she wanted to shoot

Wally, well, then she'd be in a real pickle, because that's when her black heart would finally be exposed.

What would esteemed psychiatrist, behavioral therapist, and criminal profiling consultant Dr. Janice Lemmon think of her when she said that not only did she want to kill Wally, but she liked it? And more than that, in the weeks since it happened, that she desperately missed the satisfaction she got from it.

She still remembered watching the light fade from the old man's eyes just before his weathered, broken body sagged in on itself. It had given her such a thrill to know that she was responsible for extinguishing that light. How would Dr. Lemmon respond to that tidbit?

She wondered if this was what drove her father to kill. Xander Thurman, better known as the Ozarks Executioner, was the familial connection between her and Jessie. He was not only their shared birth father, but he had murdered both their mothers, over half a decade apart. And when they were older, he had hunted down and killed both sets of their adoptive parents too. Did he watch the eyes of his victims, waiting for that sliver of time when they passed from this world to whatever came next? Was that the legacy he'd passed on to her?

Was that what drove Bolton Crutchfield too, a serial killer who had viewed her father as a mentor, who killed her foster parents only weeks after she lost her adoptive ones? Was he also chasing that fraction of a second between worlds, trying to share it with her, when he kidnapped her and tried to train her in his own image, tried to get her to kill Jessie as her first conquest on the path to joining him in some weird partnership of carnage?

Did she ever even have a chance at a normal life when she'd experienced all that before she was old enough to vote? Frankly, the fact that she wasn't already institutionalized or operating her own, personal human butcher shop was kind of a miracle. She almost smiled at the thought.

Of course there was one complication that made it hard to justify a total surrender to self-pity: Jessie. Her sister had been through just as much hardship as she had, maybe more. She had the same murderous father, who killed her mother too. But unlike Hannah's mom, who was killed when she was baby, and whom she had no memory of, Thurman killed Jessie's mother right in front of her. Then he left her to die, all when she was just six years old.

And then there was everything that happened to her later. For example, there was the time that her husband tried to kill her because she discovered his affair, and then tried again after their divorce. That second time he managed to kill her mentor, Garland Moses, before he went after Hannah and Ryan too, stabbing the latter and leaving him in a coma for weeks.

Despite all that, Jessie decided to make a career out of stopping people like her ex-husband, like their father, like Bolton Crutchfield, like the Night Hunter. As if that wasn't enough, she was teaching the next generation of aspiring profilers to take up the cause too. She wasn't letting her own trauma control her. She was using it to make the world a better place. Hannah could do that too.

And yet, she couldn't deny it: the dark urge to see the moment when a life was extinguished lingered in her. She imagined this was what it was like for a detoxing heroin addict, hungry for the fix, even when they know it might destroy them.

"Hannah," Dr. Lemmon said gently, ripping her from her reverie, "you were about to tell me about that night, about the thing we both know you've been holding back. I think it's finally time, don't you?"

Hannah looked back at the doctor. Her mind was racing and it took several seconds to realize that she'd been holding her breath. She allowed herself to exhale slowly. Then she answered.

"Really, Dr. Lemmon," she said earnestly, "there's nothing more to tell."

CHAPTER ELEVEN

"We're never going to make it," Jessie shouted.

"We could tell them to hold the train," Karen suggested as the car tore down Alameda Street and pulled into a loading zone parking spot in front of the main entrance of Union Station.

"No," Jessie countered as they hopped out and ran to the nearest entrance. "If we try anything like that, I'm worried that he'll get suspicious and make a run for it. At least right now we know where he's supposed to be."

Where Josh Sawyer was supposed to be was at Track 8 for the 10:34 a.m. train to San Diego, where they suspected he intended to make the short trip across the border to Tijuana, Mexico, and disappear for good.

They only knew about his plans because of Jamil. They'd asked him to track Sawyer's phone the moment they'd learned he'd gone to the Buckingham Hotel. But just as with Addison's, there was no signal for it. However, Jamil had discovered a credit card purchase, made around the time they were searching his apartment, for a one-way train ticket from Union Station to downtown San Diego on the Pacific Surfliner. That was twenty-five minutes ago.

"What time is it?" Jessie asked as they hurried onto the main concourse of the station.

"10:31," Karen said before roughly grabbing an attendant who was passing by.

"What the—?" the older, bespectacled man demanded.

"Which way to Track 8," she interrupted, "for the 10:34 Pacific Surfliner to San Diego?"

The man's face softened slightly. Apparently he was used to this kind of panicked question.

"That way," he said, pointing down a long hallway, "eighth track on your left."

"Thanks," Karen said over her shoulder as they started jogging in that direction.

"But you'll never make it," he called after them. "It's a five minute walk and they always pull out right on time."

Jessie looked over at Karen, briefly unsure of the protocol, before deciding manners weren't a priority right now.

"I've gotten back into running lately," she said. "If I really hoof it, I think I can make it."

"Go for it," Karen said, waving her ahead. "I'll catch up when I can. Just stay vigilant. We don't know what this guy is capable of."

Jessie nodded and broke into a sprint. She was glad she'd worn her sneakers today. After her last major case, in which she'd chased a personal trainer through a backyard and used a trampoline to not quite leap a fence, she'd promised herself that function would always trump fashion on the job.

She pumped her arms hard as she fixed her attention on the overhead signs indicating the upcoming tracks. She could see the sign for Track 8 in the distance, well over a hundred yards away. Glancing down at her watch, she caught the time: 10:33.

Under normal circumstances, she would have liked to have taken a moment to appreciate the historic train station. But right now, all the ceiling designs and intricate floor patterns blurred together as she ignored the ache in her calves and fixed her attention on the turnstile offering entry to Track 8.

When she got there, she jumped the turnstile barrier and transitioned into a rapid, but hopefully not noticeable, walk. She took slow, deep breaths to hide her heavy breathing and tried to ignore the sweat dripping down her back just under her jacket. The train was just down the track a few hundred feet and it was possible that if Sawyer was looking in her direction, he might take notice of a woman sprinting wildly toward him.

She heard a loud whistle that she assumed indicated the train was about to start moving. Her watch read 10:34. She pulled out her phone and swiped through the photos she had of Sawyer. One was of his driver's license, but it was three years old and she didn't put much stock in it.

The other was a publicity still from his band, Loaded for Bare. In it, he had longish blond hair that partially obscured his blue eyes. He had a crooked, roguish smile and a couple of days' worth of stubble. She imagined that was closer to the guy she was looking for. As she got closer to the train, she heard an announcement over the loudspeaker.

"Final boarding call for Pacific Surfliner 572, 10:34 departure to San Diego Santa Fe Depot Station, leaving now at Track 8."

Just as the announcement ended, a man darted out from behind a pillar up onto the raised entry of the second to last car. As he moved, his long blond hair trailed behind him. He was wearing a flannel shirt and blue jeans. It was Josh Sawyer. He was quick enough that had Jessie been glancing elsewhere, she would have missed him.

The train started moving and she started running again. Behind her, she could hear Karen's voice.

"Is he on it?"

Jessie twisted back around without stopping and yelled back.

"Yes—second car from the back. I'm getting on!"

Karen shouted something in response but Jessie couldn't hear it because of the noise as the train picked up momentum. By the time she reached the end of the last car, it was going as fast as she was. She shoved her phone in her pocket, grabbed onto the safety bar, ignoring the attendant on the platform who was screaming at her to stop, and hoisted herself up.

She tried to open the door but it was locked. An attendant on the other side of the window glared at her angrily. With one hand precariously gripped the rail and her feet on the narrow platform on the outside of the door, she pulled out her ID, which was attached to a lanyard around her neck, and slammed it up against the window.

"LAPD!" she shouted.

His glare quickly switched to an expression of acquiescence as he opened the door and helped her inside. As he closed the door behind her, she took a moment to catch her breath. When she was sure she could speak without panting, she turned back to him. He was a young, black man, probably no more than twenty. And now that she was inside rather than clinging to the outside of the train, she could see that he was scared.

"There's a fugitive on the train," she informed him. "He's one car up. I need you to contact the conductor and get him to stop the train. Are you able to do that?"

"Yes, ma'am," he told her, nodding.

"Good," she said. "Reach out to him now and explain the situation. But I don't want him to actually stop until I give the go-ahead. When the train begins to stop, the fugitive will know something's up. I need to be right next to him so that I can apprehend him before he reacts. Got it?"

"I think so," he said nervously.

"What's your name?" she asked.

"Ellis."

"It's going to be okay, Ellis. I've been in situations like this before," she lied. "Now tell me, is there any law enforcement personnel on the train?"

"We have a security guard for passengers who get extra rowdy," Ellis said. "He has pepper spray and a taser, but no gun."

"In that case, I want him waiting in the car one ahead of the fugitive. He shouldn't enter the car until I've subdued him, okay?"

"Yes, ma'am," Ellis said. "Are you sure you can handle this on your own?"

"Don't worry about me," she said with a reassuring smile. "Just call your boss."

Ellis turned on his radio and did as she asked, conveying all her instructions clearly and concisely. While he did that, she texted Karen to let her know the plan. Once they were both done, they approached the door to the car where Sawyer had entered. Jessie couldn't see him through the door's window from her angle and didn't want to be too aggressive about peering around. She'd just have to hope he'd settled in somewhere near where he'd boarded.

"Okay Ellis, this is it," she said, smiling down at the kid, who was half a head shorter than her. "The fugitive is a tall, white guy in a flannel shirt with shaggy blond hair. When I find him, I'll turn to face you and tug at my left ear. That's your cue to have the train stopped. Once that happens, I'll make my move. When you see me do that, instruct the security guard to enter the car and assist me if needed. That all clear?"

"Yes, ma'am."

"You've got this, Ellis. Just stay calm and do what I said and this will turn out fine. Here I go."

She turned around and, once she was sure Ellis couldn't see her, unsnapped the cover on her gun holster. Then, after readjusting her jacket so the weapon wasn't visible, she opened the door to the train car where Josh Sawyer, fugitive from justice and potential murderer, waited.

She picked him out immediately. He was standing near the door that he'd scurried through at the last minute, with his back to her. His hands were shoved deep in his jeans pockets. He kept his head down but every few seconds, he glanced at the door at the front of the car and then back, near where she'd entered.

Jessie moved away from the door to avoid his line of sight and to get closer to him. She pulled out her phone and pretended to study it as she eased closer to him. When she got within four feet, she put her phone back in her pocket and turned back around to face Ellis. She was about to tug at her ear when she saw that he wasn't looking back at her. He was staring behind her with an expression of horror on his face.

She glanced over her shoulder and instantly understood why. Despite her instructions, the train's security guard had entered the car and was walking forcefully in their direction. Peeking at Sawyer, she saw that he, too, had noticed the guard's aggressive approach. With a mix of frustration and alarm, she looked back at Ellis and vigorously tugged her ear.

Then she turned to Sawyer, whose hands were no longer in his pockets. He was tightly clutching an overhead handrail with one of them. The other was reaching behind him for something in his waistband. She couldn't tell what it was because of his untucked shirt.

Just then, there was a loud screech as the train came to a sudden, unexpected slowdown. Sawyer glanced up as if something above him might explain what was going on. Jessie decided she couldn't wait any longer.

Taking one big step toward Sawyer with her left leg, she followed that by slamming her right knee into the back of his right leg. He immediately dropped to his knees, grunting heavily. As he turned his head back to the right to determine the source of his distress, she cupped the right side of his head with her open right palm and smashed it into the metal pole to his left. The force made a clanging noise that echoed throughout the car. The sound mixed with the screams of a woman seated across from them.

Sawyer, seemingly stunned, stayed upright for a moment, before slumping forward slightly. Jessie helped him the rest of the way, kicking him in the back and sending him sprawling onto his stomach. A moment later she was on top of him, her knee in his back, pinning him to the ground as she grabbed his right arm and yanked it behind him.

"Oww!" he howled.

Ignoring him, she yanked out her cuffs, attached them to his right wrist, and then pulled up his left to meet it. After that, she pulled up his shirt to see what he'd been reaching for in his waistband. It was a baseball cap, perhaps intended to disguise himself from the guard.

"Josh Sawyer," she said loudly, as the train finally came to a complete stop. "I think you know why I'm cuffing you. I recommend you stay down and stay quiet unless you want to feel even worse tomorrow."

As she wasn't technically a police officer, she didn't want to formally read the guy his Miranda rights. But she also didn't want him blurting out anything that could compromise a case against him.

She looked up to find both the security guard and Ellis staring at her with open mouths. It took everything she had not to ream out the guard, who had put her entire plan at risk. Instead, she focused on Ellis, who had done everything she'd asked of him.

"Great job, Ellis," she said. "Who do I talk to about getting you a raise?"

CHAPTER TWELVE

Jessie watched Sawyer sit in the interrogation room, shifting uncomfortably in his metal chair. They'd decided to let him stew for a while.

Karen had read him his rights on the drive back to the station but neither of them asked him any substantive questions at the time. They agreed that it was better to question him in the seclusion of an interrogation room, without the potential of prying ears who might report back to the Eleventh Realm.

In fact, they'd asked Detective Jim Nettles to stay in the observation room and keep the door locked. Neither had any concerns about Nettles's loyalties. Over the years as a patrol officer, he'd been offered bribes and been threatened by both the Russian mob and local street gangs. He'd never taken a dime or given an inch. He wasn't about to be intimidated by a cult that shamed people into starving themselves.

They left the observation room and joined Sawyer in the interrogation room, where he now looked even edgier than he had moments earlier. That could work to their advantage.

"You know why you're here, right?" Karen asked, leaping in without preamble.

"I can guess," he said. His words were tough but he looked genuinely terrified.

"Why don't you do that?" Karen suggested.

"Listen, I'm sorry," he insisted. "I know I was supposed to leave her alone. But I was in love. I promise I'll never go near her again. You don't have to do this. Just tell them that I won't be any trouble from now on."

Jessie and Karen exchanged a confused look.

"Tell who?" Jessie asked.

Now it was Sawyer who looked confused.

"Do I really have to say?" he pleaded.

"I'm afraid so," Karen told him.

"Tell cop," he whispered.

"What?" Jessie asked. "Which cop?"

Before she could ask anything else, Karen grabbed her forearm. From the expression on her face, it was clear that she'd had some kind of insight.

"Wait a second," the detective said slowly, "do you mean COHP, as in the Council of Harmony and Potential?"

Sawyer looked at her like she was testing him.

"Of course," he said. "Please just tell them that I won't be a problem anymore. I was already leaving town. You don't have to rough me up anymore."

Now Jessie got it too.

"Mr. Sawyer," she asked. "Do you think we work for the Eleventh Realm?"

"Don't you?"

"No." she said.

"I don't understand," he said. "Then why did you come after me like that on the train? Why do you care if I was going to see Sonny?"

He seemed lost and a little bewildered. Karen looked over at Jessie in disbelief. Jessie shrugged, equally flummoxed. She couldn't tell if this was legit or a put-on. If it was the latter, he was very convincing.

"Because Addison Rutherford was murdered last night, Mr. Sawyer," Karen said flatly, "and you are our prime suspect."

Josh Sawyer's eyes opened so wide that Jessie feared they might pop out of his skull.

"Sonny's dead?"

His wide eyes welled up with tears. He looked like was about to say something else but no words came out.

"Do you really expect us to believe you didn't kill her?" Karen asked, unimpressed with his display.

"Of course I didn't," he insisted. "I loved her."

"Why were you at her hotel suite, Mr. Sawyer?" Jessie asked, hoping that getting into more granular detail might lead them somewhere more productive. She still couldn't get a handle on whether this was all part of some elaborate ruse.

He took a few deeps breaths to collect himself before responding.

"She broke up with me on Wednesday, but didn't give me any explanation as to why. I went to her place but she was gone. There were people from the Realm waiting as I left—DRA guys—and they warned me to leave Sonny alone. They said that our relationship was no longer sanctioned by COHP."

"So you're an active member, excuse me, an Adherent, of the Eleventh Realm?" Jessie confirmed.

He didn't answer for a second, seemingly lost in the painful memory. After a moment he blinked and looked at her, registering her question for the first time.

"For three years now," he said. "I was part of the StarAll until recently."

"The StarAll?" Jessie asked.

"The Star Alliance," Karen explained. "It's the name for up and comers in the Realm, the best and the brightest. Often they're people with emerging public profiles: actors, singers, models—that type of thing."

"Right," Sawyer said. "For a while, I was at the top of the Alliance. Sonny and I were royalty. My band was doing well. She had the modeling and influencing. But in the last year, the band has stalled out while her career took off. She just got a major role in the new Toby Draper movie. It was going to be announced in the trades on Monday."

"None of this explains why you were at her hotel," Jessie reminded him.

Her comment seemed to anger him

"It does," he said hotly. "Even though the DRA goons told me not to, I kept calling. Sonny finally got back to me and said she was staying at the Buckingham to get away from all the chaos for a few days. She agreed to meet with me for 'closure.'"

"What happened then?" Karen asked.

He was quiet for a moment, as if overwhelmed by the recollection of the night before. He seemed to be toggling between fury and grief.

"We met in her suite," he finally answered, wincing as he spoke. "I begged her to get back together with me. She refused. She said she'd been told personally by Sterling Shepherd that our relationship was no longer in the service of the Realm; that she was to be paired with a better, more 'favorable' match. She told me that she had no choice but to comply, that is, if she wanted to elevate to the next Realm."

Jessie looked over at Karen, confused. The detective explained.

"Theoretically, the whole goal of the Eleventh Realm is literally in the name: to 'elevate' through a series of realms by meeting amorphous requirements determined by Sterling Shepherd and COHP, ultimately getting to that final 'Eleventh Realm,' where full self-actualized potential is achieved."

Sawyer looked at Karen quizzically.

"You seem to know a lot about this stuff," he noted.

"I've dealt with many cases involving your friends," she said quickly before moving on. "You must have been upset when Addison told you that you no longer fit into her plans for elevation."

"Of course I was upset," he admitted, heated again. "But I could tell there was no point arguing. When Sonny commits to a decision, she can't be moved...couldn't be moved. So I left. But as I was heading out, I noticed some more DRA heavies waiting for me in the lobby. They cornered me on the street and said that if I ever talked to Sonny again, if I ever even tried to approach her, it would end badly for me."

"Did they say how?" Karen asked excitedly. Jessie sensed that this might be the first time an Adherent had ever mentioned an explicit threat to their safety directly to her.

Sawyer again delayed in responding. His eyes were wistful, as if he was recalling a better time.

"Did they say how?" Karen repeated, snapping him out of his reverie.

"No," he said. "They weren't specific. But I've heard enough over the years about what they're capable of to know they were serious. So I went home. But one of their guys kept tailing me. He wasn't even trying to hide it. I texted Sonny and begged her to call them off but when she texted back, she acted like she didn't know what I was talking about. I gave up on her after that."

"So why were you on that train?" Jessie wanted to know.

"I woke up today and saw that there were still DRA guys outside my place, not just one, but multiple. That was the last straw for me. I knew something was going to happen, that I'd become more trouble to them than I was worth. So I packed a bag as fast as I could and booked a train to San Diego. I have a cousin who agreed to take me across the border to Mexico. I was going to lie low in Rosarito, hoping they'd leave me be. I seriously worried they wanted to disappear me. That's who I was running from--not the police—the Eleventh Realm."

Jessie looked over at Karen. She was no expert on the minutiae of this group's practices but based on what she'd heard, Sawyer's explanation, and just as important, his body language and comportment, were persuasive. But from her partner's expression, it was clear she was less convinced.

"That all sounds great," Karen said. "But how do we know this isn't all part of an elaborate story they told you to feed us or that you're not using them as an excuse to cover up for what you did."

Sawyer slunk in his seat, seemingly defeated. But almost as fast, he perked up.

"If you give me my phone, I can prove that Sonny was alive after I left her suite."

Jessie handed it over and watched as he pulled up a text thread with Addison.

"Remember how I said I asked her to call off the goons? I was long gone from the hotel, in my apartment, when I sent it and she responded. Look."

They stared at the screen and the exchange in question. It was simple and to the point: At 10:54 p.m., Sawyer texted *Please call them off.* Three minutes later, at 10:57, Addison replied *What do you mean?*

Jessie took back the phone.

"Give us a minute," she said to Sawyer and motioned Karen to join her outside.

Once they were in the hallway, she gave her partner a hard stare.

"This isn't going great," she said resignedly. "We'll need to confirm the text exchange when we get Addison Rutherford's phone data from Jamil, but based on what we have, it's not looking like he's our guy."

"I'm not ready to rule him out yet," Karen countered. "We don't know that she was alive to send that text. The killer could have sent it from her suite. Hell, Sawyer could have snuck back into the hotel, killed her, sent himself the text, and then replied to it in order to give himself the exact alibi he just provided to us."

Jessie nodded.

"All of that is possible," she agreed. "I've definitely seen more intricate schemes. I certainly wouldn't rule it out and we should pursue it. But there are other factors to consider. I know this isn't proof of anything, but the guy looked genuinely scared to me. I believe that he really thought we were on the take for the Eleventh Realm and that we were going to find some excuse to shoot him and claim it was self-defense."

Karen sighed.

"I hate to say it, but so do I. I've seen Adherents who are truly terrified of what the Realm will do to them. I've seen the look of fear in their eyes. And he had it."

"So where does that leave us?" Jessie asked.

Before Karen could reply, they both got a buzz on their phones. It was a text from Jamil, which read: *Got a fingerprint match from the hotel suite. Confirmed identity with video footage from last night. Subject is Logan Bauer.*

Jessie looked up from her phone to find that Karen had the same slack-jawed expression she knew was on her own face. One wouldn't know it from Jamil's matter-of-fact text, but apparently one of the people in Addison's suite last night was a man who didn't need to be described by anything other than his name.

That's because he was one of the biggest movie stars in the world.

CHAPTER THIRTEEN

Ryan was tempted to just storm in and take over.

Of course, as he sat outside the lecture hall at Southwestern Law School, he knew that would be completely counter-productive. Professor Nina Washburn, Kaylee McNulty's student adviser, was almost done with her Constitutional Criminal Procedure class anyway. Going in and ordering all the students to leave so that he and Valentine could interview Washburn immediately wouldn't advance the investigation appreciably and would probably alienate the person whose help they needed.

So he sat on the hard, wooden bench in the hallway, waiting for the class to end. Susannah Valentine seemed far less bothered by the wait. She was reviewing the crime scene photos, which Ryan had seen enough of for the time being.

"The coroner says that based on the depth and width of the cuts, the murder weapon was almost certainly a machete or something similar," she told him.

"At least that kind of knife will be harder to hide if we actually come across the killer," Ryan muttered, hunched over with his elbows on his knees and his chin in his hands.

"Hey, don't get down, Ryan," she said comfortingly. "I know cases like this don't have a great closure rate, but maybe it wasn't just some unstable homeless person who walked in off the street. It could have been a jealous fellow student or a vengeful ex. There's still hope."

"You're right," he said. "It's just depressing when someone so young, someone who was trying to make difference, is cut down like that. I'll get past it. But strangely, sometimes I prefer to solve the murders of less admirable people."

Just then, the doors opened and students began to stream out. They chatted amiably, oblivious to the fact that one of their own had been butchered only hours earlier. Ryan and Valentine stood up and waited for a lull long enough to sneak into the room. When they stepped inside, they saw Professor Washburn at the lectern, talking to an excitable young man with curly red hair and thick glasses.

They waited patiently off to the side until she'd answered his questions. She seemed to sense their presence, though she never broke eye contact with the kid. Her posture shifted, as if trying to create a zone of privacy for their conversation. That was made easier by the fact that Nina Washburn's voice was so quiet as to be almost inaudible from where they stood, fifteen feet away. But her hushed tone didn't diminish her authority at all.

In fact, though her build was slight—Ryan doubted she was more than five foot three and 110 pounds—she carried herself with cool confidence. Her skin was the kind of pale that suggested she rarely went outside and her dark hair was cut short, just below her ears. She wore black slacks, black flats, a navy top, and a black sport jacket. Had she needed to go to court right now, she wouldn't have had to change a thing. He guessed that she was in her late thirties, though he could be off by five years in either direction. She projected the aura of a woman not to be trifled with.

Once the student left, she began to pack up her briefcase without looking up. Before either Ryan or Valentine could speak or approach her, she beat them to it.

"What can I do for you, detectives?" she asked mildly.

"How did you know we were detectives?" Valentine asked as they walked over.

Washburn looked up and nodded in Ryan's direction.

"I recognize your partner from his many exploits," she said, "although I'm used to seeing him with a different brunette."

"Nice to meet you, Professor Washburn," Ryan said, extending his hand. "I'm Ryan Hernandez. Jessie Hunt is working another case today. This is Detective Susannah Valentine."

"I'd like to say it's nice to meet you too," Washburn said, snapping her briefcase shut instead of shaking his hand, "but it seems that when you visit people, Detective Hernandez, it's almost certainly because something horrific has happened to someone they know. So you'll have to forgive me if my reaction is a bit muted."

"I'm afraid that your instinct is correct, Professor," Ryan admitted.

"In that case, do you mind if we walk to my office while you fill me in? I have a call with a *pro bono* client in ten minutes and I'd like the opportunity to recover from whatever you tell me before I have to focus on him."

"Of course, "Ryan said. "Please lead the way."

She started out the door and headed down the hall at a clip that required both detectives to hustle to keep up.

"Go ahead," she said. "No point in delaying the inevitable."

Ryan glanced at Valentine, who had been mostly quiet up until now, and indicated that she should break the news. She gulped hard and started in.

"Professor, we understand that you're Kaylee McNulty's faculty adviser. Is that correct?"

Nina Washburn stopped suddenly and turned to Valentine. She fixed her unblinking blue eyes on the young woman.

"What happened to her?"

Valentine squirmed slightly, but to her credit, she didn't avoid the question.

"She was killed this morning—murdered."

Washburn looked over at Ryan, as if for confirmation. He nodded that it was true. She inhaled sharply, allowed herself the smallest of coughs, and then resumed walking.

"What exactly happened please, if you're able to share that?" she asked, her pace now even faster than before.

Ryan decided to take this one.

"She was hacked to death with a large knife in a shower stall at the downtown YWCA, where she had been regularly volunteering. That's why we're here, Professor. There's no useful video onsite. We don't anticipate much success with fingerprints or DNA in a busy locker room setting. And, as I'm sure you know, the facility is within blocks of Skid Row and multiple homeless shelters. It's very likely that someone walked in unnoticed, committed the crime, and left, leaving no discernible trace. But it's also possible that there was a more personal motive. That's where we were hoping you could be of assistance."

They had reached Washburn's office. She unlocked the door, turned on the light, and waved them in without responding. She sat down at her desk and booted up her computer. For a moment, Ryan wondered whether she was going to kick them out. Then she looked up.

"You're correct," she said, her strained voice hinting at the emotion underneath. "I was Kaylee's faculty adviser. I knew her quite well. She came to me last fall for counsel on how to develop a program to help homeless women get restraining orders against violent partners. We'd been working on it together for five months. She planned to submit it to the city council in the spring. I'm quite sure it would have gotten funding. I was well aware of her legal volunteer work at the YWCA. Just so you know, she also coached a Girls' Club youth basketball team at the Lafayette Recreation Center."

"When did she have time to study?" Valentine marveled.

"I often wondered that myself," Washburn said. "And yet, somehow she did. Not only did she get by, she was in the top three in her class, along with Saul Pryce, the young man you saw me talking to after class just now and another student, Trudy Echolls. Of course, neither of those two do much volunteering as far as I know, much less at three different places."

"She sounds amazing," Ryan said softly.

Washburn smiled at them for the first time.

"She was, Detective Hernandez," she said softly. "Kaylee was quite an extraordinary young woman. On more than one occasion, I pleaded with her to be a little more cautious and not open her heart to every wayward soul she came across. Not everyone was deserving of her kindness. Her death is an incredible loss. The ripples of her absence are incalculable. So many people whose lives would otherwise be better because of her will suffer because she's no longer with us."

Ryan was quiet for a moment. He wanted to give Kaylee's passing its due respect but he also needed answers.

"I'm very sorry," he finally said. "That's why we need to ask you, is there anyone in the campus community you think might have wanted to do her harm? A student she had a falling out with? An ex-boyfriend or girlfriend who threatened her? Someone she worked with who felt wronged or became fixated on her? Anything you can provide would be more than we know right now."

Washburn sighed deeply.

"I'm afraid not," she said. "She mentioned that some of the people she helped had mental struggles, but she was never specific. As to my students' personal lives, I didn't really involve myself in them unless it somehow pertained to their work. And as much as it pains me to say this, I have to cut this interview short. My call is about to start and my client gets a finite amount of time to discuss his case each day. Unfortunately, he's on death row and we only have three weeks until his execution. So I need to focus my attention on someone I can actually help right now. Please don't take offense."

"Of course," Ryan said, putting his card on her desk, "we understand. But if anything does come to mind, no matter how small, please don't hesitate to call."

Professor Washburn nodded and picked up the phone. Ryan opened the door for Valentine and she was just stepping through it when Washburn called after them.

"There is one thing," she said. "It's probably nothing and I hesitate to even mention it because I worry your reaction will be outsized, but under the circumstances I probably should."

"Please," Ryan said.

"I mentioned that one of the students she's in competition with for the top spot in the class is a girl named Trudy Echolls. I know that the two of them used to be close friends. They were even roommates for a while. But something happened. There was some kind of falling out."

"Do you know what it was about?" Valentine asked.

"I don't," she said. "I'm only aware of it at all because Kaylee mentioned having to find a new place to stay and then I saw that they no longer sat next to each other in class. Like I said, it seems too small to be connected to something like this. But they were both pursuing that top spot, and sometimes that can get nasty, so it might be worth looking into."

"Thank you, Professor," Ryan said. "I assure you, we absolutely will."

They weren't even down the hall before he was on the phone with the Registrar's office to get the contact information for Trudy Echolls. It wasn't much to go on. But it was more than they had two minutes ago.

CHAPTER FOURTEEN

Jessie had to finish the call quick.

They were headed up to Logan Bauer's home in the Hollywood Hills, where cell reception was notoriously bad, and their connection to Jamil could cut out at any moment. But before it did, they needed to make sure they had the most up-to-date information.

"There's nothing new since I updated you last," he told them. "We pulled clean prints from a glass on the table in her suite. They were Bauer's. I found street surveillance footage of him getting out of his car, parked a block from the hotel, at 10:06 p.m, which is within the time of death window. He was wearing blue jeans and a cap."

"But there's still no actual footage of him in the hotel?" Jessie reconfirmed.

"Nothing so far," he conceded, "but I'm still looking. And of course, if he went up to her suite during the time the cameras were out, we wouldn't find anything."

"Anything else for us before we lose you in the hills?" Karen asked.

"Just the obvious," Jamil said. "I'm sure you two are already well aware, but I've combed through Addison Rutherford's social media. She's a big Eleventh Realmer and of course, there's no more high-profile member of that...organization than Logan Bauer."

"We are aware," Karen said. "And we're looking into it. Just be careful not to share what you've learned about that with others in the department, Jamil. You never know who's a supporter of those folks and how they might react."

There was no response.

"Jamil?" Karen said.

"I think we lost the connection," Jessie told her. "That is, unless you think the Council of Harmony and Potential somehow got to him."

"You jest," Karen said, as she navigated a tight hairpin turn near the top of the hill where Bauer lived. "But against these people, sometimes paranoia is the most effective weapon."

"Noted," Jessie replied. "In the meantime, do you want to give me the non-tabloid data download on this guy so I know what I'm dealing with when we talk to him?"

"Sure," Karen said. "Logan Bauer was already a big star before he joined the Realm. But about fifteen years ago, he crashed his car into a house and got a DUI. He had to go to a treatment program to avoid jail time. An actor he'd worked with a few times when he was younger ran a very posh and secretive rehab center that was supposed to cater to celebrities. It was called Detoxibrate."

"I'm sorry, what?"

"It's a combination of 'detoxify' and 'celebrate,'" Karen explained.

"No, I get it," Jessie said. "I just can't believe that someone would put their faith in a program with that name."

"Well, if that throws you, guess who ran the program?" Karen asked as she reached a straight stretch of road that suggested they were finally near the top of the hill and Bauer's house. As they passed a "private property-no trespassing" sign, the road abruptly changed from asphalt to an expensive-looking cobblestone.

"I'm afraid to ask."

"Derek Burke," she replied, "my old boyfriend, the one who first got me involved in the Realm in the first place."

"So he moved up?"

"That's an understatement. He ran Detoxibrate fifteen years ago. Now he's right up there at the top, part of Shepherd's inner circle."

"Wait," Jessie joked, "is he part of the COHP cabal you keep talking about?"

"Actually," Karen said as she pulled up to the large metal gate that surrounded the estate beyond, "he is."

An armed guard stepped out of a small cottage just inside the gate and approached them. Both Jessie and Karen got out.

"I'm sorry ladies," the guard, who looked like a former pro football linebacker, said politely, "but this is private property, starting where the asphalt road ended about two hundred yards back. Maybe you missed the sign."

"Thanks," Jessie said with equal courteousness, hoping to maneuver past any hostility Karen might harbor. "But I'm afraid we're on official business. This is Detective Karen Bray with the LAPD and I'm Jessie Hunt, a profiling consultant for the department. We need to speak to Mr. Bauer about a pressing matter."

They both held up their IDs. The guard looked at them with mild skepticism but seemed hesitant to say anything.

"Can you tell me what this is regarding?" he asked carefully.

"I'm afraid not," Karen said, "Other than to say that Mr. Bauer's assistance is essential to an ongoing investigation. I'm sure you understand that we want to respect his privacy as much as possible."

"Hold on please," the guard said, disappearing into the cottage.

"Is this going to work?" Jessie asked quietly out of the corner of her mouth, "or are we going to have to come back with the cavalry?"

"It'll work," Karen assured her. "One thing about famous Realmers—they have a God complex. They think that each time they pass into a new Realm, they achieve greater wisdom, strength, and an almost supernatural ability to heal the world. If Bauer is innocent and thinks that we need his help to solve a case, there's no way he can leave the bait on that hook. And if he's guilty, he'll want to throw us off the scent with his air of altruistic charm. Either way, we're getting in."

As if to prove Karen right, the guard came out a moment later.

"Please proceed down the path to the house. Mr. Bauer will meet you at the front entrance."

They got back into the car and drove slowly down the path. Jessie turned to Karen.

"You never finished telling me how Bauer went from drunk driver to Eleventh Realm true believer," she reminded her.

"Right," Karen said. "So he signed up for Detoxibrate and embraced the program. It used all the same techniques as the Realm writ large. They could employ lots of the food and sleep deprivation techniques without having to couch them in the language of 'unlocking potential.' For these people, it was a matter of survival. Do as we say or you will very likely die. So folks in the program would willingly eschew meals and sleep. They would engage in hours-long therapy sessions that were really just Truth Sessions in sheep's clothing. But because the alternative to committing to Detoxibrate was going to jail or possibly relapsing, there was a built-in urgency. Some of the most devoted Realmers come through the program."

They crested a rise and Bauer's house came into view. At first glance, it wasn't as grandiose as Jessie would have guessed. It wasn't some Tudor style mansion or a wannabe castle with different wings and servants' quarters off to the side. Instead it was a modern-looking place with a muted, wood exterior that blended into the hill it was built into.

Only when they got closer did she realize that the subdued color palette acted as camouflage, hiding the fact that the home, concealed by the trees of the hill it was connected to, was actually four stories high. At the very top, she could see a glassed-in pool that appeared to be partly on the roof of the fourth floor of the house and partly carved out of the very top of the hill.

"Looks like it eventually worked out for him," she said quietly.

"Yep," Karen agreed as they approached the circular driveway, "he was as zealous about his rehab as he is with his roles. When he got out, he talked constantly about how Detoxibrate, and more generally the Eleventh Realm, had changed his life. He said he'd been on a bad path: drinking, drugs, womanizing. But with the Realm's help, he'd turned it all around."

She pulled off to the side and parked the car.

"He said Sterling Shepherd saved his life," she continued as they got out of the car and walked up to the front door. "Now they're best friends. In the years since, Bauer's career has exploded even more. He credits the Realm for all of it."

Karen rang the doorbell.

"You're not going to punch him or anything, are you?" Jessie wanted to know.

"Why?" Karen replied, "Just because the man on the other side of that door is the most vocal proponent in the entire world for a cult that nearly destroyed my life?"

Before Jessie could reply, the door opened.

CHAPTER FIFTEEN

For the first time since she'd started doing profiler work for the LAPD, Jessie was genuinely star struck.

She'd handled multiple cases involving celebrities since joining HSS, but this was different. The man standing in front of her had been a movie star since she was old enough to watch films. For most of that time, she'd been unaware of his connection to the Eleventh Realm, but she couldn't remember a time when he wasn't a part of the pop culture firmament.

"Hello ladies," he said, opening the door as wide as the smile on his face. "I understand that you could use my assistance. What can I do for you?"

Logan Bauer was even more rakishly handsome in person than onscreen. She already knew from Jamil's quick biographical sketch that he was fifty years old. But he looked closer to forty, with a chiseled jaw, dotted with a day's worth of stubble, soulful brown eyes, and closely shorn salt and pepper hair, the only obvious concession to his age.

He looked to be about the same height as Jessie at five foot ten and, at around 175 pounds, he was trim but firm. He wore a loose, olive, button-up shirt with a wide collar and black slacks. Other than the tattered sandals on his feet, he looked ready for a press junket right now.

"May we come in, Mr. Bauer?" Karen asked, rescuing Jessie. "We have a few questions of a sensitive nature."

"Of course," he said, waving them in. "Let's go to my outdoor office. It's very secluded so we can speak candidly. Will that work?"

"That sounds fine, Mr. Bauer," Karen said.

"Please, call me Logan," he said, leading them down a long hallway filled with stills from his films on the walls, but notably none including him. "May I ask who you are?"

"I'm sorry," Karen said. "My name's Karen Bray. I'm a detective with LAPD's HSS unit. We specialize in high-profile cases that tend to draw media attention. This is my colleague, Jessie Hunt. She's a criminal profi—."

"I'm familiar with Ms. Hunt," Bauer interrupted. "I actually have a production deal set up at Sovereign Studios. Ms. Hunt, I think you'll recall that last fall, the producer Miller Boatwright pitched you about a project involving your life story."

"I do," Jessie said, finally able to find her words.

"Well, what you probably didn't know was that Miller pitched you that concept at my request. I wanted my involvement kept private unless something materialized. I was very impressed with everything you've accomplished, especially in light of your tragic childhood. That has only increased recently in light of your capture and killing of the Night Hunter."

"Thank you," Jessie said as they arrived at an elevator at the end of the hallway. Bauer pushed a button and the door opened. They all entered and it shot up with surprising speed.

Jessie pretended to be thrown by the fast-moving rectangular box. It afforded her a brief moment to process her conflicting feelings. First, there was awe that such a famous actor knew who she was and wanted to make a movie about her. That was quickly followed by a surge of shame that she was awed at all, and not just because Bauer was a murder suspect.

After all, just like Miller Boatwright, Logan Bauer wanted to take the most horrible events of her life and turn them into entertainment. It seemed that her fame, or more accurately her infamy, came either from public knowledge of the traumas she'd suffered or from her capture of killers who had inflicted trauma on others. Either way, it was the suffering that seemed to interest people.

"I realize it may be inappropriate," he said, oblivious to the fast-accelerating elevator, "considering that you're obviously here for a much more serious purpose than movie talk, but I still harbor some hope that you might reconsider letting me develop your story."

Between the fast-moving elevator she feared might shoot out of the shaft into the sky above and Bauer's near-blinding white teeth, she was having trouble concentrating, but did her best to compose herself.

"I'm flattered," she said, "but I think it would be best to stick to the purpose of our visit for now."

"Fair enough," he said, with an only slightly less enthusiastic smile than before. The elevator came to an abrupt stop and the doors shot open. Light poured in, along with a dose of chilly air. "We're here."

Bauer held the door as they stepped out onto what Jessie realized was the rooftop that she noticed before. Her earlier conclusion had been correct. Most of the roof was comprised of a glassed-in pool that had been partly carved into the top of the hill the house adjoined. It was both gorgeous and appalling.

It was one thing to build his home naturally into the undulations of the hill. But he'd basically shaved off the top of the rise for his personal entertainment. Something about the sight of it cleared her head. The schoolgirl giddiness that had been clouding her judgment faded away.

"We'll have privacy up here," Bauer said, motioning to several outdoor couches surrounded by the billowing curtains of a large cabana. "Can I offer either of you a drink?"

"I'm good, thanks," Jessie said sharply, marching over and taking a seat at the edge of one sofa.

She saw Karen's head perk up and knew her partner had picked up on the change in her manner. She too declined a drink and moved quickly to take a seat. She gave Jessie a quick half smile that seemed to say "let's do this." Jessie nodded.

"Do you know why we're here, Mr. Bauer?" she asked when he sat down across from them.

He opened the seltzer water than he'd taken from the small fridge in the cabana, and took a sip before answering.

"I'm assuming it's related to Addison Rutherford's murder," he said calmly, though his voice betrayed just a hint of emotion.

Jessie had to work hard to hide her surprise.

"How do you know about that?" she asked.

He smiled gently, almost apologetically.

"I'm very well sourced in this town, Ms. Hunt." He looked like he wanted to say more, but didn't.

"Mr. Bauer," Karen jumped in, "you do realize that knowing about her murder, which has not yet been made public, casts you in a suspicious light, and that not revealing how you're aware of it only increases that suspicion."

"I do realize that," he said, unflustered. "I also realize that I'm probably under even more suspicion because I was there in her suite that night, apparently not long before she died. I'm assuming that's what brought you to my door."

Again, Jessie had to fight to keep her shock at his admission from showing.

"What makes you think we know about your visit?" she asked.

"Well, the very fact that you're here, Ms. Hunt," he said plainly. "I assume I showed up in some hotel video or something and you had to do your due diligence. Is that not right?"

74

"No, actually," Jessie said, leaning in. "Oddly enough, the video from the time you visited seems to be missing. But we did get your fingerprints from a glass in her suite."

"Ah yes, I was parched," he said. "Sonny was sweet enough to get me some water."

"Care to tell us why you were there?" Karen pressed.

Bauer leaned back against the plush sofa pillow. For the first time since Jessie had met him, the man looked slightly ill at ease.

"That's a difficult question to answer," he said slowly. "Under normal circumstances, I would simply decline to do so and leave it at that. But the situation is complicated. You have a dead girl on your hands. And while my presence there has nothing to do with that, it's hard to explain it without compromising certain closely held secrets. I don't want to deceive or mislead you, but I also don't want to betray the confidence of people who've put their faith in me."

"Mr. Bauer," Jessie said, staring into those eyes, ones that she'd seen five feet high on countless movie screens in the past. "I'm trying to give you the benefit of the doubt here. But if you didn't do this and you have information that can help our investigation *and* you hold it back because of some misplaced loyalty, that is going to reflect incredibly poorly on you. And frankly, it will probably come out in the end anyway."

He still seemed unsure. Now Karen leaned in.

"You said we had privacy up here," she said quietly. "Tell us what you know. It's only a violation of their trust if they know you've said anything and we have no intention of telling them."

He cocked his head slightly to the right.

"Who would you even tell, Detective?" he wondered.

"You know who, Logan," she said softly. "Let's not pretend. There's no Proctor up here."

Bauer's eyes widened briefly before he regained control.

"All right," he said. "I'm telling you this in confidence. I went to Sonny's suite to discuss an arrangement. She had just broken up with her long-time boyfriend on…instructions from the leadership of our Assembly. It was determined that he was no longer an amenable match. Her star was on the rise. She'd just booked a big role in a major picture. The decision was made that she and I would become a couple; that together, we would be the faces of the faith. I was there to discuss the particulars of the plan. We needed to come up with our back story: how we met, what we did on our first date, how we fell in love, the little details that sell magazines and generate clicks. We did that. Then I left."

"Didn't you resent being paired up in some arranged marriage?" Jessie asked. "What if you already had a relationship?"

"I don't," he said, "and it was for the greater good, for the benefit of the Realm. Can you imagine how many new Adherents could be brought into the fold, who could unlock their true potential, if they were inspired by our love?"

"A false love," Jessie said.

"That's your interpretation, Ms. Hunt," he said. "I chose to believe that over time, if nurtured, it would grow like a beautiful flower. In any case, now that you know, you must understand why I would have no motive to kill her. From a cold, purely practical perspective, having her by my side would only increase my relevance. And truth be told, as I'm now on the wrong side of fifty, I can use all the help I can get staying relevant. I mourn her loss. But I mourn mine almost as much."

Jessie stared at the man, unsure what to make of him. On the one hand, he'd been open and upfront, answering all their questions, admitting that he was at the hotel and why, even allowing himself to come across as callously narcissistic in the name of total truth. But something didn't sit right.

A guy like this, an actor whose life and career were defined by getting people to like him, would never allow himself to be viewed in such an unflattering light unless it suited his purposes. It was as if he was using the veneer of candor to hide something else he didn't want seen.

Despite that, they couldn't very well arrest him simply because he'd been too honest. Unless there was a legitimate smoking gun, there was no way they could haul one of the biggest stars in the world into a grubby downtown police station for an interrogation. They needed more.

Worse than that, she wasn't sure that there *was* more. While she got the distinct impression that Logan Bauer was keeping something from them, she was less confident that he was their killer. The timing of his presence in the hotel didn't seem quite right, nor did the brazenness with which he acknowledged that he was there. So if he wasn't hiding being a murderer, what was he holding back?

"Thank you for your time, Mr. Bauer," Karen said, jogging her out of her trance. "We'll see ourselves out."

He stood and wished them well as they left the cabana. As the elevator shot down toward the first floor, Jessie turned to her.

"That movie star was giving one hell of a performance," she said, "but I'm not buying it. The problem is that I have no idea what the act was really all about."

They reached the bottom floor and the doors opened. As they stepped out, Karen smiled at her.

"I don't know either, but I have an idea of someone who might. I was going to suggest that we speak with this person earlier before Jamil gave us the Bauer lead."

"Who?" Jessie asked.

"I'll tell you once we're out of this place. But if she's willing to talk to us, I'll warn you that you better strap in. With this one, it's usually a bumpy ride."

*

"How do you know her again?" Jessie asked, once they were safely off the Bauer property.

"I don't," Karen said. "I only know *of* her."

"Then what makes you think she'll even talk to us?"

"Have you ever *seen* Gabrielle DeAngelis?" Karen asked, as she started back down the hill.

"I watched her TV series, *The Princess of Powell Street*, a few times," Jessie said, mildly put off by her partner's tone, "but it wasn't really for me. What does that have to do with it?"

"If you've seen her show, then you've seen her," Karen assured her. "She's basically playing herself. She's no shrinking violet and, as you may have seen in the press lately, she's about to go on the war path."

"Against the Eleventh Realm?" Jessie asked, making sure they were on the same page.

"Right, sorry," Karen said, as she banked hard into a sharp left that made Jessie grimace. "I forgot that you don't obsess over every story about them the way I do. Yes, she left about three months ago. I heard about it through the Disavowed grapevine. She tried to keep it quiet at first, hoping for an amicable divorce that would let her lead her life without being hassled. But of course, the Realm can't let that happen."

"What did they do?" Jessie asked.

"Well, from what I hear, they tried to stop her from taking her child when she left. Plus, they threatened to sue her, claiming they were owed part of her salary from the show. So the word is that she's decided to fight back publicly, that shining a light on them is her best defense. She supposedly just signed a book deal and I was told she has a big magazine interview coming out later this month."

"That all sounds very juicy, Karen," Jessie said as diplomatically as she could, "but I don't see how it helps us with this case."

"It helps because Gabrielle and Logan Bauer were tight," Karen said, "not just 'assigned to hang out by COHP' tight, but actual friends. If there's anyone who knows what he's hiding *and* might be willing to tell us, it's her."

"Maybe, but it sounds like she's got a lot on her plate right now. I'm not convinced that trying to get hold of her is the best use of our time," Jessie countered.

"Why not?"

"Don't take offense," Jessie said as delicately as she could, "but are you sure you don't just want to talk to this woman because it's someone else who can validate your bitterness toward the people who made your life so difficult?"

Without warning. Karen pulled off onto the tiny shoulder of the road and hit the brakes hard. She slammed the car into park and turned to face Jessie.

"I *do* take offense, Jessie," she said with an unexpected intensity. "I may have my issues with these merchants of lies, but I'm also an LAPD detective trying to solve the murder of a twenty-four-year-old girl. Do you have any better ideas for where we should be going right now? I'm all ears."

Jessie hadn't ever seen Karen Bray like this. Normally she was the level-headed one and Jessie rode a wave of passion and instinct.

"I'm sorry," she said quickly. "I didn't mean to suggest you weren't being professional. That wasn't fair."

"Thank you," Karen said.

"And no."

"No what?"

"No," Jessie said, "I don't have any better ideas for where we should be going. So let's go meet Gabrielle DeAngelis."

"Fine," Karen said, still wounded.

"But could I make one request?"

"What's that?" Karen asked.

"I know we want to get there soon, but could you drive a tiny bit slower?" Jessie asked, smiling, "Because I'd really like to make it to the bottom of this canyon in one piece, unless you take offense at that request."

Karen smiled too despite herself.

"Oh, shut up," she said as she put the car back in drive and pulled back onto the road, this time at something close to the speed limit.

CHAPTER SIXTEEN

Even before she met Gabrielle DeAngelis, Jessie knew she was in for an adventure.

When they pulled up to the gates of her Beverly Hills mansion, it took both women a second to process what they were seeing. Apart from the metal gate to the property, which was painted hot pink, everything else was purple. The stone walls surrounding the estate were more of a lilac, while the driveway leading up to the home was closer to eggplant. The actual mansion was more varied—a combination of violet, lavender, and something approaching merlot.

"I'm already a little bit terrified," Jessie muttered under her breath as Karen pushed the com button by the gate.

"May I help you?" a chipper sounding young man asked.

"LAPD here to see Ms. DeAngelis," Karen said.

"Come right in," the man said. "I'll meet you out front."

There was a buzz and the gate opened. As it did, Jessie thought she heard music coming from the com box.

"Is that 'Moon River?'" she asked as they pulled through.

"I think it is," Karen said, before adding. "This might be an unusual interview."

They made the short drive up to the house and parked off to the right, next to an electric Mini Cooper. To Jessie's surprise, it was silver, not purple, which made her suspect it didn't belong to DeAngelis. As they got out, the door opened and a slim, young man stepped out. He was pale, had tight blond ringlets and wore black jeans and an aqua sport jacket over a red t-shirt that read "my abs are down here."

"Welcome to the House of Mama D!" he exclaimed, waving for them to come in without formality.

But before they could take another step, Jessie heard a loud, female, slightly nasal, New Jersey-ish accent that she recognized from *The Princess of Powell Street*.

"Do our guests want libations, Malcolm?" she asked.

A moment later, Gabrielle DeAngelis appeared in the doorway. It took all of Jessie's restraint to keep her jaw off the ground.

First of all, the woman was wearing a negligee. Yes, she had on a thin silk kimono too. But it was untied and looked more like a cape than a cover-up. The negligee, which had a boysenberry shade, was sheer, with what looked like a flower petal print. The kimono was more periwinkle, and it was dotted with doves in flight. She was also wearing four inch heels (purple, of course).

Jessie could almost understand why DeAngelis dressed this way. She had a lot to show off. Very curvy with an ample bosom, she had the dimensions of a 1940s pin-up model. She was also gorgeous in a tough broad kind of way, with long eyelashes, pouty lips, and wavy black hair that cascaded past her shoulders. To Jessie, she looked like a brunette Veronica Lake. Her smile was more of a smirk, like she was in on a joke she wasn't sure she wanted to share with you. She also had a small scar over her right eyebrow, which humanized her and somehow made her even more attractive.

"Would you ladies like drinks?" Malcolm asked, following up on his boss's question.

"I'd love some water," Karen said.

"Me too, thanks," Jessie added.

"Make it so, Malcolm!" DeAngelis barked, before letting her smirk crack wide open into a full smile. "It's an inside joke. Malcolm and I love *Star Trek: The Next Generation*. I'm his Jean-Luc Picard and he's my Number One. Come on in, ladies. I can't wait to hear what this is all about. All that my manager said was that it involved Jessie Hunt, a crime, and a group I was formerly affiliated with. Obviously that was enough to pique my interest."

"Maybe we can discuss it somewhere more private?" Jessie suggested.

"Of course," DeAngelis said. "Follow me."

They stepped inside. As DeAngelis closed the door behind them, Jessie took a moment to sneak a look at the place. As gaudy as the outside was, the inside was even more so. Instead of a chandelier in the foyer, a massive disco ball hung from the ceiling.

As she led them along a short hallway, it was hard to keep track of everything. There was leopard print wallpaper that bordered the outside of a series of different-sized mirrors that ran the entire length of the hallway.

When they entered the living room, they found several stone steps that led to a sunken sitting area with mauve, shag carpeting. All the furniture designed for sitting—from the sofas to the loveseat and chairs—were some shade of purple. The walls were covered in art, some of it seemingly intentionally tacky, other pieces quite nice, and as with everything else, all with at least some hint of purple. The place looked like the setting for the most expensive key party of 1978.

"Quite a home you have here," Jessie said as they settled into spots on the couches. "Did you design it yourself?"

"I wish," DeAngelis said. "This house used to belong to a music executive who was big-time back in the seventies. He made his money in disco. I remember driving by it as a teenager and falling in love right away. In case you couldn't tell, I have a thing for purple. It turns out that he and his wife did too. When I had some career success, I got a realtor to show me some interior photos and I loved it even more. It's so kitschy. So I told Leo—that was the producer—that whenever he was ready to sell the house, I would pay twenty percent over their asking price."

"Wow, that's generous," Karen said.

"He was such a sweetie and he had fallen on hard times a bit. I thought he deserved it. Anyway, we became good friends. He and Marie had me over all the time. When he died, she moved into an assisted living facility and offered me the house. I snapped it up. Admittedly, I modernized some of the back areas. But this section, the part I share with the world, it's like I get to go back in a time machine to when I was four years old. You know, I wanted to be Chaka Khan until I was twelve?"

"Who could blame you?" Jessie said.

"No one could, Jessie Hunt," she said definitively. "Anyway, enough about me and my décor choices—I'm here to help you. I know who you are, Miss Super Profiler Lady. Who's your pal?"

"I'm Karen Bray, Ms. DeAngelis, a detective with LAPD's Homicide Special Section. Ms. Hunt and I are working this case together."

"Okay, first things first," DeAngelis said. "I'm Gabby. I'm hoping we can keep it casual. Is that okay Karen? Jessie?"

"Sure," Karen said.

"Good. Now that that's settled, what's this investigation that my manager couldn't tell me anything specific about? From what Donna said, I gathered it's about my old friends from 'they who must not be named.' Am I right?"

"You are," Karen said. "But before we begin, we need to ask that what we're about to share stay confidential for the time being. Once it gets out, solving the case may become much more challenging."

"My lips are sealed," Gabby said, pretending to lock them and throw away an imaginary key. "Despite all appearances to the contrary, I'm very good at keeping secrets."

"Great," Karen said. Before she could continue, a small creature scurried into the room and hopped on Gabby's lap. It was a small French poodle and it was dyed lavender.

"This is Jiminy," Gabby said, not batting an eye as she stroked his back. "He's my security dog but don't worry, you're safe. He's very well trained. Don't give him a second thought."

She said it with such sincerity that Jessie stifled the urge to laugh. She felt Karen doing the same as she started up again.

"Anyway," she said, "we're investigating the murder of a young woman named Addison Rutherford. Are you familiar with her?"

Gabby sighed. For the first time, her boundless energy seemed to falter. Before responding, she took a sip of the tea that Malcolm must have left on the table for her.

"That's terrible," she said slowly, before seeming to realize she hadn't answered the question. "I knew her a little bit. She came to me for career advice on occasion. She was very ambitious, wanted to get into acting, learn everything she could. I can't say that we were close."

"Why was that?" Jessie asked.

"How can I put this tactfully?" she mused, "Especially when tact isn't really my strong suit. Let's just say that she was extremely committed to the cause of the Eleventh Realm; I'd even say devout. And she came to me right as I was questioning my part in the Realm. She was always wondering how she could use her growing fame to advance the cause. And I was looking for a way out. We weren't exactly simpatico. And while the news of her death is shocking, it's not surprising to learn that there's a murder investigation involving the Realm. They are hardcore, apparently even more than I knew."

"We understand that the Realm has made things difficult for you after you left," Jessie said.

"Before, during, after," Gabby said hotly. "The whole thing has been a nightmare. From the second I first started questioning Shep's FIC, they started giving me a hard time."

"FIC?" Jessie asked.

"Flawless Interpretation of the Creed," Karen explained. "It's the belief that only Sterling Shepherd is equipped to fully understand and interpret the tenets of the TEROTH creed and share how Adherents can elevate to succeeding realms."

Gabby stared at Karen for several seconds before responding.

"Can I safely assume that you're among the Disavowed?" she asked.

"For two decades now," Karen confirmed. "I was there in the early days; I was lucky to get out."

"Then you understand," Gabby said. "The minute I started asking questions, they had me going to daily TSs with high-level TCs. Suddenly I had a Proctor wherever I went. But none of that stopped me from pursuing answers. When I finally decided to leave, they tried to get custody of my daughter, Iris. My husband died five years ago. They had no claim on her. It was purely a power play. But that didn't stop them. Then they...you know what, this could degenerate fast. Let's stick to your case. Maybe we can discuss my personal hell another time."

"Okay," Jessie said, glad the actress had offered an escape route so she didn't have to force one upon her, "here's where we think you can help. I understand that you're close friends with Logan Bauer. Is that correct?"

Gabby leaned back. Her expression was one that Jessie hadn't seen on her face before: suspicion.

"What about him?"

"Mr. Bauer was at the hotel suite where Addison Rutherford was found dead," Jessie said simply. "He visited her within the window of time when we believe she died. He didn't deny being there. In fact, he gave us an explanation for it. We're trying to determine if it's credible, but we obviously can't speak to the COHP and expect a straight answer. So we figured that since you know him, and until very recently, you knew the inner workings of the Realm, you might be able to help us."

"Oh, Jesus," Gabby said, running her fingers through her long hair. "What the hell has my boy gotten himself into?"

"I know he's your friend, Gabby, "Jessie said, leaning forward. "But we're talking about a girl who had her skull bashed in with a lamp. Can we count on a straight answer from you?"

Gabby closed her eyes and leaned back against the sofa pillow. When she opened them, they were focused.

"I'm all about straight answers," she said. "I love Logan but I'm not going to protect him if he was involved in this. What do you want to know?"

Jessie didn't need to be asked twice.

"He claimed that he went to Addison's suite to discuss an arranged relationship," Jessie told her. "He said that the higher-ups in the Realm

84

told her to break up with her boyfriend, that she and Logan were to be the new power couple of the Realm, and that he wanted to get their stories straight. Does that sound plausible to you?"

Gabby closed her eyes again. They were still shut when she started talking.

"It does," she said. Her voice had none of the playfulness from before. She was deadly serious. "They tried to do the same thing with me. They wanted me to divorce my husband, who was a general contractor, and 'merge' with another actor who had some heat at the time. I told them to screw off, only not that nicely. So it makes sense."

"I feel like there's more to this," Jessie said, "something you're holding back."

"There is," Gabby told them, finally opening her eyes. "You know how I said earlier that I was good at keeping secrets? Well, I know a secret about Logan Bauer that probably only four or five other people in the world know. I've kept it for half a decade. And I would have kept it for many more years. But considering that this secret might be important to your case, I can't keep it anymore."

"Why might it be important?" Jessie asked.

"Because it could be a motive to commit murder."

CHAPTER SEVENTEEN

This time they didn't ask the guard to open the gate; they ordered him to.

Once on the property, Jessie, Karen, and the three police cars that accompanied them tore down the driveway toward Logan Bauer's house. He was waiting outside when they arrived, still dressed in the olive shirt and black slacks from before. He was now wearing a light, brown leather jacket as well. Only the tattered sandals were gone, replaced by sensible black loafers. It was clear that someone had tipped him off to their imminent arrival.

As they got out of the car and marched toward him, he smiled ruefully and put his hands above his head.

"I'm guessing you're not here to discuss selling me the rights to your life story," he said mildly.

Jessie didn't reply.

"Logan Bauer," Karen said. "You have the right to remain silent…"

As she continued to read him his rights, Jessie heard the sound of something approaching in the distance, just beyond the hill that had its top sliced off to make room for his pool. A few seconds later she realized what it was. A local news helicopter soared into view just over the hill and passed overhead. After making a tight turn, it returned and hovered above them as Karen led the now-cuffed movie star over to a squad car and guided him into the backseat.

*

The block around Central Station was a madhouse, with hordes of fans and media everywhere.

Just getting into the parking garage was a challenge, with news vans and paparazzi planted outside the ramp that led down inside. A group of officers had to part the crowd like it was the Red Sea, only with cameras. As a precaution, they took the service elevator up to the first floor.

When the doors opened, Jessie was happy to see that Captain Decker had fulfilled her request. The hallway with the interrogation room they planned to use had been temporarily sealed off, complete with officers at either end to prevent any looky-loos from sneaking a peek.

Decker hadn't protested when they told him about their intention to arrest Bauer in force at his home, but Jessie could tell he was nervous. He liked HSS's high profile and the media attention that came with it. But if this case went sideways, that attention could turn unflattering fast. He was taking a big risk in approving their plan, but refusing to do so would have been worse—it would have undermined his credibility with the team.

Karen marched Bauer into the same interrogation room they'd used to question Addison's ex-boyfriend, Josh Sawyer, while Jessie stopped just outside. The only people waiting for her there were Detective Jim Nettles and Officer Garrett Dooley, a straw-haired, gangly, overly enthusiastic, young officer whom Jessie implicitly trusted after working multiple cases with his assistance. From their conversations, Jessie knew that the kid, about six-foot-three but maybe 175 pounds dripping wet, was devoted to three things: his family, his faith, and the LAPD. There was no room in there for fancy acronyms or talk of Realm elevation.

"You guys got this?" Jessie asked the men, whom she'd briefed in a call on the way over.

"Nobody will be in that observation room but me," Nettles assured her. "Jamil is the only one who'll have access to the recording. Dooley will plant himself out here between both rooms. Other than the three of us and Decker, this area will be off limits until you're done."

"Thanks," Jessie said. "We'll move as fast as we can under the circumstances. And remember, Bauer's lawyers are probably scrambling to get here ASAP. The second you get word that they're in the building, give me the heads up. I know Decker is going to try to stall them, but I doubt that will work for long."

With everyone on the same page, she joined Karen in the interrogation room. Bauer had already been cuffed to the bolted-down table. There was a bottled water and a doughnut on a paper plate in front of him. Jessie sat down across from him. Karen remained standing. The actor flashed his patented smile.

"I don't suppose this doughnut is gluten free?" he asked with unexpected lightheartedness considering the circumstances.

"You do understand that you're under arrest for murder, Mr. Bauer?" Jessie asked.

"Of course," he said. "Sometimes I joke when I'm in intense situations. I realize it's inappropriate."

"Listen," Jessie said, cutting to the chase, "We're not going to waste any time playing games with you. We have some direct questions for you. You've already been read your rights so you know that you don't have to answer them. But I'm assuming your big-time Eleventh Realm lawyers are already on their way here and that means that if you have anything worthwhile to share, this is the time. Once the attorneys get here, the process starts. You'll be formally arrested. It's almost 2.p.m. on a Friday afternoon so you'll likely spend the weekend in jail before they can get you bail. A judge might deny it entirely because of your wealth and the flight risk. So I'm guessing we have ten minutes, maybe fifteen at most, for you to convince us that you didn't kill Addison Rutherford."

He sat with that information for a moment before responding.

"In light of all that," he said, "May I ask you a question?"

"Sure."

"What changed from when you left my place the first time that has me suddenly at the top of your suspect list?"

Jessie looked up at Karen to see if she wanted to take this one. She nodded that she did. The detective sat down in the chair next to Jessie, leaned in close, and indicated that Bauer should do the same. When the actor was only inches away, she whispered in his ear.

"We know about France."

Bauer reeled back in his chair. He looked stunned.

"What did you say?"

"We know all about the villa in France," she repeated, barely audible. "That's not all. We know about Claire, and Chloe too."

"How?"

"That's not important," Karen told him, her voice still a soft murmur. "The point is that we know you have a secret girlfriend in France named Claire, who's not an Eleventh Realm Adherent. We know you two have a daughter, a toddler named Chloe. We know that you've been keeping them off the radar from everyone, including the Realm, and that only about a half dozen people in the world knew about them, at least prior to today."

"I don't understand—," he started to protest.

"Keep your voice down, Mr. Bauer," Jessie growled quietly. "We're being recorded. And for the time being at least, we're trying to protect your privacy on the off chance that you're innocent. But you can see how this looks from our perspective. You are instructed by Realm leadership to begin a sham relationship with a young starlet, when you have what amounts to a secret family abroad. It's not hard to imagine how, in a moment of panic, you eliminated the woman who was about to blow up your clandestine life, so that you could keep living it."

"That's not what happened," he insisted, trying to keep his volume down and mostly failing.

"Then tell us what *did* happen," Jessie told him.

Logan Bauer looked at her, and then Karen, with helplessness in his eyes.

"If I tell you the truth," he whispered, "and it gets out, it could destroy me in more ways than you know."

"Mr. Bauer," Jessie said, not unkindly. "From where I sit, it doesn't seem like you have much choice. You can trust us, tell us everything, and hope that we can help you get out of this, or you wait for the lawyers to arrive. They'll shut this down. Then we'll have to go public with what we know and you'll have a front row seat as your life goes up in flames. I'm going to be straight with you: if you killed Addison— and right now it sure looks like you did—you should keep your mouth shut. But if you didn't, this is the moment of truth. Come clean. And do it fast."

He sat quietly for a moment, his eyes focused on the doughnut in front of him. When he looked up, they were set.

"Okay," he said, "but can we do this off the record?"

"Not off the record," Karen said. "But we can stop the recording briefly if that reassures you."

"It helps."

"Then you need to verbally consent to that on camera," she instructed.

"All right," he said, looking in the one way-mirror where he rightly assumed one of the cameras was set," I verbally consent to temporarily suspending recording."

Karen glanced back over her shoulder, mimed slitting her throat and called out, "You heard him. We'll let you know when to hit record again."

"Should I start?" Bauer asked after a few seconds. "Can I talk normally now?"

"Go ahead," Karen said.

"Okay, you're right. I do have a girlfriend in France named Claire. We met when I was shooting a film in Paris four years ago. It became romantic. I bought a villa just outside the city so that we could meet without prying eyes, from either the media or the Realm. But pretty quickly, it became clear to both of us that this was more than a fling.

We decided we wanted to be together. But like you said, she's not an Adherent, which I knew would be a problem, so we kept it secret. I bought a different place—a very remote country house, through a shell company so it would be harder to trace."

"And she was okay with that?' Jessie asked, "Being so isolated?"

"She's a painter and an introvert, so she didn't care where she lived or worked," he explained. "In fact, the idea of being involved with someone so well-known was her main concern. She didn't want her life upended, so she actually preferred the arrangement. I told almost no one. I worried that if it got out, I'd be forced to leave her and I couldn't bear that. And then she got pregnant. Chloe was born eighteen months ago and she's the light of my life."

"Is that why you've made so many movies in Europe the last few years?" Karen asked, "To be closer to them?"

"Exactly," he said. "It was easier to justify travel in and around the region than to explain repeated transatlantic flights unconnected to work. Also, the Realm's presence isn't as strong in Europe. It's harder for them to track me there. And the truth, which only two people knew until now, was that I was planning to leave the Realm."

"You were?" Karen asked, unable to hide her shock.

"Yes," he said. "I wanted to make a clean break, much like my old friend Gabby DeAngelis did. I was inspired by her bravery. But I had a problem. I needed to get all my ducks in a row before going and I knew they were getting suspicious."

"About your commitment to the Creed?" Karen asked.

"Yes," he said, raising his eyebrows at her obvious familiarity with the language of the Realm. "I knew that if they discovered what I was planning, they'd come at me hard with everything I had revealed to them over the years in my Truth Sessions. I've done some pretty objectionable stuff. But I was ready for that. I'd already made my peace with the possibility that it might end my career. I've told Claire everything and she's forgiven me. That's all that matters. As long as I have her and Chloe, then nothing they can do to me will make a difference. As long as my family's safe and together, I can withstand whatever they throw at me. I just needed to be fully prepared for the onslaught."

Jessie looked at the clock on the wall behind Bauer. It was 2:06. They'd been in this interview for almost ten minutes. Time was running short. This was a compelling story but it didn't do anything to suggest his innocence.

"Not to rush you," she said, "but I need you to get to the part where you offer proof that you didn't kill Addison to keep your family safe and together."

"Right," he said. "Here's the thing: I never would have killed her, but as far as the motive you mentioned, I didn't *need* to kill her. I admit that I didn't really go to that suite to discuss the back story for our fake relationship. I went there to convince Addison *not* to have a fake relationship at all. I pleaded with her to make a united front with me and refuse to let the Realm dictate our personal lives."

"And how did she react?" Jessie asked.

"That's what I've wanted to tell you," he said with more passion than she'd ever seen in his movies. "She agreed with me. She told me she wanted to leave, to finally get out for good. She wanted to escape the Realm too."

Jessie and Karen looked at each other, both of them temporarily stunned into silence.

CHAPTER EIGHTEEN

It was Karen who recovered first. After a couple of seconds, she turned back to Bauer.

"You expect us to believe that?" she asked. "Everything we've heard is that she was a true believer, among the most devoted Adherents to the Creed."

"That's what I thought too," he said. "I was just as surprised as you are now. But she said that Sterling Shepherd himself had insisted on our union. She said he'd met with her privately and claimed that it was crucial to grow the Creed. He was grooming us as the first couple of the Eleventh Realm, able to win over a new generation of Adherents."

"I thought you and Shepherd were besties," Jessie said. "Why didn't he tell you himself?"

"We are friends," he said with a laugh, "but that's not how our relationship works. Shep would never directly order me to do anything. He likes to keep everything between us upbeat, sociable. He lets his COHP cronies do his dirty work. That's what he did with this—he sent Inara Reynolds to give me the news."

"That's the marathon girl?" Jessie asked Karen, remembering the unusual first name.

Karen nodded that it was.

"How do you know—?" Bauer started to ask.

"Please continue," Jessie interrupted. "You were saying Addison wanted to leave."

"Yes," he said. "She told me that she loved her boyfriend and that being ordered to break up with him and pretend to be involved with someone she barely knew was the last straw. She wanted to leave. So I let her know I had the same desire. I told her about France—."

"You told her about your family?" Karen asked, shocked.

"No, I didn't get that specific," he said. "I was worried that she might lose her nerve, back out, and tell a Proctor what I was planning. I just said that I was planning to leave for France soon, maybe for good, and offered her a ride on my plane."

"What did she say?" Jessie asked.

"She said that doing that was huge move, that she had to think about it. I told her I planned to leave soon, maybe by the end of this weekend, before word got back to Shep that I wasn't doing the First Couple thing. She said she'd let me know by today. But then I learned this morning that she'd been killed and I knew something had gone terribly wrong."

"Who told you?" Karen wanted to know

"That's the proof that I didn't kill her," he said intensely. "I was hoping not to involve this person because I didn't want him to get in trouble. But a bellboy named Eli told me."

"Eli Almeida?" Jessie asked, recalling the kid who had described the mystery man on the tenth floor as wearing blue jeans and a baseball cap.

"That's right," Bauer said. "I saw him outside the hotel on a smoke break when I went to see Sonny. He recognized me. I asked him for a favor and offered him $1000 in cash if he'd do it."

"What was the favor?"

"I asked if he could shut down the security cameras in an elevator and on Sonny's floor so that there wouldn't be any record of me visiting her and then let me in through a side door. I didn't want any paparazzi to find me there. I was also worried there might be DRA Proctors in the lobby or bar. He agreed and a few minutes later I was in. He took me up to her suite and waited just outside while I talked to her. I asked him to stick around to help me get out without being noticed. He was there when I left her suite. He was standing right there in the hallway when we kissed on the cheek and said goodbye. He saw that she was alive when I left. I was so pleased with how it went that I gave him my cell number and told him to call me if he ever wanted to go to a movie premiere."

Jessie looked over at Karen. If this was true, then their case against Bauer was kaput and they'd just spent the last couple of hours on a wild, useless goose chase.

"Why didn't you tell us this before?" the detective demanded.

"Because I didn't kill her and I thought that this would all blow over when you found out who did," he said. "I didn't want to throw that kid under the bus if I could help it. He snuck me into the hotel. He cut the feed on those cameras for me. And then he called me this morning to tell me that Addison was dead. I figured he'd lose his job for sure if the hotel found out."

"You really kept all this from us to protect a bellboy you barely knew?" Jessie demanded. That just didn't feel credible to her.

"No," he admitted. "That wasn't the only reason. I was also scared."

"Of what?" Jessie asked.

"Of them," Karen answered for him.

"Is that true?" Jessie wanted to know, staring at Bauer hard, trying to get a read on him.

"Yes," he said, suddenly looking much older than his fifty years. "You have to understand: once I found that she was dead, and how, I was terrified. I didn't know who did it but I could guess. Sonny and I had just discussed leaving the Realm and then she turned up dead. How could I be sure they didn't have recording equipment in that suite, that they hadn't heard everything, and decided they had to take drastic action? How could I be certain that I wasn't next?"

"You thought that the Eleventh Realm would have one of the biggest stars in the world murdered?" Jessie asked.

"Is that so crazy?" he shot back, "If they were willing to take her out, why not me? With the things I know, they may have decided it was safer to just get rid of me. Who knows? Maybe killing her was a warning to me, about what could happen if I really tried to leave. I couldn't risk it after that. If they did bug the room and heard me mention France, then it's only a matter of time before they learn about the country house and who's there. I can't put my loved ones at risk. If their goal was to shut me up, it worked. Or at least it was going to, until you picked me up."

Jessie studied the man's face. She's seen it onscreen so many times, but this was different. Those were always fictional roles, in which, by the very nature of acting, he was lying to the audience, making them believe he was someone he was not.

Before today, she'd never had cause to try to read the actor, to determine if he was telling the truth. This was someone who'd won one Oscar and been nominated for three others. He received awards for his ability to deceive.

But with his lawyers on their way—maybe even already at the station for all she knew—there wasn't time to deliberatively evaluate whether he could be believed. She had to assess whether one of the most celebrated actors in the world was playing them. And she had to make a choice right now. In the end, it wasn't much of a choice at all.

"You said that if their goal was to shut you up, it worked," she reminded Bauer. "What if it didn't?"

"What do you mean?"

"We're going to offer you a deal," she said, looking at Karen to see if she was on board. The detective had no reason to go along, but she nodded that she would.

"What deal?" he asked.

"Assuming your story with the bellboy holds up, we'll honor this deal. But I need your word, here and now, that you will too."

"What am I agreeing to?" he wanted to know.

"Most of our conversation hasn't been recorded," she reminded him. "It's all been kept in this room, among us. We promise to keep your France situation quiet. We won't reveal that you told us anything about the Realm, now or in the future. We'll use your information but won't identify you as the source. That way you can walk out of here claiming you kept your mouth shut, that you were loyal to the Realm. That should afford you the opportunity to avoid scrutiny until you're ready to make your escape."

"What do I have to do to get all that?" he asked.

"Two things: first you have to agree not to criticize the department in general or Homicide Special Section in particular when you go. Be vague when questioned by your lawyers and especially by the media. Say this was all a misunderstanding. No one was at fault. You have great respect for the LAPD and HSS. There are no hard feelings. You're sure this will all be cleared up in the end. Remember, good publicity is important to cops too."

She didn't mention that it was particularly important to Captain Decker.

"And second?" he asked.

"You need to tell us everything you know about the Realm's misdeeds and you need to do it fast. We need you to put it in a written statement in the event that we ever need it."

"If you aren't going identify me as the source, when would you ever need it?" he demanded.

"In case you're killed," Jessie said flatly.

Bauer didn't have a comeback for that one. Instead he had a question.

"What misdeeds are you asking about?"

"A little while ago, you said that with the things you know, the Realm leadership may have decided it was safer to just get rid of you," she said. "What things do you know, Mr. Bauer?"

The man paused for a moment. Jessie gave him the time. After all, what he decided next could alter the course of his life forever. As he mulled it over, both her phone and Karen's buzzed. She looked down. It was a text from Nettles that read: *the lawyers are in the building.* Her head popped up.

"Time's up," she said urgently. "Your attorneys have arrived at the station. It's now or never."

That seemed to clinch it for him.

"Okay, deal," he said quickly, diving in, "Here's what I know: the Realm engages in a pattern of harassment against the Disavowed. They have a whole playbook."

"That's not breaking news," Karen said. "We already know about Rightful Targeting."

"Sure. But I'm not being metaphorical. I'm talking about an actual, physical playbook, copies printed and distributed to a select group of Adherents from the Department of Restricted Activities."

"You've seen it?" Karen asked.

"No," he said, as if the suggestion was ridiculous. "I'm not that high up. I've only heard about it third-hand. I've also heard that the book has a special name but I'm not privy to it. What I *do* know is that it lists methods and techniques to use. I'm no lawyer, but a lot of them sure seemed illegal to me."

Jessie doubted that a third-hand description of this supposed book would hold any weight with the District Attorney or in court but she didn't want to slow him down by saying that, so she moved past it.

"Okay, what else?" she asked, looking up at the ticking second hand on the wall clock behind him.

"Then there are the disappearances," he said. "Lots of Adherents are sent on what are called M&Ms, which are solo 'meditation missions' intended to help them unlock their potential. The Adherent is dropped off in an unforgiving environment, often an isolated part of a desert or forest—alone—with almost no supplies."

"I've heard of these," Karen said. "Sort of a test of faith and trial by fire rolled into one."

"Right," Bauer said. "And they're required to sign a waiver before going out, absolving the Realm of any responsibility should anything happen to them. The problem is that a surprisingly high number of Adherents never come back. And invariably, they're people who had expressed misgivings about the Realm just before being sent on the M&M."

"What else?" Jessie demanded. Her internal clock was ticking loudly.

"Well, there's the trafficking."

Jessie felt her jaw drop open involuntarily. Only the buzzing of her phone snapped her out of her shock. She looked at the message from

Nettles: *Lawyers in the hallway. Decker is trying to hold them off. Not working. You've got seconds.*

"What trafficking?" she asked hurriedly.

"They don't call it that," Bauer said, sensing her urgency and talking even faster. "Hell, the women might not even comprehend what's happening to them. But when it comes right down to it, it's basically sexual slavery."

Before Jessie could get more details, the door burst open. In stormed not one lawyer, but three. Two were men and one was an extremely tall woman. The older, shorter male lawyer stepped forward.

"My name is Walter Serra," he barked, focusing his attention on Jessie and Karen. "I represent Mr. Bauer and this interview is over. Don't say another word, Logan."

Bauer's mouth was already closed tight and he kept it that way. Serra continued.

"Unless you intend to arrest our client, which I suggest you think about very carefully, we'll *all* be leaving now."

Bauer looked from the lawyer back to Jessie. His eyes were bulging with fear. She stood up slowly, giving herself some extra time to think. This had to be handled just right.

"You might as well take him anyway," she said, feigning disgust. "He barely said anything as it was. All we got out of him was that he doesn't eat doughnuts with gluten. But I assure you, we're not done with your client."

"I wouldn't be so sure," Serra retorted haughtily. "Please uncuff him."

As Karen wordlessly removed the handcuffs, Bauer surreptitiously mouthed the words "thank you" to Jessie. In lieu of nodding, she merely blinked. The actor stood up, made a display of brushing himself off, and then headed for the door. He stopped just before leaving and turned around.

"I have enormous respect for all the work you do here," he said. "I just wanted to let you know that I don't hold grudges and once this is all cleared up, I hope we can all move forward toward our full potential."

He left without another word. His attorneys followed, as did Decker. As they walked down the hallway, Jessie heard the captain say something to Serra about the department being well within its rights. She and Karen were left alone in the interrogation room.

"We never got that written statement," Karen said as she plopped down in the chair that Bauer had occupied only moments earlier.

"Nope," Jessie agreed, her mind racing even as she spoke in a measured tone. "And now we may never have the chance to get it."

"I know what you're thinking," Karen said, apparently sensing that Jessie wasn't saying everything in her head.

"What?" Jessie asked as she sat down too.

"I've worked with you enough to know your next move," Karen said. "Since we don't have anything official from Bauer, you want to go big to shake things up."

"How would I do that?" Jessie asked, trying not to smile.

"You want to go directly at Sterling Shepherd and use the allegations about sex trafficking to unnerve him, and then hit him with questions about Addison Rutherford's murder to see if he reveals anything, verbally or through body language."

"Is that such a bad idea?" Jessie asked, impressed at how right on the detective was.

"I actually love it," Karen said. "I want a front row seat. But you have no idea of the hell that will rain down on us if you if you take Shepherd on. He, his lawyers, and the DRA will try to destroy you, to destroy both of us. And to be honest, as much as I despise them, I'm not sure I can go there. It's one thing to investigate a murder. It's another to make a direct attack on the leader of the Eleventh Realm. I have a family to think of. I have a little boy."

Jessie nodded. She was actually surprised this hadn't come up earlier. Karen Bray was a great detective but she wasn't used to having her life threatened or having to go into hiding. Not many people were, and facing the potential of ongoing, unspecified danger was something that, unlike her, Karen hadn't become inured to. Frankly, those were calluses Jessie didn't wish for anyone to develop.

"I understand," she said. "Let's take a breath. First, we'll verify Bauer's story about the bellboy. If that bears out, we'll have some confidence that Addison Rutherford *was* trying to leave the Realm. If she was, then Sterling Shepherd would have had a strong motive to prevent that, maybe even strong enough to have her killed. But we don't have to go at him head on. Between the two of us, and with an assist from Jamil, maybe we can find another way to determine his involvement, a back door that doesn't put you or your family at risk. Trust me."

"It's not you I'm worried about, Jessie," Karen said. "It's everyone else."

CHAPTER NINETEEN

Trudy Echolls, Kaylee McNulty's one-time friend, didn't live on campus.

Ryan and Valentine pulled up in front of the address they'd gotten from the registrar. It was an unassuming four-story apartment complex a few blocks from campus. Ryan was curious to know more about Echolls's background before they questioned her and, for what wasn't the first time, he considered calling Jamil to get a biographical breakdown. But he'd heard the news of Logan Bauer's arrest just like everyone else and knew the researcher was probably up to his eyeballs in that case. They'd have to get the details on their own.

They weren't even sure Echolls was at home but her schedule said her only class today wasn't until this evening so it was a decent guess. Besides, he didn't want to call ahead to give her time to prep. They waited until someone left the building to enter so they didn't have to buzz up to her unit. There was no elevator so they had to traipse up the stairs to the fourth floor.

Even though Ryan considered himself almost completely recovered from the stabbing and coma that had cost him more than half a year, he still struggled with stairs. By the time they reached the top, he was winded and his right thigh was throbbing.

"You okay?" Valentine asked.

"I will be," he panted. "Sometimes my body just likes to remind me not to get too cocky."

"I still can't believe that you're this far along after what happened to you," she said. "I read up on your kinds of injuries and the general consensus was that it takes between a year and eighteen months to be really functional again. You destroyed that timetable."

"Yeah, well, it doesn't feel that way right now," he said, hoping his thigh would settle down."

"Do you want me to take point on the interview?' she asked. "Just until you get your bearings."

"Sure."

"All right, then let's do it, old man," Valentine said, walking over to the door.

"I'm like two years older than you," he said.

She only smiled in return before knocking on Echolls's door.

After a few seconds, the light in the peephole disappeared and someone replied.

"Who is it?"

"Gertrude Echolls, this is the LAPD," Valentine said. "We have a few questions for you about a fellow student at Southwestern. Can you open the door please?"

"Can I see your badges please?" was the immediate reply.

They both held them up in front of the peephole. Echolls unlocked and opened the door. Ryan studied her without trying to be obvious about it.

The girl was cute in a mousy kind of way. She was slim and pale, with glasses and black hair tied back in a ponytail. She wore corduroy pants, a gray turtleneck sweater, and slippers.

"What's this about?" she asked.

"We're pursuing a report involving a student named Kaylee McNulty," Valetine said, as if the report might be about an overdue library book. "Our understanding is that you two used to be roommates. Is that correct?"

Echolls scrunched up her nose in surprise but answered anyway.

"We were roommates last semester, but she moved out over winter break. Did she do something?"

"What would make you think that?" Valentine wondered.

"Actually, nothing would," she said. "I'd be stunned if Kaylee had done anything remotely illegal."

"Why did she move out?" Valentine pressed.

"Is that what this is about?" Echolls demanded, sounding irked for the first time. "Did she sic the cops on me for being a bad person or something?"

"Why would she do that?" Valentine asked. "Did you do something bad?"

Echolls laughed bitterly.

"I guess that depends on who you ask. Am I evil if agreed to accept an internship at an oil and gas company this summer? Because Kaylee sure thought I was."

"Is that why she moved out?" Ryan asked, speaking for the first time.

"Pretty much," Echolls replied. "I think the phrase she used was something like 'I can't in good conscience live with someone who is actively ruining the world instead of trying to better it.' That's almost verbatim. Are my choices a crime now?"

Ryan fought the urge to offer a snarky answer. Instead he went with a question.

"Ms. Echolls, where were you this morning between 8:30 and 9:15?"

Trudy Echolls's self-righteous express immediately vanished.

"Why? Did something happen to Kaylee?"

Ryan looked over at Susannah Valentine and nodded. When they worked together, Jessie always liked him to deliver news of a victim's death to a potential suspect so that she could watch their reaction. Now he intended to use Valentine for the same purpose. The detective turned to Echolls and answered simply.

"Kaylee McNulty was found murdered this morning."

For a second, Echolls didn't seem to hear her. Then her legs wobbled slightly.

"Oh, Jesus," she muttered as she started to crumple to the ground.

Ryan stepped forward and managed to grab her by the shoulders before she completely collapsed. He straightened her up and guided her to a nearby barstool. Her eyes were cloudy and her skin was clammy. There were beads of sweat on her forehead. He felt a little bad doing it, but there was no better time to push her.

"Where were you this morning, Ms. Echolls?" he repeated.

She looked at him, and though she still didn't seem all there, she answered. Her voice was flat and emotionless.

"I was in the law library from about 8 a.m. until lunchtime. I'm struggling with a unit we're doing on federal securities regulation and wanted to bear down on it. There are cameras everywhere in there. You should be able to confirm it," she said, then reluctantly asked, "How did she die?"

Ryan felt his heart sink as their only potential lead dried up in one answer. Assuming they could verify what Echolls said and she was eliminated as a suspect, they had nowhere to go once they left this apartment. It took him a second to realize that the girl was still waiting for an answer and that Valentine wasn't sure if they should give her one. He sighed.

"If you cared about her at all," he said, "you're probably better off not knowing."

An emotional numbness took hold of him as he started for the door. As Valentine followed him out, he heard her offer Echolls her card and tell her to call if she thought of anything else. Once out in the hall, he stared down at the daunting stairwell. His leg had only just stopped aching and now he had to traverse the steps again.

"What now?" Valentine asked, pulling him back into thoughts of the case. He'd been enjoying the brief respite when all he had to worry about was managing a challenging physical task.

"To be honest," he said, turning to face her. "I'm at a loss. This was always a long shot. We knew the attack was probably some random, disturbed walk-in at the facility. Part of me hoped we'd have some 'eureka!' moment but I find that those are pretty rare these days."

"Hey," she said, moving closer and playfully punching him in the shoulder. "Don't get too down. You never know what will turn up. Maybe someone will report a person walking into a Starbucks with a bloody machete."

"Wouldn't that be nice?"

She put her finger under his chin and lifted it so that they were at eye level.

"Does someone need a lolly?" she asked playfully.

Ryan's malaise melted away. Something about her response felt inappropriately intimate. He sensed his face flushing and stepped quickly back.

"You know I'm involved, right Valentine?" he said, perhaps more forcefully than he'd intended.

Her eyes went wide for a second before she broke into a cackle.

"Yeah, I know, Detective Hernandez. Your engagement is front page scuttlebutt at the station. I think you misunderstood. I was just trying to be silly and lift your spirits in a tough moment. No offense, but first of all, I don't mix business and pleasure. And even if I did, you're not my type."

His face stayed red, but now it was for a different reason.

"Okay, sorry," he said. "I guess I misjudged your intentions there."

"You're not *that* charming," she told him.

"I get it," he said, holding up his hands in surrender. "Now you're just being mean."

Valentine looked ready to fling another barb his way when his phone rang, rescuing him. He answered without even looking to see who it was.

"Hernandez," he said.

There was a long pause. He thought it might have been a misdial and was about to hang up when an automated female voice came on the line. It said, "Collect call from Twin Towers Correctional Facility-Women's Forensic In-Patient Unit. Will you accept a collect call from—?" The voice paused. A moment later a human one replaced it to say "Andrea Robinson." He recognized both the name and the voice immediately.

"Yes," he said, though he wasn't sure he should. After another second, he heard the loud background noise so familiar to a prison, and then she began to speak.

"Hello, Detective," Andy Robinson said. "Thank you for taking my call. I know you could have declined."

"What do you want?" he asked, refusing to play games. He knew that Robinson was hoping to get moved to a better facility in exchange for helping Jessie in some yet-to-be-made-clear way. But he was dubious about her motives and didn't see why she was calling him.

"I'll be brief," she said. "I know your time is precious and they only allot a few minutes for these calls. I think I may have information that could be valuable to the case you're investigating."

"You've got the wrong person," Ryan told her dismissively. "I'm not working the big movie star investigation with Jessie."

"I'm not talking about that case, Detective," she replied coolly, "Although I am intrigued by it. I'm referring to yours, the one involving the young woman who was chopped up."

"How do you know about that?" he demanded.

"Why wouldn't I?' she asked, sounding surprised. "They allow us to watch television in here—certain channels at least—and I just saw it on the news."

Ryan cursed silently to himself. If it was on the news, that likely meant someone had leaked it and that the murderer, if they watched TV too, would know they were being pursued. Valentine looked at him, perplexed. Since he couldn't think of a reason not to, he put the call on speaker.

"What information do you have about the case?" he asked.

"I'm afraid that's where I draw the line, Detective," she replied coyly. "I assume Jessie told you about the offer I made a while back. I have to keep some kind of bargaining chip, don't I?"

"How do I know you're not just blowing smoke?" he asked. "You see a story on the news. You decide to co-opt it for your own purposes. Prove you're legit."

"I see why she likes you so much," she replied coquettishly. "You're so virile and manly, even over the phone. All right, Detective. How's this for legit? One word: machete."

Ryan glanced at Valentine, who looked as shocked as he felt.

"What about it?" he managed to ask in a mostly normal voice.

"I'm sorry, detective. That's all the information I can provide at this time. If you want more, I'd be willing to discuss it, but not with you. Tell your lovely fiancée that I'd like to make a date in the prison visiting area. And tell her the clock is ticking."

CHAPTER TWENTY

Jessie couldn't find a back door.

After almost an hour of searching for an indirect way to approach Sterling Shepherd, one that might prove as effective as just shell-shocking him with what they knew, they'd come up empty. Karen took a break and went to look for a snack. Jessie stood up to stretch as best as she could in the small confines of the research department. Jamil, who rarely seemed to need food, drink, or rest, continued to type away.

"Maybe we're wasting our time," Jessie said, as much to herself as to the dogged researcher. "After all these years, with the help of his lawyers and his DRA minions, it wouldn't be stunning if Sterling had found a way to patch all his vulnerabilities. I wouldn't be surprised if he had his opposition research people doing work on him, just to keep ahead of any allegations that might come his way."

"You're right," Jamil said.

"I am?" Jessie said, surprised that the kid was willing to give up. Jamil never gave up.

"Not about wasting our time," he said. "But I think you're right that he's had so long to cover up all his transgressions that it may impossible for us to untangle them now—but maybe not for everyone."

"What do you mean?" Jessie asked.

She recognized the inflection in Jamil's voice. It was the one he got when he thought he had a good idea but didn't want to say so outright in case he'd misjudged.

"I think we're coming to this too late," he told her. "But I keep coming across someone who's been investigating the Eleventh Realm since the very beginning, before anyone else started looking into them. He may have found some incriminating stuff before they could bury it."

"Who?" Jessie asked, perking up.

"Huell Valcheck," Jamil said enthusiastically.

Jessie's own enthusiasm faded as fast as it had arrived.

"That guy?" she said skeptically. "I read some of his stuff in the research, *and* some of the stuff about him. Frankly, he struck me as a kind of nut job conspiracy theorist."

"Ms. Hunt," Jamil said, turning around in his chair. "Who do you think paid for and circulated those stories about him, the ones that undermined his credibility?"

Jessie thought about it and was briefly embarrassed that the source of the stories about him hadn't occurred to her. She still wasn't as adept as she'd like at comprehending just how far the Realm's tentacles stretched.

"Are you sure about that?" she asked.

"I have detailed records," he told her. "A bunch of these articles were commissioned by Realm-friendly publications and then aggregated like crazy so that now it's hard to discern the original sources. But the more I dig, the more I find that every hit piece on him comes from a writer or outlet with connections to the group."

"But wasn't the guy institutionalized?" she asked.

"Briefly," Jamil said. "I haven't been able to find out what that was about. Listen, I'm not saying this guy is Bob Woodward, but you've got to wonder: If Valchek was already such an erratic, unhinged hack, why did the Realm put so much money and effort into trying to shut him up?"

Jessie felt a flicker of excitement return to her chest.

"That's a really good question, Jamil," she said. "And I don't have an answer. I assume you have his address?"

*

Jessie went alone.

Karen was already on edge and interviewing a potentially unreliable gadfly reporter seemed like something she could skip. So while she stayed at the station to follow up on Bauer's alibi involving Eli the bellboy and to check back with Forensics for any updates, Jessie made the solo trip to Mar Vista, a small Westside neighborhood nestled between Culver City and Venice.

She pulled up at the address Jamil had given her, then double-checked that she had it right. This didn't seem like the kind of place that a relentlessly hounded and largely discredited one-time journalist would set up camp. The house was a large, two-story, Craftsman-style home with green pillars and trim. The otherwise brown exterior was designed to look like a log cabin. A tall wooden fence surrounded the property, which sat on an incline at the corner of a residential intersection across from an elementary school.

Jessie noticed that six inches above the wooden fence, all the way around the house, was a thick metal cord that she suspected might be electrified. That seemed more in keeping with her assumptions about the guy. There were also multiple "private residence-no trespassing" signs. She parked, got out, and walked to the front gate. Across the street, dozens of kids at recess were squealing with delight as they played.

Unlike the rest of the fence, the entry gate door was made of what looked like iron. There was a large slot in the center of it that she assumed was for dropping off packages. She stood out front, unsure how to proceed. Jamil hadn't found a working phone number for Huell Valchek. He had an e-mail address but hadn't responded to the message Jamil sent.

She would have used the gate buzzer but there wasn't one. There was a camera affixed to the top of the fence looking down on her, but it seemed like it might be broken. It was dented and there were cobwebs on it. She was about to bang on the gate door when a static-y voice spoke from a com speaker that she hadn't previously noticed. It was inside the slot for passing packages through.

"This is private property," the voice, male and distant, said. "State your business."

Jessie decided to be straight. She didn't know what resources this guy had at his disposal or what he already knew about the case. Any attempt at deception would surely ruin what remote chance she might have to get something useful out of him.

"Hi, Mr. Valchek," she said, leaning awkwardly toward the slot. "My name is Jessie Hunt. I'm a consulting criminal profiler for the Los Angeles Police Department. I'm investigating a case involving the murder of a young woman who was an Eleventh Realm Adherent. We think her death may be tied to the group, and potentially its founder, Sterling Shepherd."

She paused for a response. After several seconds, the static-y voice replied.

"I don't hear a question in there."

Jessie tried not to smile. He was being difficult but at least he hadn't dismissed her outright.

"We've hit a bit of a dead end," she said before lowering her voice. "We've gotten off-the- record reports of harassment of Disavowed members, as well as brainwashing of Adherents, some of whom have mysteriously disappeared, others of whom may have been trafficked in some way. We think this murder may be connected to those allegations, but any useful records on those matters seem to be sealed up tight. I was hoping that you might have accessed some of them before the Realm became expert at covering its tracks. I need your help, sir."

There was another long pause. She started to wonder whether the intercom was working.

"Mr. Valchek?"

"Don't move please," the static-y voice requested. "This will only take a moment."

Jessie was tempted to bail. What exactly was "this?" Was he planning to shoot some poisoned dart at her or have the walkway beneath her slide out to drop her in a moat?

None of that happened. After another five seconds, a buzzer sounded and the iron gate door unlocked.

"You may enter," the voice said. "Proceed to the front door. Once you remove your shoes and your weapon and place them in the lockbox by the entrance, you may enter."

"I can't hand over my weapon, Mr. Valchek," she told him.

"Then I'm afraid we can't continue. You aren't fully vetted. I'm not allowing a stranger, even a famous one, in my home without some guarantee of security. It's your decision."

Jessie sighed. Of course the one time she didn't bring a partner, she was being asked to unilaterally disarm.

"Fine," she said. "But if I see a cattle prod or a syringe, this is going to get very ugly."

"Please proceed," he said, promising nothing.

She pushed open the iron door to find a surprisingly well-maintained interior courtyard, complete with a vegetable garden, surrounded by a larger drought-tolerant succulent garden. She noticed that the walkway to the front door was covered in leaves, even though there was no tree overhanging the yard. She could guess why. It was a security precaution. Her feet crunching on them as she approached the door echoed throughout the courtyard.

She found the lockbox, did as he asked, and then grabbed the doorknob. It was unlocked. She stepped inside the house, closed the door, and put the box down beside it. As she did, she heard the door lock click.

The place was dusty and dark. As her eyes adjusted, she noted that that she was in a small foyer with a stairwell directly in front of her. To the left was a dining room with a low-hanging chandelier. To the right was a sitting room with a fireplace. Oddly, there was almost no furniture in either room.

She heard another click and saw a door to what she assumed was a coat closet open under the stairwell. Out stepped a man who looked vaguely recognizable from the long-ago photos of him in the stories that had turned him into a laughingstock. He moved toward her slowly, with his hands out at his sides, as if to show he meant no harm. Still, his halting, unnatural walk was unsettling. It looked like, at any moment, he might fall down or charge at her.

"Huell Valchek?' she said.

The man stopped about five feet in front of her. He was a little shorter than her, but his tangled, gray hair was longer than hers. He had a wispy gray beard and an equally unimpressive mustache. He wore thick, black glasses that looked like they would have been better suited to a man in a 1950s Brylcreem ad. He had on tan cargo shorts and a pullover sweatshirt with a San Diego Clippers logo on it. Everything about this guy was vintage.

"Ms. Hunt," he said, "had I known you were coming, I would have made some tea."

"That's okay," she replied. "If you have information I can use, I can do without the hospitality."

"In that case," he said, motioning back toward the door under the stairs. "Would you like to proceed directly to my lair?"

CHAPTER TWENTY ONE

"Lair" was only a slight overstatement.

It turned out that the door under the stairs didn't lead to a coat closet at all. Instead, a stairwell led down to a whole third level of the house.

"Not many L.A. homes have basements, these days," she said, trying to muster up some small talk as she walked down carefully. She glanced over her shoulder repeatedly, just to make sure he wasn't about to shove her down the rest of the way.

"This place wasn't built in 'these days,'" he told her. "It's been in my family for generations. The basement was originally intended as a bunker during World War Two, when my grandparents worried about potential Japanese bombing raids after Pearl Harbor. I've made a few adjustments."

He was being modest. From where she stood at the foot of the stairs, it looked like he'd turned the entire sub-level into both a living and workspace. There were no walls, so she could see a corner with a bed and a dresser, another section with a couch and a big screen TV, and a kitchen nook, complete with a fridge, stove, oven, microwave, and a small table.

"Do you live upstairs at all?" she asked.

"No, the rest of the house is just for appearances," he admitted.

"Then, I've got to tell you, you need to do a better job of keeping up appearances. You're not fooling anyone. The place looks vacant."

He chuckled, though he didn't say anything. She looked around the rest of the space. The other half of the floor was populated with multiple desks littered with computer monitors and hard drives. A dedicated section had multiple bookshelves with more files than she could count. In the back corner was a small section that appeared to be cordoned off. It was barren, other than a desk, with one computer on it.

What drew her attention wasn't its isolated location or the sparseness of the area. It was that the area was cordoned off by a metal cage. The apprehension that she felt when first seeing Valchek come out of the upstairs hallway closet and again going down the stairs suddenly returned, only exponentially stronger. It wasn't lost on her that she was in the basement of a potentially disturbed man, alone, and unarmed.

"Um, care to explain that?" she asked, pointing at the cage.

Valchek looked in that direction.

"Oh, don't worry," he said, waving dismissively. "I'm not planning to lock you up. It's not a dungeon. It's a homemade Faraday cage."

"I'm sorry—a what?"

"It's just an area constructed to block electromagnetic signals. It makes it harder for snoopers to track my work. It's like a dead zone that they can't access, much harder to hack. I use the cage for my computer but there are smaller versions too. Some people have Faraday bags like this," he said, holding up a small innocuous-looking pouch that was sitting on a nearby table. "They use them to block signals to and from their cell phones."

"Wow," Jessie marveled. "Considering that you've got one of those cages, I'm surprised that you didn't check me for a wire before I came down here."

"I did," he said. "How do you think I knew you were carrying a weapon? That 'iron' door you entered through on the way in isn't just decorative. It's a scanning device, as effective as anything they have at airport security. I knew you weren't a risk on that front. The question is: are you a human intelligence risk?"

"What do you mean?" Jessie asked.

"How can I be sure you haven't been co-opted by the Realm and aren't just here as some kind of spy?"

The question was not asked playfully, so she treated it with the gravity he seemed to think it deserved.

"I assume you wouldn't have let me through your front door, much less down here, if you were really worried about that. My life, much to my dismay, is largely an open book. You don't have to be an investigative journalist to see what I'm about."

"Maybe not," he countered. "But from what I know of you, you've been through a hell of a lot of trauma in your life, both as a child and in recent years. The Realm feeds on people like that, those in search of an easy Band-Aid to cover up wounds that won't heal on their own. Who's to say you didn't encounter them and find yourself drawn to their easy answers? How can I be sure you're not a plant, designed to gain my trust and then destroy all my work?"

Jessie sighed deeply. Looking around, she saw an uncomfortable looking, metal folding chair next to the wall.

"May I?" she asked, pointing at it. He nodded yes. Once seated, she replied. "First of all, Mr. Valchek, I hate to break it to you but your work has already been destroyed. The Realm has been largely successful in ruining your credibility. Hell, even I was hesitant to approach you until our police researcher showed me that all the hit pieces on you came from Realm affiliates. So the 'you plan to secretly destroy my work' ship has long since sailed."

Valchek nodded. He didn't seem offended. It was as if she was confirming something he already knew but preferred to forget.

"You said first of all," he reminded her. "What's the second of all?"

"It's this: I'm not looking to use a Band-Aid to cover up my wounds, emotional or physical. Those wounds help define me. They're what drive me to do this job, to face down the ugliness in the world. I've seen it up close and if I can catch bad people, so that fewer good people have to go through what I have, then that's the only salve I need. You can believe me or not. If you don't, I'll be on my way. If you do, then I have some questions I need answered, and the sooner the better."

Valchek played with his wispy beard for a few seconds, then seemed to make up his mind. He pulled his desk chair over to face hers and sat down.

"What do you want to know?" he asked.

Jessie exhaled. She hadn't realized she'd been holding her breath. Maybe now they could finally get somewhere.

"What do you know about the case I'm working?" she asked.

"You're investigating the murder of Addison Rutherford, a Realm Adherent. I have some familiarity with her. You questioned the actor Logan Bauer but let him go. Was that your decision or was it forced upon you?"

She wanted to tell him about Bauer's apparent change of heart to explain her choice, but couldn't violate her promise to keep it secret.

"Despite our initial suspicions, it doesn't look like Bauer is our killer."

Valchek looked unconvinced.

"Whether he's responsible for this girl's death or not, I can assure you that a lot of young people have had their lives ruined because of his advocacy on behalf of that destructive organization."

"I have no doubt," Jessie said, "but right now, I'm trying to solve the murder of one particular person. If it's somehow connected to the Realm, that may actually impact them in some larger way. Either way, my goal here is the truth. I'm hoping you can help me. But it needs to

112

be through credible information, not supposition or unverifiable accusations. That will only undermine the case. Can you do that?"

"I can," he assured her. "Tell me what you need."

"Okay," Jessie said, diving in. "Addison Rutherford was apparently being groomed for a major role as a face of the Realm. But it's possible that she was considering leaving the group. I'm trying to determine just how far they might go to keep her quiet. Not rumors. Not innuendo. But possibilities based on facts, prior similar examples. Do you have those?"

"Sure," Valcheck said, getting up and walking to the bookshelves. "The most notorious example was seventeen years ago. The Realm was looking to get tax-exempt status from the government. But I got word that one of their top accountants had left, along with a bunch of documents that proved a vast, tax-avoidance scheme. He planned to testify before Congress. A date was scheduled. But the week before his testimony, his car went off a cliff and exploded in a massive fireball. The preliminary determination was that his brakes had given out but no foul play could be proven and the investigation was closed. His documents were never found and the Realm got its tax-exempt status a few months later."

"What about Rightful Targeting?" Jessie asked. "I've heard that some of their methods crossed the line from nuisance harassment into illegal activities and that there may be hard copies of an actual book that describes approved methods."

"There are," Valcheck told her. "They're called Red Books. I've seen photos of one, taken surreptitiously. They're printed on red paper, so they can't be easily copied and there are only five printed books in total. Each is kept in their archives and is only checked out to authorized DRA members for finite periods. The location of every book is always tracked and they never leave the Heartbeat Hub, which means no one from the outside is going to see them. That's the thing people don't get about the Eleventh Realm Headquarters. The facility doesn't have all that expensive, elaborate security to keep people out. It's designed to keep people in. The place looks majestic but when you get down to it, the Hub is really just a gleaming, architectural prison."

"Okay, as troubling as that is, I get them not letting people leave," Jessie said, "but why keep such a tight grip on the books?"

"Because the book lists techniques that go far beyond traditional harassment, including everything from cutting home gas lines of the Disavowed, to staging car accidents with them so they can sue the person, to hacking someone's computer and putting kiddie porn on it, to swatting their home. But that's been impossible to prove too. They leave no fingerprints, real or digital. Like I said, I saw a photo of the cover of a Red Book. But I've never seen the inside pages, much less seen a copy in person. All my intelligence comes from Disavowed who want to get the word out, but none of it would hold up in court."

They were on a roll now. Jessie kept going.

"What about the disappearances of difficult Adherents while on Meditation Missions?"

Valchek looked impressed.

"You've been doing your homework," he said. "I've done extensive background research on M&M missing persons and they are very much a real thing. I have the police reports to prove it. But as with so many things Realm-related, there are complications."

"Like?"

"With the disappearances, there are two main issues," he explained. "One is that all the Adherents signed waivers before going, absolving the Realm and anyone associated with it should anything go wrong. The waivers are very specific about the risks. They're pretty ironclad. The other is one of volume."

"What does that mean?"

"After the first few years of M&Ms, the COHP came up with a clever idea. They flooded the zone with M&Ms. By that I mean they intentionally had a ton of people go on them. It wasn't that hard a sell. Most M&Ms aren't that intense, the equivalent of a weekend backpacking trip. So Adherents would clamor to go on them to prove their mettle. The higher ups would save the really brutal ones as punishment for Adherents who got out of line. But the overall stats didn't look that bad."

"The stats?" Jessie repeated, surprised that there was statistical component to the endeavor.

"Yes, my most recent tally, which I acknowledge is incomplete, has Adherents going on over 4,300 total M&Ms in the last quarter century. Records show a total of thirty-six confirmed disappearances in that time. That's less than one percent, so it doesn't seem that suspicious at first glance. It's only when you dig down that you learn that all thirty-six who disappeared had actively questioned the Realm, some publicly. According to my research, at least half were seriously considering leaving at the time they went on their M&M. But there's never been enough evidence to bring charges. In most cases, a body was never even found, making it hard to assert these incidents were anything other than unfortunate accidents."

Jessie was about to move on to the trafficking when, without warning, Valchek's eyes closed and he groaned loudly. His whole body convulsed in a sudden violent spasm. Then his eyes shot open. He stared at her with intense, unblinking eyes. Jessie wondered if he was dead.

CHAPTER TWENTY TWO

Multiple thoughts popped into her head at once.

Was he having a stroke? Had he taken some kind of suicide pill that was just taking effect now? Did some Realm operative somehow sneak in behind her when she'd entered the house and fire a poisoned dart at him from the stairwell behind her?

She was about to leap out of the folding chair when the papers he was holding slipped from his fingers and fell to the floor. It looked like he might too. At the last second, he managed to grip the arms of his desk chair and steady himself. His eyes finally, mercifully, blinked.

"What the h—?" Jessie started to ask.

"Cerebral palsy," he said quickly. "It used to be mild. But it's gotten worse in recent years. The doctors think that my overuse of mind-altering drugs a number of years back probably didn't help either."

Jessie recalled his halting walking style in the upstairs hallway, which made more sense now. She decided to hold off on her planned question and go with another one that had been eating at her.

"Is that why you were institutionalized—the drugs?" she asked.

He smiled bitterly at the question.

"That hurt my reputation almost as much as those 'profiles' of me back in the day," he said, leaning back in the chair. "But I wasn't placed there. I actually committed myself to the hospital."

"Why?" Jessie asked, surprised.

"I had just lost my job after the Realm put on full court pressure with their concerted attack machine. My good name was in tatters. My wife left me, taking our four-year-old daughter with her. She actually took up with an Adherent who, unbeknownst to me, had been whispering in her ear—both sweet nothings and subtle attacks on my character. I was almost broke. I was drinking too much, taking too many psychedelics. I felt like I was coming apart at the seams. I worried that I might hurt myself. So I took a mental break from everything. I committed myself to a hospital, stayed there for six weeks, got clean, got therapy, got new medication to help with the CP, and then checked out. I managed to regroup enough to function and to get back to my work. But my time there became a permanent part of my story, one that's trotted out every time I release a new piece on the Realm or do an interview. I'm accused of being a paranoid, escaped mental patient spinning fantasies on the internet."

Jessie tried to lighten the mood a little.

"I have to say, you do seem *a little* paranoid."

"That part is true," he admitted. "You have no idea, actually. Sometimes it's with good cause and sometimes my suspicions go…badly."

"Like how?"

"Like when I pepper sprayed the new mailman because I thought he was a secret DRA operative," he said sheepishly. "It turned out that my normal mail carrier was on vacation and this guy was a new hire, subbing for veterans until he got his own route. I felt bad."

"But you said that sometimes it's with good cause?" Jessie noted, hoping to steer him away from the bad memory.

"Yes," Valchek said, brightening. "The Realm obviously knows where I live. My security measures have kept them from getting in but that doesn't stop them from sending people to keep tabs on me. They change them out periodically so it's sometimes hard to identify them. A few are sloppy. I might catch one taking pictures of me in the supermarket or getting too close when they follow me around town. But often, they'll just park on the street out there for hours at a time, waiting for me to go somewhere or just staying put to keep me off balance. That's why living next to the school is so helpful."

"What do you mean?" Jessie asked.

"I have hidden cameras placed everywhere around the block, not just on my property. And if I note an occupied car that's been parked nearby for too long, I'll call it in to the police. They tend not to like random people loitering in cars near elementary schools for no apparent reason."

"So you do a little of your own Rightful Targeting?" Jessie said, smiling.

"That's one way to put it."

"Okay, then let's get back to the Realm," she said. "Tell me about the trafficking."

He sighed heavily.

"Are you sure you really want to get into that?" he asked.

"I wouldn't be here if I didn't," she told him.

"Okay," he said, "Tell me what you know so far."

"Almost nothing," she admitted, recalling what Bauer had said hurriedly before his lawyers burst into the interrogation room. "Just that

117

women in the Realm are being trafficked, that it's potentially some kind of sexual slavery, and that they might not even realize what's happening to them."

Valchek nodded.

"As little as you know, that's more than 99.9% of the population is aware of," he said. "I should warn you that we're now entering the world of hearsay. I only have my interviews with two victims for reference. Both were conducted in secrecy and I've guaranteed them anonymity. I can't violate that without their express consent. Do you still want to hear this, even if it won't directly help any prosecution?"

"It might help in other ways," Jessie said. "So, yes."

"Okay," Valchek said with a shrug. "Then here we go. Sterling Shepherd is a sexual addict and a predator too. Some have suggested that's the reason he started this whole endeavor in the first place, to cultivate a collection of young women willing to do his bidding. Whether that's true or his needs became insatiable once he gained power, I don't know. But I have it on good authority that he churns through women, often keeping what he allegedly calls a "stable" of them available for whatever mood he's in or activity he's into at a given time."

Jessie had handled cases of sexual degradation before, one involving a billionaire who traveled to foreign countries to engage in behavior that would get him arrested here. But the idea of a collection of women kept at someone's disposal, available to pick out like baseball trading cards, was new to her. She couldn't help but wonder if at some point, Addison Rutherford had ended up in his so-called stable.

"And these women were willing participants?" she asked in disbelief.

"'Willing' is a complicated word in this situation," Valchek said. "Remember, all of them are Adherents. All of them view Shepherd as something approaching a god in their very presence. To be asked to be with him sexually would be considered an honor, a spiritual experience, a way to elevate to the next Realm, to maybe finally reach the vaunted Eleventh Realm."

"Has anyone ever even reached the Eleventh Realm?" Jessie asked.

"No. According the Creed, once one elevates to the Eleventh Realm, they have finally unlocked their potential. In that moment, their body returns to stardust and they merge with the universe in everlasting harmony and love. From what I understand, that's what the Eleventh Realm ultimately is: an eternal sanctuary comprised of pure love. Obviously, not even Shepherd has gotten there yet. But he has purportedly reached the Tenth. And a select few have reached the Ninth Realm."

"Who?"

"Supposedly a couple of members of the Council of Harmony and Potential have gotten there, as well as a select group of 'chosen' ones. Conveniently, those few include only the most devoted female Adherents, who have given their spirits and their bodies over to the Realm, via its representative on Earth, Sterling Shepherd."

"Is there any way to find out who those women are?" Jessie asked. "Maybe one of them could be coaxed into talking."

"Don't hold your breath," Valchek said. "The very thing that makes them valuable as witnesses is what makes them unlikely to talk. They are loyal to the Realm, and to Shepherd above all else, and they are very secretive. The only thing I ever learned about them was the cryptic maxim they used: 'those on the cusp of elevating to the Tenth Realm will bare it to the world.' That's a direct quote I got from one of the women who served as Shepherd's plaything for a while. But as she hadn't even gotten past the Fifth Realm, she didn't know what it meant."

Jessie tried to keep her thoughts clear. She didn't want to become overwhelmed by the enormity of the crimes this group was capable of, especially when it didn't seem like anything she'd heard was getting her closer to finding Addison's killer. Upon reflection, she wasn't even sure anything she'd heard was legally actionable.

"You know," she said, uncomfortable even voicing the thought she'd just had, "as awful as all this is, I don't know that it would hold up in court as trafficking or sexual slavery."

Valchek laughed cynically.

"I agree," he said. "Unfortunately, that wasn't all there was to it. Once Shepherd got tired of a girl, he would farm her out to other powerful Adherents. Though I can't prove it, I've even heard rumors that he would send girls out to service non-Adherents for money. If true, he's basically running a prostitution ring. The sickest part is that these women, even the ones doing the bidding of non-Adherents for cash, think that they're improving their chances of being elevated to the next Realm. So they'll do anything and say nothing. It's grotesque. Maybe that's why Addison wanted to leave."

"What do you mean?" Jessie demanded.

"Well, you said that Shepherd was grooming her as a public face of the Realm. Maybe that's not all he was grooming her for. And maybe she was resistant to what was being asked of her privately. If she was having second thoughts about the Realm, it wouldn't be the first time."

"Wait, what?" Jessie asked, not sure she had heard him correctly.

Valchek seemed to realize that he had been holding back information that might have been useful earlier.

"Sorry," he said. "In retrospect, maybe I should have led with this. But we started getting into the weeds and—."

"Just tell me!" Jessie shouted.

He was briefly startled by her outburst but quickly recovered.

"You may recall that I said earlier that I had some familiarity with Addison Rutherford," he said, handing over one of the files he'd pulled from the shelves earlier. "That's because she supposedly tried to leave once before."

"How do you know this?" Jessie pressed, grabbing the file, which was labeled "Dessler, M." It was very thin.

"Because I spoke to the woman she asked for help," he said. "Her name is Miranda Dessler."

"Was she an Adherent too?" Jessie asked as she flipped through the file. There were only three pages total. She took photos of each one with her phone.

"No," Valcheck said. "She knew Addison before she joined the Realm. I don't remember all the particulars. And you can see that the file isn't much help. That's not why she talked to me anyway."

"Why then?"

"Because after she tried to help Addison, the Realm sicced the DRA on her, using their techniques to scare her into submission. She came to me asking for help. She had read some of my pieces and wanted to know how she could protect herself from them. I gave her some suggestions. I'm hoping they worked because I never heard from her again."

"How long ago was this?"

"Two years ago," he said.

"Are you sure you didn't hear from her again because of your suggestions and not because the DRA got to her somehow?"

"No," he confessed. "I'm not sure at all. I guess it's up to you to find out."

"It almost always is," she said, resignedly, standing up. There didn't seem to be much more to discuss.

"One last thing," he warned as they headed back to the stairwell. "If it's not already obvious, then let me make it so. These people aren't just vindictive. They're not just power hungry. They're dangerous, to you and the people you love."

"What are you saying exactly?" she asked as they reached the foot of the stairs.

"I'm saying that while I've told you all these things, you should think carefully before acting on them. It's one thing to investigate this girl's death. That's defensible up to a point—even they can't officially balk at it. But if you start digging deeper, trying to unearth the Realm's deepest, darkest secrets, you could be putting everything you care about at risk. Take it from someone's who's been there. It's not worth it."

"Thanks for the advice," she said with an appreciative smile.

As she started up the stairs ahead of him, she didn't say what she was really thinking. If Huell Valchek had known her better, he would have realized that cautioning her not to pursue something was a sure-fire way to get the opposite reaction. Without meaning to, he'd only strengthened her resolve.

She was going to solve Addison's murder. And she was going to get these people too. As for now, she had to find a ghost named Miranda Dessler.

CHAPTER TWENTY THREE

The apartment wasn't much to look at.

Jessie had confirmed with Jamil that the address Valchek gave her was still the record of residence for Miranda Dessler. According to the landlord, the rent had been paid regularly every month since she moved in, including the last two years.

Jessie got out and stared at the place from across the street. The unit was visible from where she stood. It was on the second floor of a small, two-story complex on Fountain Avenue between Fairfax and La Brea called The Carver Arms. The building, which looked like a converted motel, was like a thousand others in this part of West Hollywood— 'protected' by an ineffectual metal gate, painted eggshell white, and with an exterior staircase of questionable sturdiness.

She walked across the busy street, ignoring the honk of a driver, frustrated that he had to slow down for half a second to let her pass. She traversed the lawn in front, which was more dirt than grass, and was about to buzz the building manager's office when she saw that the gate was slightly open. She stepped inside and tried to close it, only to find that the latch was broken.

Jessie was surprised that, after what Miranda Dessler had been through, she would continue to live in a place like this. As she walked quietly along the path to the stairs, she recalled the little information that Jamil had been able to pull up on the woman during the drive over.

Though the rent was paid in full every month, there was no phone, electric, or water service at the unit. Nor could he find any record of an active cell phone, e-mail, or any social media accounts. It was like she'd decided to go off the grid in the middle of a huge city.

Jessie made way her up the stairs and came to Dessler's unit. The curtains over the window were drawn and there wasn't any sound coming from inside. She knocked on the door. There was no answer. She tried again and announced herself.

"Miranda Dessler, this is the LAPD," she said, which wasn't entirely accurate. "May I speak with you?"

Still nothing. She checked the door and found it locked. As she and Karen had done at Josh Sawyer's apartment, she checked the single window at the front of the unit. Unlike at Sawyer's place, it was locked.

She decided now was an ideal time to take advantage of the fact that she was technically *not* in the employ of the LAPD, but rather a consultant. Glancing around and seeing no one nearby, she pressed herself up close to the door and quickly used a technique Ryan had showed her to pick the lock. She had some initial trouble, but eventually got it open. After hearing the soft click as the door opened, she quickly stepped inside and closed it.

The apartment reeked like something, or someone, had died in here. She prepared herself for the possibility that Miranda Dessler's long-dead body was somewhere in the unit. Looking around, it was clear that no one had been in the apartment in a while. Dust covered everything. Clothes were strewn over the floor as if someone had either left in a hurry, sloppily searched the place, or maybe both.

She moved to the kitchen and opened the refrigerator. It was immediately apparent that it was the source of the smell. There was a carton of milk with an expiration date from two years ago. In addition, the crisper held what seemed to have once been a head of lettuce but was now mostly just a mushy, brown blob.

She tried not to gag as she closed the door. She told herself that if the smell came from the fridge, then at least that meant there was a chance that no one was dead in here. She headed for the bedroom, pushing the door open with her shoe.

She didn't see a body. The bed was unmade and there were books and some framed photos on the dresser. Jessie recognized Miranda from a few. Two abstract art posters hung on the walls and the closet was filled with clothes.

Jessie moved to the bathroom. The counter was bare except for a nearly empty toothpaste bottle and a leftover facial cleanser package. A towel hung from the shower pole. She opened the medicine cabinet to find a few packaged alcohol swabs and an empty bottle of aspirin. That was it.

She was just closing the cabinet when she heard a click in the living room. It was the same sound she'd heard when she'd opened the front door. Her back stiffened involuntarily. Had she not completely closed the door? Or had someone opened it?

Ignoring her heartbeat, which had suddenly quickened, she peeked out into the bedroom, but she couldn't see into the living room from her angle. Moving as quietly as possible, she darted over to the door, hoping to hide behind it until she knew for sure if she was alone. As she went, she undid the holster on her gun.

Jessie was just reaching the door when he stepped inside—a huge man with a full beard. She barely had time to process his surprised face because her attention was fixed on the taser in his right hand. There wasn't time to pull out her gun.

Instead, she reached out and grabbed the man's forearm just as she saw him press the taser trigger. With all the force she could muster, she shoved his hand back toward his own body. The current made contact with his chest. He grunted and doubled over, dropping the taser.

Without taking time to think, Jessie put both hands on his bent over back and gave him a hard shove, sending him toppling to the floor. Then she kicked the taser under the bed. He grunted again.

For the briefest of moments, she debated whether to try to cuff and arrest him. But then she thought better of it. She didn't know who this guy was, though she had an idea who he was affiliated with. Under the circumstances, and considering his size, it was probably best to just get out.

Breathing fast and shallow, she hurried out of the bedroom and rushed toward the front door, which was half open. She yanked it the rest of the way to find another man standing right out front. He was facing away from the apartment, as if he was a lookout, ready to warn his partner if anyone came by.

The man, who was shorter and leaner than his compatriot, must have heard the door open because he turned around immediately. Jessie didn't wait to see what he wanted. As before, she had no time to go for her weapon so she settled for kicking the guy in the right knee, imagining smashing the kneecap through his leg so that it fell out the back.

He howled loudly, gripping the second floor railing to try to stay upright. Jessie stepped forward and kicked him in the ankle of his left leg, which was supporting his weight. The ankle bent sharply to the side and his leg shot out from under him as he yelped in pain, his voice echoing through the courtyard. He fell backward, hitting the back of his head on the hard surface. He didn't seem to notice, as he was still screaming from the knee thing.

A shout from inside the apartment told her that the other guy had regrouped enough to belatedly warn his buddy. Worried that he might charge out at any second, she decided not to stick around.

She dashed over to the stairwell and took the steps two at a time. She paused for a moment at the broken gate door, glancing around to make sure there was no one else waiting for her. The only person on the street was an older lady walking her small dog.

She looked back up and saw that the bigger guy had managed to exit the apartment. He was looking around for her, oblivious to the shrieks of the man lying at his feet. She couldn't wait any longer.

She opened the broken gate door and sprinted across the unkempt, brown lawn in front of the complex. Taking only a second to check for oncoming cars, she tore across the street and got into her own. Only after she had started it and pulled out into traffic, did she allow herself to look over at the building she'd just left. The large man had just shoved open the gate and was charging across the dead grass in her direction.

She punched the accelerator and left him behind. He was yelling something but she didn't even bother to listen. Her mind was racing. Assuming these goons were from the Eleventh Realm—and that was the only logical assumption—that meant that Sterling Shepherd, COHP, the DRA, and his entire army of acronyms were escalating things massively.

They had to know who she was. And yet they'd come after her anyway. That meant they were desperate to hide something, so desperate that they were willing to harm—or worse—a high-profile representative of the LAPD. What could make them so reckless?

Jessie couldn't help but think that it was about more than just the death of one girl. She still had every intention of finding Addison Rutherford's killer. But this was bigger than that now. It was about a group that used indoctrination, intimidation, and violence to victimize anyone in their path. And she intended to stop them.

Once Jessie rounded the corner down the block, she pulled out her phone. She had a call to make.

CHAPTER TWENTY FOUR

The ride share dropped Hannah off at the convenience store two blocks from the house.

She could have had it take her straight home, but she wanted to get some gum and, besides, the walk would do her good. She'd been sitting too long anyway.

After leaving Dr. Lemmon's office, she had caught a ride to the Los Angeles Central Library, which was only a few minutes away by car. Though she didn't have school today because of the teacher in-service, she had been given a bunch of homework yesterday to finish over the long weekend. Rather than do it all at home, she decided to shake it up and study in a more inspiring location.

She'd loved the Central Library since visiting on a field trip in fifth grade. On a subsequent, voluntary trip she had found a nice, quiet nook overlooking a central atrium. Whenever she needed a break from the material, she could simply glance down and do a little people watching. That was how she had spent most of the day, studying and spying.

But now, as she got out of the car and headed toward the convenience store, she was dealing with the consequences of sitting in a hard-backed, wooden chair for hours on end. Her seventeen-year-old leg muscles were aching much more than they should. She hoped the walk home would loosen things up.

Once inside the store, she decided to get a drink too. She passed the guy working the register, a distracted-looking, heavyset dude in his thirties who was reading a comic book, and headed to the sports drink refrigerators at the back. As she looked over her options, she heard a voice whisper harshly from a few aisles over.

"Do it, you little wuss, or you'll be sorry."

Glancing over, she saw the blacked-haired head of a guy who looked to be about her age. He was staring menacingly down at someone who was clearly much smaller. She couldn't quite hear what the other person, who was speaking much more quietly, said beyond the word "arrested."

"If you don't," the black-haired guy growled, "you'll wish you got arrested. That'll be less painful than what you get."

126

Hannah had two simultaneous reactions to those words. First, her face flushed in anger. Second, she got the butterflies that always arrived when she knew something out of the ordinary was about to happen, usually at her hand.

Without turning overtly in their direction, she ambled over and planted herself in front of the fridge at the back of the aisle where the incident was occurring. From there she could get a decent view in the reflection of the fridge window.

Facing the black-haired guy was another teenager, who was a head shorter and looked to be in his early teens. The older guy was holding something in his hands that he repeatedly pushed at the younger one.

"Please," the smaller kid pleaded, "just leave me alone. If you want the beer so bad, just sneak it out yourself."

"This is your last chance," the bigger guy said, stepping right into the little one's personal space. "Do this now or the rest of the school year is going to be your personal hell."

Hannah vividly recalled her most recent session with Dr. Lemmon, only hours earlier. They had discussed how much of her work in therapy had been about not making rash choices, even though they often gave her the quick rush of emotion that she found so hard to muster in normal human interactions. This was an opportunity to put that work into practice and not just react.

She turned to face the pair. The younger boy, who was skinny with a mess of blond hair, stared back at her. Now that she could see him clearly, she could tell that he was probably fourteen or fifteen, likely a freshman at the school with his tormenter. He looked terrified.

The older guy followed the kid's gaze and turned around. Hannah finally got a good look at him. He was about the same height as her, with a blockish build. She guessed he had thirty or forty pounds on her. His hair was greasy and his face was covered in acne. He had on black jeans with a pocket chain attached. Under his jacket was a black Insane Clown Posse t-shirt. He was holding a malt liquor bottle. When he saw her, he sneered at her lasciviously.

"If you stick around, maybe I'll let you have a taste of what I've got," he offered nastily.

Hannah wrestled down the urge to throw up in her mouth and took another step forward.

"You're a big boy," she said sweetly. "Why don't you buy your own beer?"

His hungry leer changed in an instant.

"Why don't you shut your whore mouth?" he growled.

Out of the corner of her eye, Hannah noticed that to the right of the big guy was a shelf filled with oversized bottles of cheap wine. She pictured herself flitting over, grabbing one, and smashing it on the shelf. She imagined the wine splattering to the floor as she held the broken, jagged–edged bottle to the guy's neck. She visualized the fear in his eyes just before she jammed the sharp glass into his jugular vein, pulling it out and plunging it in again. She could almost feel his warm blood spurting over her as it shot out of his body and he crumpled to the floor.

"Why don't you shut it for me?" she asked, unable to hide the anticipation in her voice.

The guy looked startled at her comment. As he struggled with a comeback, she relished the moment. She could also almost taste the charge of adrenaline she could feel coming on. It was the same one she'd gotten when she shot the Night Hunter. It was the feeling she'd been missing ever since that night. She was desperate to recapture it. She had to know if this was her path to finding it again.

"Maybe I will," he said, stepping forward.

She barely heard him over the voices arguing in her head. Suddenly one emerged, louder than the other, and it was clear: *You can't do this. If you go down this road, there's no turning back. Is that what you want?*

In that moment, she realized she didn't want to know the answer to that question. She suddenly understood that she was more afraid of learning the truth about what depths she was capable of than she was scared of hurting someone else.

Her focus shifted back to the situation she was in. The black-haired guy was in *her* personal space now. She could smell his sour breath and it required effort not to flinch at it. She cocked her head around him so that she could see the younger boy.

"Get out of here, kid," she said calmly.

The boy didn't need to be told twice, turning and running out of the store without a word.

"I guess it's just you and me," the black-haired guy said.

"I guess so," Hannah replied.

She still felt the rush nipping at the edge of her brain and decided that there was another way to unleash it. She gave the guy one more, sweet smile and then puckered her lips as if to kiss him. He looked genuinely stunned. That was when she did it.

"Stop touching me!" she screamed as loud as she could, pulling up her top to expose her bra. "Help! This guy is groping me. He won't let me go! Please, someone help me."

The guy's jaw dropped open.

From somewhere near the register, they both heard a male voice say, "What the hell!" The black-haired guy glanced around. He appeared frozen in place. A moment later, the heavyset comics fan appeared with a baseball bat in his hands. He marched toward the black-haired guy. Hannah began to 'cry' as she covered her exposed chest with one arm while she pointed at the guy with the other.

"It was him!" she wailed.

That seemed to snap the guy out of his frozen moment. He rushed past Hannah to the back of the store, dropping the malt liquor bottle, which smashed on the floor. She moved out of the way so the man with the bat could follow. As she watched, the teenager made a beeline for the front door with the employee right behind, making surprisingly good time considering his considerable size. They both disappeared from sight.

Hannah pulled down her top, smiled to herself, and went back to get that sports drink.

CHAPTER TWENTY FIVE

Jessie knew they wouldn't like her plan, so she waited as long as she could to share it.

Back at the station after the incident at Miranda Dessler's apartment, Karen, Jamil, and Detective Jim Nettles, who had come on to assist with the case, had all listened intently as she described what happened there.

"But you're okay?" Nettles confirmed, as Jamil turned to his screen and tried to pull up cameras in the area around The Carver Arms.

"I'm good," she assured them. "*They're* the ones who will be feeling it."

"Maybe next time call for backup when you decide to visit a sketchy apartment?" Karen suggested.

"I didn't realize how sketchy it was until it was too late," Jessie countered, noting the obvious frustration on Jamil's face as he did his search.

"Dammit," he muttered quietly. That was about as crude as Jamil Winslow got. She understood why. He was upset because there were no cameras in the immediate vicinity of the complex. Since Jessie didn't know what car her assailants drove, there was nothing to go on.

She quickly moved on to explain what she'd learned from Huell Valchek, hoping to distract the kid from his disappointment. Once she explained the key points he'd shared, including how it appeared that Addison had tried to leave the Realm once before and the possibility that she was being groomed as Sterling Shepherd's personal, human sex doll, she came to the big finish she knew they'd hate.

"So I have an idea," she said.

"Why do I already despise it, even though I haven't even heard it yet?" Karen asked.

"Because you're a smart lady," Jessie told her. "But we're running out of options. At this point, we have no idea what happened to Miranda Dessler. And Addison's boyfriend, Josh Sawyer, was eliminated as a suspect."

"So was Logan Bauer, by the way," Karen noted. "We corroborated his alibi with Eli the bellboy."

"And then we verified the bellboy's whereabouts for good measure too," Nettles added.

"That clinches it," Jessie replied. "Now that you've confirmed Bauer's alibi and he knows he's in the clear, he's got no incentive to go on the record about the sex trafficking stuff."

"That's not entirely true," Karen reminded her, cryptically referencing the man's France situation.

"We're not going there," Jessie said. "We made a promise. And unless there's no other way to get what we need, I intend to keep it. That's why I came up with this other idea."

"What?" Jamil asked.

"Based on what we know, there's one obvious suspect out there that we haven't talked to, someone who clearly had the motive to kill Addison Rutherford and the resources to make it happen. We can't pussyfoot around it anymore. We have to talk to Sterling Shepherd."

Karen shook her head violently.

"No way," she said. "First of all, we don't need that kind of heat. Furthermore, there's no way to get close to him. His lawyers would never let us in the same room. We'd be showing our hand without getting anything in return."

Jessie smiled.

"O ye of little faith," she said.

"What do you mean?" Karen asked apprehensively.

"I called Jamil on my way back to the station and asked him to do a little checking," she said, turning her attention to the researcher. "You want to tell them what you found?"

He nodded, clearly proud of what he'd discovered.

"Shepherd is doing a seminar this afternoon," he said. "They've rented out the Dolby Theater for it."

"Where they hold the Oscars?" Nettles asked incredulously.

"That's not surprising," Karen said. "The Realm likes to go big. But Jessie, please tell me you're not thinking about going to this thing and confronting him in person."

"No," Jessie assured her. "I'm not thinking about it. I've already made the decision. Jamil got me a ticket under…what was the name again?"

"Jennifer Chase," Jamil said. "I thought I'd have some fun with it. Get it—Chase, Hunt?"

"It's a little on the nose but I like it," Jessie told him. "So I'll be attending Sterling Shepherd's 5 p.m. seminar on "Elevating Your

131

Game: Unlocking your Full Potential through Harmony and Love."
Wow, that title really uses *all* the buzzwords, huh?"

"Jessie," Karen said intensely, leaning forward in her chair. "I think you're being a little too blasé about all this, especially after what just happened to you. You were attacked, almost certainly by thugs acting on orders from the man you want to confront. You can't just stride into some theater and expect to take him down. He has layers of protection at his disposal."

Jessie smiled at her friend's concern.

"Karen, believe me, I know exactly what I'm up against," she said. "That attack at the apartment is *why* I'm taking the direct approach. I'm not going to let another case make me pull my punches or go into hiding. I can't be looking over my shoulder anymore. I'm going at this guy and I'm taking him down."

"But we don't know for sure that he's responsible for Rutherford's death," Karen protested.

"You're right," Jessie conceded. "But we have enough for a meaningful chat—motive, opportunity, and one more thing: I looked at some photos of him recently. In case you didn't notice, he fits the description that Eli the bellboy gave of the guy on the tenth floor pretty well too. He's trim with salt and pepper hair. He's about fifty. Hell, he could easily pass for Logan Bauer's less attractive cousin. He could have gone right up to her suite and, with those cameras out, we'd never know about it."

"True," Nettles said. "But he might also have an ironclad alibi."

"Something I'd be happy to discuss with him in person," Jessie countered.

"But what if he does have an alibi?" Karen pressed. "Even if he's responsible for this, do you really think he did it himself? He has lackeys for that. If we charge him with murder and it doesn't stick, then he walks out of here a living martyr, more powerful than he ever was before."

"I'll admit that's a concern," Jessie said. "But we all know this guy is dirty. Once we get him under pressure, I'm confident that we can make something stick. This may be the only chance to apply that pressure. I don't want to waste it."

"What happens if he doesn't crack under the pressure?" Karen wondered.

"Then we escalate things."

"What does that mean?"

"I'll explain later," Jessie dodged. "Right now, we've got some planning to do and not much time to do it. That seminar starts in forty-five minutes. Let's get moving."

CHAPTER TWENTY SIX

Ryan sat in the uncomfortable chair and waited.

He knew this was a long shot but he didn't have much choice. There was no way he was going to bother Jessie when she was in the middle of a murder investigation, especially one that already involved a major movie star and now, apparently, a powerful cult.

That's why he was the one sitting in the visitor area of the Twin Towers Correctional Facility's Female Forensic In-Patient Psychiatric Unit. He wondered if he was waiting at the same window where Jessie had met with Andy Robinson just a week ago, when the convicted killer had offered to trade valuable information for a transfer to a less objectionable facility.

While he waited, he silently acknowledged to himself that there was another reason he was here instead of Jessie. And it was a reason he couldn't tell his fiancée. He was worried about her.

Andrea Robinson was in here for murdering the wife of her lover. Her scheme had been brilliant and she had almost gotten away with it, had it not been for Jessie's keen intellect and sharp instincts. But by the time she'd uncovered what the woman had done, Robinson had already poisoned her. She'd barely survived the encounter.

And the truth was that Jessie ended up in that situation because Andy Robinson had played her. The woman was a rich socialite, but she didn't act like one. Instead, she easily assumed the persona of a chill, self-deprecating regular gal who knew all the trappings of wealth and pageantry were ridiculous and worthy of mockery.

It was Jessie's first case for the LAPD, one she worked with him, and she was very green. That partly explained why she allowed herself to become friendly with a woman who seemed to be a witness and not a suspect. It might also have been why, after the case appeared to have been closed with another suspect arrested, Jessie went to Andy's home for a girls' "movie and mojitos" night.

But inexperience couldn't explain it all away. Part of what got Jessie in trouble was how clever and manipulative Andy Robinson was. At her trial, she had been diagnosed as a sociopath who hid her amorality under a facade of charm. Prosecutors believed, though they could never prove, that she had committed other crimes before the one that ultimately got her caught.

And for whatever reason, Jessie seemed particularly susceptible to Andy's brand of disarming charm. Ryan worried that even wearing a prison jumpsuit and separated by a bulletproof window, the woman might find a way to worm her way into Jessie's head, to play on her insecurities.

Of course, he could never say that to the woman he loved. She wouldn't take kindly to hearing that he had any doubts about her. She'd say she'd come a long way since then, which was true. She'd say he should have more faith in her ability to see through Robinson's manipulations, which was true as well.

But none of that stopped him from worrying. And if he could spare her from dealing with Andy Robinson's games, it was worth a shot. So he sat in the hard chair, shifting around, trying to find a way to get comfortable and failing.

The door on the prisoners' side of the visitor area opened. For a moment no one entered. It was if the new entrant was allowing everyone to prepare themselves for her arrival. That's how Ryan knew it would be her. Sure enough, a second later Andy Robinson walked through the door.

She was wearing the official uniform assigned to inmates with mental health issue designations: a yellow shirt and blue, loose-fitting pants. Despite the dressed-down style, she looked pretty good, all things considered. Andy had a blandly attractive, if unmemorable face, which effectively masked the darkness in her. She was of average height and weight. Her blonde hair was in a loose ponytail. There was nothing about her that screamed "sociopathic killer," except maybe for an insinuation in the eyes.

They were a bright, blazing blue, almost too intense to be called beautiful. Were she not a convicted murderer, those eyes would probably be described as striking. But under the current circumstances, the phrase that came to Ryan's mind was soul-penetrating.

She glanced around at the visitor windows until those eyes fell on him. It was obvious that she recognized him, even before she gave him a pitying smile. Walking over slowly, she took him in, never blinking once. Neither did he. When she sat down, she stared at him for several seconds before picking up the phone receiver on the wall beside her. He did the same.

"Congratulations on your engagement, Ryan," she said, without even attempting to sound sincere.

"Thank you," he replied. "You're looking well. No snot in the hair or visible, unwanted tattoos."

"You look good too," she noted, with barely disguised viciousness. "Sitting upright, breathing on your own, fully conscious. Kudos."

"Thanks," he said, refusing to give her the satisfaction of a reaction. "So you said on the phone that you had some information that could be helpful to my case. I guess whether you get a new wardrobe is dependent on what that information is. What can you tell me?"

Andy leaned back languorously and gave him a torpid smile.

"I don't think so, Ryan," she replied. "You knew the rules when I called. That information is for Jessie alone."

"I'm afraid she's unavoidably detained at the moment," he told her. "If you saw my case on the news, then you surely saw hers. She's up to her ears in cults and movie stars. She doesn't have any spare time to stop by just now. But as it's *my* case, I'll happily hear what you have to share."

"Nope," she said pertly. "Rules are rules."

He could feel the opportunity slipping away, if he ever had a grip on it in the first place, and tried again.

"Here's the thing, Andy. This case is time-sensitive. If you wait to talk to Jessie and some killer out there with a machete uses it on someone else when you could have prevented it, that won't bode well for your transfer request."

Andy offered a condescending smile, as if she was about to explain something to a dull child.

"That's not how I see it, Detective Hernandez. From my perspective, I'm offering you valuable information and all I'm asking is to deliver it directly to Jessie Hunt. If this killer takes another life and it comes out that you could have prevented it by facilitating a simple conversation and refused, who do you think will be blamed by Captain Roy Decker? By the media? By your sexy new partner, Susannah Valentine?" She paused an extra beat after that last line before continuing. "As for me, I'll be no worse off than I was before, still stuck in this place. But maybe next time I hear about some crime I can help with, I'll demand more than just a transfer. Maybe I'll insist on a private meal with your lady love. How does that sound?"

By the time she was finished, her blue eyes were glowing with such passion that Ryan thought she might be able to light up the room all on her own.

"You know, Andy," he said, leaning in close to the window, "you're not doing much to convince me that you're rehabilitated."

Andy leaned in too. Only she came closer and pressed her lips to the glass.

"No touching the window!" a guard behind her yelled.

She pulled back, leaving lips marks and the misty residue of her hot breath. When she spoke, her voice was low and measured.

"Jessie Hunt in this room—make it a reality. And I'd move quickly. Based on what I know, I'd say it's only a matter of hours before you're staring at more chunks of machete-hacked human meat. If that happens, the next victim's on you, Ryan."

With that, she stood up, turned on her heel and walked to the exit door. Once she left, he sat there a few minutes more, trying to ignore his churning stomach as he silently turned over his options. He didn't seem to have many good ones.

He could call Andy's bluff and proceed as he had been. But they had no leads to speak of. And what if it wasn't a bluff? Andy had somehow known about the Night Hunter's plans to use Kat Gentry to get to Jessie.

If she had gained access to the plans of a secretive serial killer who she didn't even know, was it that hard to believe that after a year in city lockup, she might have gleaned some information about a local murderer? Was he willing to take the chance that she was pulling a con job in order to protect a woman who might not need it and definitely didn't want it?

As he got up and shuffled out of the room, he knew that, as a cop, there was an obvious answer. But he wasn't just a cop. He was a man who'd seen the woman he loved go through more torment in thirty years than most people suffer in ten lifetimes. He didn't want to intentionally subject her to more.

And then, almost against his wishes, he had one more thought. What if the situation was reversed? What would Jessie do in his shoes? The answer to that was clear. And once he had it, he knew what he had to do.

CHAPTER TWENTY SEVEN

Jessie pretended not to be nervous.

As she waited in line outside the Dolby Theater, she could see members of the team that had been assembled. Captain Decker, despite his understandable misgivings, had approved a unit to help at the seminar. Initially, he'd been hesitant to be so bold in pursuit of a well-funded, politically-connected target right after having to release a major celebrity, but Jessie had convinced him.

"Remember," she'd told him back at the station, "Bauer never badmouthed us after he was released. He was even complimentary. We're not taking any major press hits right now. And this Shepherd guy is bad news. You know it, Captain. Doesn't it eat at you that he and his minions have gotten away with so much for so long? How many times have you been told to let something slide that you knew should have been charged? Now *you* get to make the decision. Please, make the right one."

He did. Unspoken was their shared awareness that if he had said no, any chance that Jessie might return to HSS full-time was likely out the window. He had to know that if he didn't back her on this, there was no way she would commit to him in the future. His job offer wasn't something that hadn't been top of mind for her since this case started, but apparently he hadn't forgotten about it.

As a result of his decision to go all in to support her, the crowd outside the theater was littered with plain clothes cops, all hand-picked by Decker as officers he knew could be trusted, who wouldn't leak their presence to the Realm.

Officer Garrett Dooley was a few spots in line behind Jessie. With his goofy, excitable demeanor, Karen said that he already had the vibe of an ideal target for Realm indoctrination. After they dressed him in a tie-dyed t-shirt and bell-bottomed jeans, he looked more like a lamb to the slaughter. He would be the only other LAPD representative inside the theater with Jessie.

Karen had also given her some fashion advice.

"Dress unknowingly sexy," she said. "You want Shepherd to notice you, to be intrigued by you, but not to view you as too worldly. He has to think you can be molded into what he likes."

That's why she was wearing jeans tight enough to make her worry about her circulation. It was also why, under her jacket, she had on a floral, spaghetti-strapped top that was cut much lower than she would wear in normal life. She had even let someone from the Vice unit style her brown hair so that it was extra bouncy around her bare shoulders.

Right now the revealing attire was covered by her bulky jacket and her hair was hidden under her jacket hood, which she was using to hide her recognizable face. A point would come soon when she would have to take off that layer off physical—and emotional—protection, but not yet.

"Testing, testing," she said quietly into her concealed microphone wire as she neared the ticket taker. "I'm close to entry. Everyone in place?"

"We're all good down here," Jamil said through the tiny earpiece she wore. He was stationed in a van out front on Hollywood Boulevard. Karen and Nettles, both loitering a few dozen feet away, nodded that all was well with them too.

The ticket taker scanned her phone and Jessie went to her seat. Dooley took his across the aisle a few rows up from her. The theater was filling up fast. By 5 p.m., there didn't appear to be an empty seat in the place. That seemed odd, considering that she and Dooley had been able to secure decent seats barely an hour before show time. She had a sneaking suspicion that the unfilled seats were being occupied by Adherents. The overhead lights flickered, indicating the two-minute warning.

An announcement asked everyone to take their seats, mute their phones, and prepare for a life-changing experience. Soon thereafter, the theater went dark. Portentous music began to play and images appeared on a screen at the front of the theater.

They showed choked traffic, gas spewing from factory smokestacks, skeletal children in Africa, flood waters pouring through city streets, and a continuing array of horrors as the music got louder, all culminating in a nuclear mushroom cloud.

Then the music shifted into something softer and more hopeful as a different set of scenes played across the screen: children running at a playground, a mom beaming at her equally happy baby, flowers blooming in a field, a couple holding hands, good Samaritans building a house. Interspersed among those shots were others, all of smiling people, all wearing shirts with the logo for the Eleventh Realm, which was an "11" with what looked like a small suspension bridge between the digits that formed a kind of smile.

139

After a minute of that nonsense, the music changed once again as the phrase "We Can Change the World—Together" appeared on the screen. The new melody started quietly, but grew louder fast. It was intended to be inspirational and sounded to Jessie like a knockoff of the theme from the movie "Rocky." As the volume increased, a spotlight appeared in the middle of the stage and a female voice came over the speakers.

"Good afternoon everyone and thank you for joining us for 'Elevating Your Game: Unlocking your Full Potential through Harmony and Love.' It is now my great honor to bring to the stage, the author of the book, *The Purifying Power of Potential: A New Creed for a New Era,* better known as *P3*, which has sold over fifty million copies worldwide, the man responsible for feeding twelve million unfed children and housing seven million unhoused families, and the founder of The Eleventh Realm—please welcome Sterling Shepherd!"

The crowd broke into cheers and applause as a man jogged from offstage to the circle of light. He was dressed business casual, in khaki slacks, a blue button-down shirt and brown loafers. He had on a headset wireless microphone. For a new messiah, he was playing it pretty conservative. It was hard to reconcile the man on the stage with Karen's twenty-year-old description of a guy with shaggy hair and stubble, who might be mistaken for a stoned surfer.

He may not have been Logan Bauer, but he was definitely a good-looking guy. Jessie guessed that he was a little taller than her. He was lean and athletic, clearly in good shape for a fifty-year-old. His dark brown hair was well-dotted with gray and his tan face was starting to wrinkle a bit. It gave him a devil-may-care unpretentiousness, as if he couldn't be bothered with worldly things like aging. Even before he spoke, Jessie could feel a magnetism emanating from him.

"Love is the way!" he shouted.

"The way is love!" came the enthusiastic reply from at least half the crowd.

"Thank you so much for coming," he said, motioning for folks to end their applause. "I know it's tough to take time out during your busy lives, so I really appreciate it."

There was a second, shorter round of cheers.

"Hey," he said, as if suddenly having an unexpected thought. "Why don't we bring up the house lights, if that's okay with everyone? I don't want today to be a lecture. I want it to be a conversation."

There were more cheers as the lights came up, almost as if the lighting tech had known the request was coming. Shepherd held up his hand to quiet the crowd again.

"My name is Sterling Shepherd, but I'd love it if you all would call me Shep."

More cheers. It went on like that for a while, Shepherd saying something charming or self-deprecating to whoops and hollers of enthusiasm that seemed outsized for the moment. Eventually he settled into a groove. Despite his assertion that he didn't want to lecture the audience, he expounded on why so many of people's efforts at self-improvement failed. No one seemed to mind. Then he transitioned into what made the Eleventh Realm different. But after a little while, it became apparent to Jessie that something was missing.

Shepherd talked at length about the Realm's good works around the world, giving a dizzying array of examples. He talked inspirationally about how people could achieve amazing things, and consequently, maximize their potential, by working together and sacrificing for the greater good. But he barely mentioned the philosophy of the Eleventh Realm.

There was no discussion of elevating from one realm to the next and how it was achieved. There was certainly no mention of bodies becoming stardust again and merging with the universe in everlasting harmony and love when they got to that Eleventh Realm. It was all pious platitudes, amorphous and non-threatening.

The reference to "sacrifice" was the closest he ever got to suggesting that potential joiners—he didn't use the term Adherents—might have to give anything up for all they would get in return. Apparently Shep didn't think he could sell spending tons of money on courses and seminars that didn't offer tangible results. Nor did he see fit to reference food and sleep deprivation or potential harassment if a person ever left. Funnily enough, sexual slavery never came up either.

After an hour of his spiel, Jessie had more than her fill. Maybe she was just too cynical, but there was no point during his talk that she felt remotely intrigued by what he was promoting. Of course, her knowledge of what was lurking under the hood may have had something to do with that.

It wasn't lost on her that, though she and Sterling Shepherd were very different, the reaction of the most devoted people in this audience wasn't all that different from the more enthusiastic students in her seminars. She knew that some of them came, not because of any interest in criminal profiling, but because of her celebrity. Others seemed to treat her with a kind of hero-worship that she found disconcertingly similar to the vibe in this theater. For now, she chose to ignore that parallel.

Just as she was starting to doubt if he'd ever take questions, he wrapped up and opened the floor to 'the curious and the questioning.' Jessie hurried to get in line at one of the standing microphones. From her new vantage point, she noticed something she hadn't seen earlier. Just beyond the far side of the stage, partially obscured by a curtain, were two men. She recognized them immediately. They were the guys who'd attacked her at Miranda Dessler's apartment. The big guy with the beard looked the same but the smaller man seemed to be favoring his left leg.

Her suspicions that they'd been Realm heavies confirmed, she was tempted to whisper something into her microphone to alert the others. But she feared the people around her might hear her. Besides, any attempt to round those guys up would undermine the operation. For the time being, she had to let them go.

While she waited for her turn, she tried her best to project innocent excitement, something she wasn't even sure she was truly capable of anymore. As time ticked away and she listened to question after question—some legitimate, some fawning and from obvious plants— she began to worry that the seminar would end before they got to her. Then, just before the ninety-minute mark, the usher near her indicated for her to step up to the microphone stand.

Even though it was cold in the theater, Jessie took off her hooded jacket and adjusted her plunging top to full effect. For this to work, she needed Sterling Shepherd to be more focused on her body than her question. She could only hope that he didn't recognize her before she asked it.

"My name is Jennifer. Thank you for taking my question, Mr. Shepherd," she said, trying to sound nervous and thrilled at the same time. It wasn't hard. All she had to do was channel her real feelings of anxiety and disgust and tweak them with a smile.

"Please, call me Shep," he insisted, "and have we ever met? You look very familiar to me."

"I wish," she said, leaning over and letting her hair fall in her face. The last thing she needed was to get called out before she even started. "But I had two questions, if that's okay. They're quick."

"Go ahead," he said, smiling warmly to make her feel comfortable.

"Thanks. My first question is: did you ever want to do something else before you started on this journey to helping people unlock their potential?"

She wanted to butter him up before her next question.

"Well," he said, happy for the softball, "like a lot of kids, I wanted to be a fireman for a while, and then an astronaut. But once I got old enough to take the question more seriously, I'm ashamed to say that for a number of years there, I mostly focused on getting mine. I tried real estate, acting. I even sold knives door to door for a while. But it was only when I started to put other people's well-being ahead of my own that I began to feel any kind of fulfillment. Making a difference made me feel different."

Once the applause died down, he nodded at her.

"You had a second question?"

"Yes, Shep," she said, feeling a pit materialize in her gut, "I was just wondering what your involvement was in the death of one of the Eleventh Realm's most devoted Adherents, Addison Rutherford, who was murdered in a hotel not far from here?"

To his credit, Sterling Shepherd managed to mostly keep it together, maintaining the perfect veil of poise that was his hallmark. He didn't grimace or scowl or show any overt sign of guilt. He did look shocked however and, though she didn't know him at all, Jessie thought she saw a little fear too.

There were gasps in the crowd. While her eyes were fixed on Shepherd, Jessie noted movement all around her as dozens of cameras were whipped out and began to record. Shepherd noticed it too and quickly adjusted to the situation.

"Now I know where I recognize you from," Shepherd said. "You're the famed profiler, Jessie Hunt. Wasn't it just a few hours ago that you were harassing one of our most admired members, Logan Bauer, about this very matter?"

As he spoke, Jessie saw several security guards making their way to her. She also saw the goons backstage whispering furiously to each other. People close to her were murmuring. Others were hissing at her.

"Get in position, guys," she muttered under her breath into the police wire, using the crowd noise to mask her words. "I'm about to pull the trigger on this."

"And now you come here," Shepherd continued, "to an event designed to help people, in order to make unfounded allegations against me too. I have to say, Ms. Hunt, that's beneath you."

Everyone turned to get her response. Jessie paused a second for dramatic effect.

"Did you kill Addison Rutherford, sir?" she demanded. "Did you order her death?"

A young woman with curly blonde hair a few rows in front of her stood up and pointed at her.

"Hatemonger!" she shouted. Within seconds she was joined by a chorus of others, mostly female, mostly younger.

One of the security guards was just reaching out for her when a series of doors to the theater burst open. More than a dozen cops, half of them in plainclothes, poured in. Nettles, who had entered near the stage, headed straight for Shepherd. The security guard closest to Jessie, a big, sweaty guy with a meticulously curated goatee, grabbed hold of her arm and tugged hard.

"You don't want to do that," she warned him.

"Why the hell not?" he spat at her.

"Because of this," Officer Garrett Dooley said, suddenly appearing beside her with his police shield extended for the guard to see. "Take your hand off her or you'll be spending the weekend behind bars."

The guard hesitated, but only for a second. He let go of Jessie and retreated into the crowd, the rest of which didn't seem as chastened by Dooley's warning. They were pushing closer, furious and full of catcalls.

"We should probably get out of here," the officer muttered to her.

Jessie looked around for the best exit. Down on the stage, Sterling Shepherd was being handcuffed by Nettles. Karen was reading him his rights. Two uniformed officers were holding back several young women who were trying to lie down, hoping to block any path to extract Shepherd. They were all screaming "the way is love" at the top of their lungs. One was stripping naked. Jessie noticed that she had a tattoo in the same spot on her left breast that Addison did, though she couldn't identify what it was from this distance. The goons from the apartment attack were nowhere to be found.

Jessie could feel the throng, hot with self-righteous fury, closing in. She had a weapon and knew that Dooley did too. But pulling it out would be a massive escalation and likely a catastrophic mistake.

Still, she wasn't sure what to do. All the other cops were either helping secure Shepherd or distracted by their own collection of screaming Adherents. The people near Jessie and Dooley were either civilians trying to get away fast or Adherents out for blood, now within striking distance.

144

They were trapped.

CHAPTER TWENTY EIGHT

Jessie looked over at Dooley. His face was set with determination but there was panic in his eyes. He started to reach for his weapon.

"Don't," she instructed.

He moved his hand away. Jessie forced herself to consider their options. Running was pointless. It might drive the crowd encircling them into a bigger frenzy and they were unlikely to get away from the dozens of people surrounding them. She decided she had to change the dynamic.

"Watch my back," she instructed the officer, before grabbing the microphone stand and leaping up into the nearest chair. The mic was still in the clip and she prayed no one had thought to turn it off or she might have to start swinging the metal stand around to defend herself. She blew into the microphone and heard her own breath over the speakers.

"Stop!" she yelled at the people around her. Her voice echoed throughout the theater. "I know you're all upset but you are interfering in a lawful arrest."

The people advancing on her paused, more out of surprise than assent. She didn't wait for them to regroup.

"Protest outside the police station if you want, but if you touch me or any of the police officers doing their job in this theater, that's assault. Do you really want to go to jail over this today? Do you want to go on trial for attacking a law enforcement officer as part of some riot?"

She saw some of the people closest to her look at each other hesitantly, unsure of the answer to that question. She pressed on.

"Do you think it will help your movement to been seen on the six o'clock news, assaulting people who are trying to solve a girl's murder? Does that help advance the Creed? Is that how you elevate to the next Realm?"

Now the people near her were murmuring to each other.

"Breathe for a moment," she said, lowering her voice, "Then take a step back and realize that what you do now could destroy both your own future and that of TEROTH."

She worried that using an Adherents-only term for the group might incite more anger but it seemed to have the opposite effect. She saw a few people stare at her, both surprised and impressed.

"We're going to do our jobs," she announced. "Then you can make your voices heard the right way. Now let us pass."

Jessie got off the chair and put the mic stand on the floor beside her. The people around her stared but didn't move, as if stuck in suspended animation. She turned to Dooley and spoke in a forceful but calm voice.

"Let's go, Officer."

Then she turned and walked up the aisle to the exit with Dooley right behind her, hoping that they'd make it there in one piece.

*

He didn't say a word.

Sterling Shepherd didn't speak in the car on the way to the station, nor as he was being booked. And so far, not in the interrogation room where Jessie and Detective Jim Nettles had been peppering him with questions for the last ten minutes. Nettles had stepped in at the last minute for Karen, who had gotten cold feet.

"After reading him his rights," she had said once they arrived at the station, "I saw him staring at me, trying to place where he recognized me from. My name has changed and I look different, but maybe not enough. If he identifies me and this doesn't pan out, I'm worried that he'll have his minions start Rightful Targeting me again."

It was a legitimate worry. Jessie remembered how her partner had expressed fear for her son's safety mere hours earlier. Back then, her concerns had seemed slightly hyperbolic. But now, Jessie realized just how justifiable they were. That was why Karen was currently watching everything from the observation room. But there wasn't much for her to see.

Shepherd hadn't asked for a lawyer or invoked his right to silence, which is why they kept going. But it was becoming clear that he knew his attorneys would be arriving soon and was happy to spend the intervening time watching them get worked up without success. Jessie looked over at Nettles and motioned for them to go outside. Once they stepped out, Karen met them in the hall.

"This clearly isn't working," Jessie said. "He's just toying with us."

"You have to keep trying," Karen insisted. "Once his lawyers get here, they'll shut you down and we'll never get another chance at him."

Jessie could sense the desperation in her voice and felt for her. Jessie had only been pursuing Sterling Shepherd for one day and she despised him. Karen had been dealing with the man's odiousness for almost twenty years. Now she had him in her sights. She could taste victory. But suddenly a man who made his living through the power of his words and personality might escape justice by going silent. It was infuriating.

"He's not going anywhere," Jessie assured her. "He's been arrested for murder and it's a Friday evening. Not even Sterling Shepherd is getting bail tonight. I think we let him stew and see what Jamil has turned up while we've been wasting our time in that room."

Both Karen and Nettles nodded, but before they could go to research, a flurry of people poured into the hallway. Captain Decker was among them. So was Logan Bauer's lawyer from this afternoon, Walter Serra. He marched right toward Jessie and pointed his finger in her face.

"This is harassment, pure and simple," he seethed before turning to Decker. "You need to release my client right now or prepare to face a lawsuit that will bankrupt this department."

Decker looked unfazed by the threat.

"I'm afraid we can't release a suspect who's under arrest for murder, Mr. Serra," he said coolly. "But you're welcome to speak with your client. He's in the same room where you found Mr. Bauer earlier.'"

Jessie couldn't help but be impressed with how unperturbed the captain seemed and how unflinchingly he had their backs.

"Maybe you can convince Mr. Shepherd to explain where he was last night that *wasn't* in the hotel suite of a murdered Adherent," Karen baited.

"I can do that for you right now," Serra said petulantly. "He was at the Heartbeat Hub all night for a private event celebrating our recently elevated female Adherents. We can produce a dozen eyewitnesses who will verify that alibi. Would you like names and numbers?"

"That would be super," Jessie said, though she didn't put much stock in what these women might say. After seeing how they threw themselves on the stage, chanting "the way is love" like a bible verse and ripping off their clothes, she suspected that they'd say whatever they were told if it pleased the prophet who provided the Flawless Interpretation of the Creed.

"I'll have a full list within the hour," Serra said, "now may I please speak to my client privately?"

"Of course," Jessie said stepping aside to let him pass. He was almost to the door when she added, "Just one question, Counsel. You haven't had a chance to speak to Shepherd yet. How could you possibly know his alibi already?"

Serra looked briefly flummoxed before replying.

"I guess I'm just a great lawyer."

He opened the door and disappeared from sight. Jessie didn't want to waste any more time and turned to go to Jamil's research office. To her surprise, standing at the end of the hall was her fiancé. He wasn't smiling.

"I'll catch up to you and Jamil in a minute," she told Karen. Her partner nodded and hurried off, not wanting to get in the middle of whatever was about to happen. Ryan walked over.

"What's wrong?" Jessie asked. "Is Hannah okay?"

"She's fine," Ryan swore. "Didn't you see her text?"

Jessie pulled out her phone and saw that she'd missed multiple texts from Hannah and three voicemails, all from him.

"Damn," she said, "I put my phone on silent during that seminar and forgot to turn it back on. Can you update me please?"

"Of course," he said, taking her gently by the arm. "Let's go to the courtyard for a little privacy."

That only made her more nervous but she held her tongue until they were outside. The sun had set and the chilly day had turned into a genuinely cold evening. They moved over to the same bench where Jessie had spoken with Karen earlier. Only then did Ryan talk.

"First thing first—Hannah's great. She finished her homework at the Central Library today after her session with Dr. Lemmon. Since you weren't responding to her messages for obvious reasons, I told her she should expect to eat alone tonight. She asked if she could go to the coffeehouse for a few hours afterward. I told her that it was okay unless you said otherwise when you were back in touch. You cool with that?"

"Yes," Jessie said, texting her sister exactly that, along with an apology for being out of touch. "So I see that you left me some voicemails. You want to tell me what's going on? Do I need to sit down?"

"It's not that bad," he said. "But it's not great either. I didn't want to come to you but I don't think I have any other choice. I need your help with my case."

"Me?" Jessie asked, genuinely surprised. "Isn't Valentine up to the task?"

149

"It's not that," he said, and then added, "Maybe we *should* sit down."

He took a seat on the bench and she joined him.

"You're starting to scare me," she said. "Just tell me what it is."

"Okay," he said. "I didn't want to bother you. I know your case is blowing up right now. But I think you're the only one who can help. We've hit a dead end in the machete murder. We have zero leads. But someone else might. And she'll only talk to you."

Jessie sighed in understanding. Now it was clear. Just as she had with the Night Hunter case, Andy Robinson had reached out on this one too. She must have claimed to have information vital to the investigation. But she'd only tell Jessie, and only in exchange for a transfer to a nicer facility.

Jessie had been putting off giving the woman an answer on the potential deal for a week now and apparently Andy had decided she was tired of waiting. In retrospect, it was foolish to have assumed someone like Andrea Robinson would just patiently wait to hear back.

"What is she saying?" she asked. There was no need to use her name.

"Not much, at least not to me," Ryan said. "Just that she has information that could be helpful. She knew the murder weapon, even though that hasn't been made public. And she hinted that this might not be a one-time-only thing, which I suspect as well. Normally, I wouldn't ask you to re-engage with that viper. We both know what she did to you. And I'm pretty sure that she's more interested in screwing with your head than actually transferring facilities. But if there's a chance that she can provide information that could save a life, I had to come to you."

Jessie stood up. Ryan did too.

"But like I said," he continued before she could reply, "I know this Eleventh Realm thing is out of control. I don't expect that you can just take a break from interrogating that self-appointed prophet in the middle of the investigation."

"Funny you should say that," she told him. "We're at a bit of an impasse right now. I think I can sneak away for a few minutes. Karen, Nettles, and Jamil can hold down the fort for a while. Maybe they'll make some brilliant discovery while I'm gone."

"Are you sure?" he asked.

Jessie took his hands in hers, leaned in, and gave him a kiss. Then she stepped back and fixed him with her most confident smile.

"Can you give a girl a ride?"

CHAPTER TWENTY NINE

It was well past visiting hours.

As a result, Jessie had to wait in a small room intended for therapy sessions between prisoners and facility doctors. It was nothing like Dr. Lemmon's well-appointed office. Spartan and uncomfortably cold, it looked more like an interrogation room than a place to bare your soul to a medical professional. The room was comprised of two bolted-down chairs, one table with a loop for manacles, and a single framed poster on the wall of a beautiful, unnamed beach.

Jessie was staring at it, wondering if was intended to soothe prisoners in distress, when the door opened. A guard, stepped in, followed by Andy Robinson, and then a second guard. She looked the same as the last time they met except that her blonde hair was down now. She sat in the chair opposite Jessie, expressionless, and extended her arms so one guard could slide the manacle chain through the slot in the table. The first guard left the room.

"In or out?" the second one asked.

"What?" Jessie said.

"Do you want me in the room or out? It's your choice."

Jessie looked at Andy, who shrugged.

"I would prefer a little privacy, so we can speak openly," she said. "I promise not to make any sudden moves."

"Out is fine," Jessie said. "Just don't go too far."

"I'll be right outside," he said before closing the door.

Alone now, the two women stared at each other for a while. Andy finally broke the silence.

"Feel safe enough?" she asked.

"Safe is a relative term, Andy," Jessie replied. "So I understand you have some information to share with me."

"Good to know your strapping messenger boy did my bidding," Andy noted. "I was worried that he might be too taken with his new partner, Detective Valentine, to stay on task."

Jessie marveled at the woman's ability to go straight for the jugular, and under other circumstances it might have been effective. But tonight, stressed out, exhausted, and short on time, she didn't have the energy to worry about the motives or impact of HSS's newest addition.

151

"Forgive my brusqueness," she said, "but I'm trying to prevent a murder and solve an unrelated case, all before bedtime. So maybe we can dispense with the psychological games for once and just cut to the chase? What have you got for me?"

"What about our deal?" Andy asked.

Jessie had been expecting the question. And though she wasn't happy about it, she was prepared with an answer.

"If you give straightforward information on this case—not some cryptic hint—and it proves useful in apprehending the perpetrator of this crime, I will write a letter supporting your transfer to a different, maximum security facility, but one with a better track record for inmate care. However, as I told you previously, I can't control whether my recommendation will make any difference. I'm sure it will be impactful but I don't make the final decision."

"Understood," Andy said. She seemed confident that a letter from the woman she tried to kill would be sufficient.

"If the transfer *is* approved," Jessie continued, "you'll need to provide additional intelligence in other cases. If you do that on a regular basis, you can remain at the new facility. If not, then you come back here. Clear?"

"What if my leads dry up?" Andy asked. "Not everyone likes to chat with the village gossip."

"Not my problem," Jessie said. "My part of the deal is to provide the letter. Yours is to keep the intel coming. I don't want there to be any confusion on that point."

Andy seemed to ponder the offer. It was several seconds before she replied.

"Can I read your letter before you send it?" she asked.

"Yes, but you can't suggest changes. It is what it is. And I don't sit down at a keyboard until this machete killer is caught. Do we have a deal?"

Andy fixed those intense blue eyes on her, as if she was doing an x-ray on her soul.

"I'm trusting you, Jessie Hunt," she said. "That's a big deal for me. Please don't let me down."

"Said the woman who tried to poison me," Jessie retorted.

Andy smiled. For whatever reason, the comment seemed to satisfy her concerns.

"I talk to a lot of fellow inmates," she said. "It can get pretty boring in here, so listening to the rantings of some of the more creative patients can be intermittently entertaining. A few months ago, one of them told me about a recurring fantasy she had. Her father had gifted her a machete that he used to clear brush back on his ranch. She's homeless so she kept it in a locker at the train station, along with all her other prized possessions. She said that once she got out of here, she was going to get that machete and chop up the first person she could find who didn't deserve it. She said that she would scoop up some of her victim's blood and drink it, as a way to cleanse her own sins. That inmate was released a week ago."

In addition to being horrified, Jessie had questions, but didn't want to interrupt Andy when she was on a roll so she said nothing. Andy didn't even notice.

"I didn't think much of it," she continued. "It was just another violent daydream among many I'd heard. But when I saw the news today and heard about the crime, it felt familiar. They didn't mention a machete but they did say the victim had been hacked to death. When I heard that the girl worked as a volunteer at the very place where she was killed, other pieces fell into place: violent murder, likely with a big knife. Victim was an innocent. And the location of that YWCA is within blocks of the homeless encampment on San Pedro Street where this woman said she normally hung out. It didn't seem like a coincidence."

"What's her name, Andy?" Jessie asked.

"Livia Bucco."

Jessie stood up.

"Thank you," she said. "If this pans out, I'll write you the letter."

"I have no doubt," Andy replied.

"We'll have to dispense with the elaborate goodbyes. I have to get this name out there now."

She started for the door and was just about to knock for the guard to open it when Andy called after her.

"One more thing, Jessie," she said. "You better get your man to hurry. When Livia told me about her fantasy, she said that once she started, she would never stop. She said that was her primary principle."

CHAPTER THIRTY

Ryan was getting desperate.

He and Valentine had been at the encampment that Andy told Jessie about for twenty minutes now, asking around and showing Livia Bucco's mug shot to anyone who would look. But no one who would talk recognized her. At least that's what they said.

It wasn't shocking that these folks weren't especially forthcoming about the whereabouts of one of their own with a pair of cops. But as Livia Bucco had no regular address, they didn't have much choice but to continue to ask around and hope. They knew that she'd been hired as a bagger a local grocery store but apparently she'd quit this afternoon, after only two days of work. So they were left with the encampment.

He was just about to give up when Valentine texted that she'd had some luck. He hurried over to where she was waving at him, past a row of tents on the sidewalk. She was with an older man sitting on an overturned paint bucket, taking a long hit from a homemade bong. Ryan pretended not to notice.

"What have we got?' he asked.

"Don here says he knows Livia. Isn't that right, Don?"

Don nodded.

"You were just about to tell me something about where she likes to hang out sometimes, right?"

Don nodded again, before succumbing to a loud hacking cough. It was half a minute before he could speak.

"She likes her privacy," he rasped. "So she goes to the Pearly. She sits up on the roof and watches the night twinkles."

"The Pearly," Ryan repeated. "Do you mean the Pearl Hotel over on San Julian Street?"

Don nodded.

"That's where she goes most nights," he said, "when her head starts telling her bad thoughts."

Valentine looked at Ryan. She obviously didn't get the reference.

"The Pearl Hotel is two blocks over. It shut down about a year ago, scheduled for demolition next month. It's all boarded up, but if someone was motivated, they could probably find a way in."

"Then let's go check it out," Valentine suggested, before turning to the wizened man on the bucket. "Thanks, Don."

Even at Ryan's still slow jogging pace, which Valentine graciously matched, they got to the hotel in less than three minutes. It didn't take long to find the likely spot where Livia Bucco snuck in. A lower, corner section of the metal fence designed to keep people out had been cut and bent back, making it easy to slide through.

They maneuvered through it quickly, discovered a section of one boarded-up door that had been ripped off and entered the hotel to find themselves at a side entrance of the lobby. They moved as fast they could without making noise, until they came to the door of a stairwell near a bank of unmoving elevators.

"More stairs," Ryan muttered. "Great."

"How many stories is it?" Valentine asked.

"Six, I think," Ryan said, pulling out his gun and flashlight. "Let's not assume she's up top watching the night twinkles. She might be on the other side of that door with her machete."

Valentine nodded and removed her weapon too. Then she pulled open the stairwell door for Ryan. He darted in, pointing his light and gun at the stairs. They were empty.

The two of them made their way up slowly, rounding each corner carefully until, ten minutes later, they were at the door to the roof. Ryan eased it open, hoping it wouldn't creak. It stayed mercifully silent and Valentine stepped through, looking in every direction for movement. Ryan joined her and did the same, watching for any sign of Livia Bucco. It was hard to get his bearings on the exposed roof, with so many tall, brightly lit buildings competing for his attention.

They came to a short flight of stairs that led from the door down to the main section of the roof. Valentine led the way while Ryan covered her. She took the first step down when a loud metallic clanging reverberated in the air. Valentine looked down.

Ryan didn't need to do the same to know what had happened. Livia had placed something on the top stair—probably nails and screws—to alert her if anyone was approaching. Any element of surprise they'd had was now gone.

At the far corner of the roof, he saw someone stand up from behind a rooftop unit and look their way. Though he couldn't see her face at this distance, he was sure it was Bucco. She was holding something in her hand. When she moved, it gleamed in the moonlight.

"Hi Livia," he said loudly, deciding that de-escalation was the best option at this point. "My name's Ryan and this is Susannah. We're from the city and we're here to help you. Can we talk?"

"You're cops, right?" Bucco asked, taking a step forward into the light.

She was a big woman, larger than Ryan even. But she looked sloppy and worn down. According to her file, she was about thirty-five but she appeared closer to fifty. Her face was a bright red, as if she'd been badly sunburned. In her right hand was the machete, resting comfortably against her thigh.

"We are," he admitted. "We know about Kaylee. We were hoping you could explain why that happened. We want to hear you out. Is that okay?"

"You've got guns," Bucco noted.

"I can holster my weapon, Livia," Ryan said, doing just that as he walked down the stairs so that he was on the same section of roof as her. He nodded for Susannah to do the same before adding, "We're just trying to understand what happened."

"It's hard to explain," Bucco said, taking a tentative step forward. "I'd like to, but I don't think you'd get it."

"Does it have something to do with your primary principle?" Ryan asked.

Livia stopped moving and her face darkened.

"Where did you hear that?" she demanded.

"Someone at the prison hospital you were released from mentioned it," he said. "Can you explain what that's about for me?"

The woman's expression had changed. It was like a light had been switched on in her head. Where before there had been uncertainty and something approaching guilt, now there was grim purposefulness. Ryan wasn't sure what was different.

"I can't explain," she said. "I shouldn't have said I would try. It would be a violation for you to know."

"A violation of what?" he asked.

She looked at him as if he was small child who had yet to learn the basics of the world. There was pity in her eyes.

"A violation of the Principles," she said simply.

"What are the Principles?" he wanted to know.

Bucco turned away from him and stared out at the city nightscape.

"They're too vast for you to comprehend," she said.

"Try me."

Suddenly she took a large step up onto the brick edge of the roof and looked down below. Susannah gasped.

"Livia, stop!" Ryan shouted. "Don't do that. We can discuss this."

Bucco turned her head and looked over at him.

"My mind is my strongest tool. It can take me anywhere if I let it."

"What does that mean, Livia?" Ryan asked, trying to keep his voice steady. "Please come down and explain it to me."

She smiled at him. Whatever doubts had been troubling her before seemed gone now. She turned back to face the vast emptiness in front of her.

"It means my work here is done," she said.

Then, without warning, she gripped the machete in both hands, extended it out in front of her, and then swung it back hard toward her. It made contact, the blade smashing into her forehead with a sick thwack.

"No!" Ryan shouted.

Her arms dropped to her sides. For a long moment, her body rocked, as if she might topple backward onto the roof. But then her weight slumped forward as her knees buckled and in an instant, she fell, dropping out of sight.

CHAPTER THIRTY ONE

Jessie thought she was in the clear.

Because of the crowd of protestors outside Central Station's main entrance and the garage driveway, she had the cab driver drop her off a block from a side entrance where Officer Dooley was waiting to let her in. She had just texted Dooley that she was half a block away when they accosted her.

Three women charged at her from across the street, shrieking like banshees. It only took a second to process that these were the girls who had tried to stop Shepherd's arrest at the theater by blocking his exit using their prone, naked bodies.

They were in her face before she had time to act, screaming profanities and calling her their favorite epithet, a hatemonger. Mixed in with that was the occasional claim that "the way is love," which she found ironic considering their behavior. She swerved to avoid them and banged on the side door.

"Dooley, let me in," she yelled, turning around and adopting a boxing stance as she growled, "back off!"

Two seemed to take the hint, stopping their forward movements, if not the verbal attacks. But one kept coming, oblivious to her shredded blouse, which exposed half of her chest. Jessie suddenly realized this was the girl from the stage with the tattoo like Addison's. The marking on her breast was now clearly visible. It was in the exact same spot as the dead girl, only this one was much shorter than Addison's. It said merely: *t.*

The girl was almost on her, with a flailing fist coming her way, when the door opened. Officer Dooley yanked Jessie back behind him, caught the girl's forearm and twisted it behind her back. The girl winced before rediscovering her voice.

"Assault!" she screamed. "Assault under color of law!"

"Go back to the front of the station now," Dooley warned, "unless you want to spend the weekend in a small cell with a bunch of hookers and addicts."

He gave her a shove and slammed the door without waiting for a response.

"You okay?" he asked once they'd both caught their breath.

"That depends," she said. "Has Shepherd confessed?"

"Afraid not," he told her as they walked down the hall. "He hasn't said a word. Decker had him put in a private cell. He didn't want to leave him in general population in case something happened. He doesn't want another lawsuit threat. Plus, he's hoping the solitude might make an impact."

"So that's what we're reduced to?" Jessie asked as they approached the research department. "Hoping that a time out in the corner is going to break him? If that's the best we've got, then Karen was right. I may have only made things worse by having the guy arrested."

"There is *some* good news," Dooley told her when they got to the door to Research.

"What?"

"Why don't you ask Winslow," he said, opening the door for her. "He's the one who figured it out. He should get the credit."

Jessie stepped into the room, where Jamil, Karen, and Nettles were each reviewing different documents. They all looked up as she entered.

"I hear you made a breakthrough," she said to Jamil.

"Just now actually," he said.

"Convenient for you, Hunt," Karen teased. "You leave for almost an hour, we do all the heavy lifting and you show up just in time for the gold nugget."

"We're not sure that it's gold yet," Jamil cautioned.

"Please, Jamil," Jessie pleaded as she shut the door, "I don't care if it's gold, silver, or cubic zirconium. Just tell me what you have."

"I found Miranda Dessler," he said, beaming. "Only that's not her name anymore. Now she goes by Skyler Montgomery."

Jessie leaned back against the door, unsure how excited she should get about this development.

"Where is she?" she asked.

"Not that far from here, actually," he told her. "She's got a loft in the Arts District, above the gallery where most of her work is displayed."

"She's a working artist?" Jessie asked.

"Yep, pretty successful too," he said, "which might explain how she's been able to pay the rent on that apartment on Fountain for the last two years. I'm assuming she kept that place in order to keep the Realm from looking for her elsewhere. Regardless, living where she is now, she can still be in the city, but never have to go up to the Hollywood area where someone might recognize her, although recognizing her might be hard."

"What do you mean?"

He swiveled around to face his monitor and punched up a screen. A driver's license popped up, showing a woman with short, dyed blonde hair and black glasses. It was hard to reconcile her with Miranda Dessler, whose most recent photos showed a long-haired brunette without glasses.

"I did a facial recognition search on the off chance that she'd done something like this," Jamil explained. "Reading about folks that the DRA did Rightful Targeting on, I noticed that a lot of them changed names, entire identities even. Lots changed their look. A few had plastic surgery, anything to get off the Realm's radar. It's not Witness Protection Program level stuff, but she did a pretty solid job. She got new bank accounts, a new social security number. She hasn't contacted any old family or friends since 'Miranda' dropped off the grid. To the rest of the world, she's shy, secretive Skyler Montgomery, an up-and-coming artist who doesn't do interviews or go to her own gallery shows. I was impressed."

"Me too," Jessie agreed, allowing some hope to grow in her chest, "and I can't wait to meet her and find out what happened when Addison came to her for help. Can I get the address?"

"Sending it to you now," he replied.

"Send it to me too," Karen said.

Jessie turned to her, surprised.

"Are you sure you're up for this?" she asked. "The Realm has research people too. By now, they have to know that you're the same Karen who bailed on them all those years ago. They might come after you again."

"I know," Karen said. "But I've decided that part of taking care of my son is teaching him to do the right thing, even when it's hard. I want him to be proud of his mommy. Hell, *I* want to be proud of his mommy. So I'm in."

Both their phones pinged, indicating the arrival of Jamil's text with the address.

"Then I guess we should get going," Jessie said.

*

They got to the Arts District in five minutes.

Jessie checked the time. It was 8:03 p.m. Late enough that Dessler should be home but not too late to pay a visit.

After finding the right warehouse and waiting for a resident to exit the building, they snuck in before the door closed and made their way to Dessler's second floor loft. After everything the woman had been through, it wouldn't be a shock if she had an emergency escape route. The less time she had to activate it, the more likely they were to actually find her, which was why they didn't buzz her unit to request entry.

They came to her graffiti-covered, barn-style, sliding steel door. Jessie liked the woman's style. Not only did it look artsy-edgy, but it afforded an extra layer of security without being obvious about it.

"You ready?" she asked Karen.

"I guess. Let's just hope that she doesn't drop electrified netting on us or something."

Jessie almost hoped she did, just out of curiosity, but didn't say so. Instead she knocked on the door, which created a clanging echo throughout the hallway. After that there was silence for a solid thirty seconds.

Jessie was sure they were being watched on a camera they couldn't see. She imagined the woman panicking and leaping into some tunnel slide hidden in her unit, one that shot out through a vent at the back of the warehouse and allowed her to run off into the night. The image was interrupted by a female voice on a box to the left of the steel door.

"Can I help you?" the woman asked with trepidation.

Jessie had thought about how best to approach this moment and decided that anything other than complete honesty was likely to backfire.

"I hope so, Ms. Montgomery," she said. "My name is Jessie Hunt. I'm a criminal profiler with the LAPD. I'm here with Detective Karen Bray. What I'm about to tell you might be hard to hear so I wanted you to be prepared."

There was no answer.

"Are you still there?" she asked.

"Go on," the woman said.

Jessie looked over at Karen who shrugged. This was better than radio silence at least. Jessie continued.

"We're investigating the murder of Addison Rutherford. She was killed at the Buckingham Sunset Hotel in West Hollywood last night. We think her death may have something to do with her affiliation with the Eleventh Realm and the possibility that she was trying to leave that group."

"Okay," the voice said. "Why are you telling me all this?"

Jessie steeled herself, well aware that this was the make or break moment.

"Because in the course of our investigation, I spoke to the journalist, Huell Valchek, who told me that Addison may have tried, unsuccessfully, to leave the Realm once before and enlisted the help of a woman named Miranda Dessler. Unfortunately, it didn't work out and Dessler was harassed relentlessly by the Realm's Department of Restricted Activities. She eventually dropped off the radar completely. But our research team has learned that you, Ms. Montgomery, might...have knowledge of Ms. Dessler's thinking and experience back at that time and be able to fill us in on what happened then. It could prove helpful as we try to bring Addison's killer to justice. Would you be willing to talk with us?"

"Um, what makes you think I would know anything about this Dessler woman?" the voice asked.

"Ms. Montgomery," Jessie said patiently, keeping the charade going. "We're not here to cause you any trouble. We're not looking to upend the life you've built. We don't need you to testify to anything in court. But right now, we have Sterling Shepherd in custody. We think he may have killed Addison or at least ordered her death. But we're at an impasse and we're concerned that he may walk. It's our hope that you might be able to shed some light on what happened between Addison and Miranda two years ago. It could be the key that unlocks this case. We're asking for your help. Please."

There was another interminable silence. Finally, they heard a click, then a sliding sound. A moment later the steel door slid open to reveal Skyler Montgomery, formerly Miranda Dessler.

CHAPTER THIRTY TWO

They waited until she was settled.

First she offered them tea, which they accepted. Then they all took seats on her couch, which was massive and circled around to make a full "C." The big couch made the already smallish woman seem tiny. She had a frail, bird-like build and it looked like a loud word might knock her over. She still seemed nervous so Jessie and Karen waited for her speak first.

"So I guess we can dispense with the pretense," she said, with unexpected poise and a hint of resignation. "You obviously know who I really am."

"Yes," Karen told her. "But only a tight circle of us is aware and we intend to keep it that way."

"You're not going to arrest me for getting a false identity?" she asked.

"That's not our priority right now," Karen said. "If you want to go by Skyler for now, that's okay with us."

"I think I would," she said. "Miranda Dessler has been dead to me for a while."

"That's fine," Jessie said.

"Thank you. So what do you need to know?"

"If you could just tell us the circumstances of how Addison came to you," Jessie suggested, "what she wanted, and how it played out. Anything you can remember would be helpful."

"Okay," Skyler said, hiking her legs up onto the couch and tucking her feet under her. "Sonny and I went to college together for a while at Pepperdine. We were freshman roommates and stayed friends in sophomore year. But she dropped out at some point during junior year. I'd heard that she'd gotten mixed up with some cult but didn't know the details. I tried to reach out to her a few times but never heard back, so I eventually gave up."

"But she got in touch at some point?" Karen asked.

"Yes, the year after I graduated, she called me out of the blue. She said she'd gotten involved in the Eleventh Realm; that it had done wonders for her personal growth, but now she wanted out but didn't have anywhere to stay. She asked if she could crash with me for a little while under she got her life together."

"And you said yes?" Jessie confirmed.

"Yeah," Skyler said. "I didn't know much about the Realm, just that a girl I used to be close to was asking for help. My couch pulled out into a bed so I figured why not."

"So what happened next?" Jessie asked.

"I drove to their headquarters in Hollywood, the Heartbeat Hub, to help her pack up her things and give her a ride. I was prepared to call 911 if anyone gave me a hard time."

"But they didn't," Karen said knowingly.

"No," Skyler confirmed. "At first, they actually seemed really nice. A few of them offered to help pack up her stuff. They invited us both to the dining hall to have a bite for the road. When we got there, they were all singing songs and playing games. It felt like summer camp. Sonny started singing along a bit and invited me to join in. I was polite and did a little, but eventually said I had to get going."

"They were okay with that?" Karen asked.

"They said they were but then they took us to some room for her 'exit interview.' They started talking about much they'd love for Sonny to stay, how much she brought to the community. I could see her resolve weakening. They told her that she was on the verge of unlocking her potential or something like that and then they told me that I could too. They started in with the hard sell and the red flags went up for me."

"What kind of red flags?" Jessie asked.

Skyler sighed, as if the idea of recalling the experience might be too much for her. But then she seemed to recover and continued.

"First of all, they just wouldn't let up with the pressure, trying to get me to stay. They were tag-teaming me. At one point, there were three different people up close, taking turns trying to wear me down. And then I started noticing things I missed at first."

"Like what?" Karen wanted to know.

"Most of the doors were locked from the outside. If you were inside, you had to have someone with a keycard open it for you and there were only a few people with that kind of authority. There were cameras everywhere and they weren't stationary. They tracked movements through a room. Also, all the windows had bars on them. They were fancy so they looked decorative from the outside. But they were still bars. I saw barbed wire at the top of the fences, which seemed excessive to me. There were armed guards patrolling the perimeter of the complex. I even saw a few in the halls. And everyone there wore a bracelet with a blinking light. I don't know this for sure, but I think they were for tracking purposes. After I took all that in, I'd had enough."

"So what did you do?" Karen pressed.

"I took Sonny aside and said I wasn't comfortable there, that I wanted to leave right then, and if she still wanted a place to crash, she needed to come too."

"Did she?" Jessie asked, knowing the answer.

"She said she would but that she didn't want to be rude to her friends. She would just stick around a little longer. But I knew then that it was over. They had sucked her back in. So I told her I was leaving. She pleaded with me not to leave her but she wouldn't come with me, so I had no choice. I walked out on my own and thought that was the end of it."

"But it wasn't," Karen said.

"Not by a long shot," Skyler said. "First I got calls from her asking me to come back to get her. I said she had my address and could take a cab to my place. Then I started getting calls from other Adherents, trying to get me to attend events. After that, they even showed up at my door. They had cookies and flyers and invited me to come to some seminar. They said there was a picnic as well and that they could take me right then. I got freaked out and said that I didn't want them bothering me again or I'd need to involve the authorities."

"How did that go over?" Karen asked.

"Not well," she said, "In retrospect, I wonder if that's why they changed tactics. Would they have eventually left me alone if I hadn't threatened to fight back? I guess I'll never know for sure but that's when the harassment really amped up."

"In what way?" Jessie asked.

"First they warned me that they had the cops in their pocket," Skyler told them. "I actually thought you two might be on their payroll until I realized you were the same people I saw on the news, cuffing both Logan Bauer and Shepherd."

"Yeah," Karen assured her. "We're definitely not on Team Realm. In fact, they're probably prepping their Rightful Targeting plans for us as we speak. But you were telling us about what they did to you."

"Right," Skyler continued. "After that, they said I better not contact Sonny or they'd press for a restraining order against me. The idea of reaching out to her again had never even occurred to me. It escalated from there. I got calls at all hours of the night. They'd leave messages saying 'the way is love' but their tone wasn't very loving. My tires got slashed. I was working at a gallery at the time and a group of them came in and accused me of being a pedophile in front of clients. They didn't refer to any incident. They just kept yelling 'pedophile' over and over. I got fired because I 'contributed to a disruptive environment.' They followed me everywhere—the grocery store, the movies, one even showed up in my gynecologist's waiting room. When I was called back to a room, she stood up too, said 'the way is love,' and walked out. But even after all that, it took finding my car window smashed with a dead bunny in the passenger seat to take the measures that, well, that have you at Skyler Montgomery's loft. When you knocked, I thought they'd finally found me."

"To the best of our knowledge, they have no idea who you are," Jessie reassured her, "and we intend to keep it that way. Is there anything else you can tell us about your interactions with Sonny during that time?"

Skyler thought about it for a moment.

"I can't think of anything else," she said apologetically.

"That's all right," Jessie said, standing up. "We'll leave you be."

Skyler escorted them to the door.

"I'm really sorry I couldn't be more help," she said as she opened it. "And I really do hope you nail Shepherd. That guy is a cancer."

"I couldn't agree more," Karen said. "Unfortunately, not everyone can see it so clearly."

Jessie wanted to offer some reassuring platitude, but the truth was that nothing Skyler had told them, while awful, appeared to implicate Shepherd in Addison Rutherford's death. If anything, her story seemed to suggest Addison was still in Shepherd's thrall the last time Skyler saw her, still a long way from leaving the Realm. Skyler was just closing the steel door when a thought popped into Jessie's head.

"Hey," she asked. "Did Sonny have a tattoo on her chest when you saw her, on her left breast?"

"Sure," Skyler said. "She said it was a sign of her devotion to the Creed or something. She mentioned wanting to have it removed with a laser when she left."

"Did she tell you what it was about, what *twil* meant?"

Skyler looked perplexed.

"No," she said. "She said it was a secret—that she could bare the image to the world but not the meaning. But I don't remember it saying *twil*."

Something about that response made Jessie's brain tingle, though she couldn't quite identify why.

"What did it say?" she asked.

Skyler's brow furrowed as she tried to remember.

"I'm not positive but I think it was just *twi*. There was no '*l*.' Does that mean something?"

"Probably not," Jessie lied. "Anyway, thanks for your time."

Skyler nodded and slammed the steel door securely behind them, rattling Jessie's bones. Karen waited until they were outside the warehouse to ask her question.

"Something's obviously percolating in that mind of yours," she said. "You want to fill me in?"

Jessie hadn't totally formulated her thoughts but decided to share what she was thinking anyway.

"I'm not sure," she said as they hurried to the car to get out of the cutting wind. "It's just that after hearing Skyler's story, I can't help but notice a pattern. How many times has Addison Rutherford suggested that she wanted to leave the Realm, only to pull back?"

"I don't know," Karen said as they got in. "But it's not unusual to have false starts. I view it almost like rehab. There are going to be relapses. It might take a few attempts to finally get clean."

"I get that," Jessie said as Karen started the car and pulled out, "but what if something else is going on?"

"What do you mean?"

"I'm just thinking about what Skyler said about Addison's tattoo, that it was a sign of devotion to the Creed; that it was about baring it to the world."

"What about it?" Karen said.

"It reminds me of something Huell Valchek told me. He said that apparently no one has elevated to the Eleventh Realm yet. He said that Shepherd had reached the Tenth, and that a select few had gotten to the Ninth, including some members of COHP and…"

She paused, pulling out her phone to check her notes from their conversation. She scrolled to the relevant moment and continued.

"Here it is," she said. "He said that according to what he'd been told, some members of COHP and a select group of 'chosen' ones had gotten to the Ninth Realm, within two levels of elevating to the Eleventh Realm. Those 'chosen' included only the most devoted female Adherents, who have given their spirits and their bodies over to the Realm, via its representative on Earth, Sterling Shepherd."

"Okay," Karen said. "I heard stories about that too—women who hoped to elevate by giving Shepherd pleasure. I'm still not following the point, though."

Jessie wasn't sure she was either but kept going anyway.

"When I asked Valchek if there was any way to identify the 'chosen' women, he said that all he knew about them was that they followed a cryptic maxim: 'those on the cusp of elevating to the Tenth Realm will bare it to the world.' I'm wondering if they bared their devotion to the Creed through a tattoo."

"You think that's what they're about?" Karen asked skeptically.

"Why not? They *are* baring themselves to the world when they expose those letters on their breasts. Addison had them. One of the girls who stripped at the theater had a '*t*' in the same place as Addison's. I saw it up close when she tried to attack me outside the station. According to Skyler, Addison's '*twil*' was once a '*twi*.' What if they get a new letter every time they elevate to another Realm? If so, that means the girl from the theater was still pretty low on the totem pole. If I'm right, then Addison used to be at a lower level and moved up—adding an '*l*' sometime in the two years from when she asked Skyler for help until she was killed."

"Okay, that's not a crazy theory," Karen conceded. "But how can we possibly know how close to the top Addison got? What word are they ultimately spelling? Twilight? Is that ten letters?"

"I think it's possible that they don't start getting the letters until they reach a certain level—I'm guessing the sixth," Jessie suggested.

"How could you possibly know that?" Karen demanded.

"Because I think we already know what the letters mean," Jessie told her.

Karen pulled over on the side of the road and turned off the car.

"Please don't keep me in suspense."

Jessie wasn't sure she was right but couldn't come up with a reason that she was wrong, so she spilled.

"The girls screaming in the theater, the people leaving the harassing voicemails on Skyler's phone—they all said the same thing: the way is love—T-W-I-L. I think that's what the tattoo stands for. And I think once you get that "L," it means you've made it to the Ninth Realm, that you're one of the 'chosen,' on the verge of joining Shepherd himself. I think Addison was in COHP, or at least as important as those who were."

Karen sat with the thought for a moment. The fact that she didn't protest told Jessie that she wasn't completely off base.

"Okay. Let's say that's true, "Karen proposed. "So what are you saying—that once she overcame her moments of doubt and recommitted to the Realm, Addison Rutherford became even more hardcore?"

"No," Jessie said. "I don't think she ever *had* a moment of doubt. I think that your initial suspicion about her when you first saw Shepherd's book in her hotel suite was right. I think she was a true believer from the get go. I think she was a double agent."

CHAPTER THIRTY THREE

Karen was quiet.

She looked like she wanted to ask about five different questions. Instead, she started the car again, and pulled out, making sure to drive extra slow the rest of the way back to the station. Finally she spoke.

"Obviously, if your theory validates my brilliance as an investigator, I'm listening," she said.

Okay," Jessie continued. She was on a roll now and didn't want to stop. "I have doubts that Addison ever really considered leaving. Think about it. She tells Miranda Dessler that she wants to leave, but it looks to me like she was more interested in pulling her old friend into the Realm than getting herself out. It reminded me of how they tried to use you all those years ago to get new Adherents when you were a student at Occidental. Maybe they wanted Addison to do the same thing with her circle from Pepperdine."

"But why not just have Addison stay at school and recruit people from within?" Karen asked.

"My guess is that by the time they determined that she could be an asset, she'd already dropped out and lost touch with her old friends. Maybe Miranda was the first step to reconnecting with everyone. But it wasn't just her. Again and again, Addison gave the impression that she was going to leave, only to remain with the Realm. She did it with her boyfriend, Josh Sawyer. She suggested it to Logan Bauer. I have a theory on that one."

"Of course you do," Karen said. "Spit it out."

"Sure. What if Shepherd and COHP were already worried about Bauer's loyalty? What if this whole boyfriend breakup/ hotel suite situation was a test, a way to gauge Bauer's true intentions? Shepherd assigns him and Addison to be the official 'it' couple of the Realm, then instructs Addison to act upset over her forced breakup and express reservations to see how Bauer reacts. He reveals his own doubts and offers to help her get out. Once he leaves, she reports that back to COHP. Now they know where their big star really stands and how they can use it against him. They also know that France is important to him, even if they don't know why. Addison has done her job."

"You think it was all part of some master plan?" Karen asked.

"Yes," Jessie said, more confident the longer she thought about it. "I don't think Addison Rutherford ever had any intention of leaving the Realm. I think that tattoo shows that she was among the most trusted, devoted Adherents they had. I think Sterling Shepherd made her his secret weapon. She could repeatedly pretend to leave as a tactic to pull in new recruits or to smoke out potential turncoats. I think she died a zealot."

Karen rounded the corner to the police station. There was still a crowd of protesters but it had thinned out considerably. They were able to access the parking garage without too much trouble.

"There's a problem with all this," Karen said as she entered the garage. "We know that even if he found out that Addison was playing him, Bauer didn't kill her. And if your theory is right, it removes the obvious motive for Shepherd to have her killed. If she wasn't planning to leave, if she was really secretly working for the Realm, there would be no reason to harm her."

"I know," Jessie said. "I was hesitant to say it, because I know how badly we both want to get this guy. But if I'm right, it's hard to explain why Shepherd would want her dead. I'd be willing to bet that he's as upset about it as anyone."

Karen parked the car and turned off the headlights. She turned to face Jessie. It was obvious what she was thinking.

"If we can't pin him to this murder, he walks," she said. "Then he leaves this place as a victim and a hero. It'll be exactly what I feared. He'll be even more powerful than when we brought him in."

Jessie could sense the anxiety radiating off her partner. This was what Karen had warned against and now it was happening, just as she'd feared.

"I know," Jessie said, the guilt swelling up in her. "But I could be wrong. And even if I'm not, that doesn't mean we have to let him go yet. Until we find another credible suspect, we can hold him, at least through the weekend. Who knows what will turn up between now and then?"

"That's just delaying the inevitable," Karen said, her voice thick with despair. "It's just a matter of time at this point."

"Karen," Jessie said, lowering her voice even though it was just the two of them in the car. "No one else needs to know about this. We obviously still have to pursue other leads because if Shepherd and the Realm aren't responsible for this, there's a murderer out there who needs to be caught. But in the meantime, Shepherd stays in jail until we have no choice but to let him go. Deal?"

Karen nodded but without enthusiasm. Her whole demeanor had changed and it was hard to blame her. She didn't speak on the elevator ride up to the main floor or as they walked down the hall to the research department. When they arrived, Jamil was typing away. Nettles had crashed on the couch. Seeming to sense their arrival, his eyes popped open. He stretched his arms and sat up.

"Get anything good?" he asked through a yawn.

"No smoking guns, but we're still hopeful," Jessie said, deciding that neither man needed to know everything just yet. "Which is why, until something breaks with Shepherd, I think we need to use the time that he's indisposed to pursue other theories."

"You don't think he's our guy anymore?" Nettles asked pointedly.

"I didn't say that," Jessie insisted. "I just want to cover all our bases. I don't want his lawyers to credibly accuse us of having tunnel vision on this, to claim that once we honed in on him, we dropped all other avenues of investigation."

"I didn't know we *had* any other avenues of investigation," Jamil said.

"That's why I think we need to broaden our suspect pool. We've looked at everyone who might want to shut Addison up if she was leaving the Realm. I think we need to go the other way, just to be safe, in case Decker asks."

"Go the other way?" Nettles repeated. "What does that mean?"

"It means that we should consider the possibility that Addison's change of heart regarding the Realm was such a well-guarded secret that maybe someone thought she was still a devout Adherent and resented her for it. We know that she convinced a lot of people to join up. What if a former Adherent who had their life destroyed when they were Disavowed blamed her for it? What if a friend or family member of an Adherent was upset after they lost a loved one to the Realm or if they disappeared after an M&M?"

Nettles looked suspicious about this new line of inquiry but said nothing. Jamil, on the other hand, dived right in.

"I could set up a search to track anyone who filed complaints about the Realm lately or anyone who was charged with a crime in relation to them," he offered.

"That's great," Jessie said. "Maybe expand it to include people she went to college with, as well as folks that the Realm requested restraining orders against."

Jamil nodded, inputting the data into the computer. Karen spoke up for the first time since entering the room.

172

"Just be aware that a lot of the Realm's restraining orders are intended as harassment. You'll have to filter those out."

"How?" Jamil asked.

"Look for orders requested by either Walter Serra or one of the other lawyers who came here to get Bauer earlier. The nuisance requests would be filed by junior attorneys. But the serious ones, where they were legitimately concerned about someone who posed a real threat to them, would be filed by one of their big guns. They wouldn't leave anything that important to lackeys."

Jessie was glad that Karen was starting to re-engage with the case. Anything that got her out of her doldrums was a positive. Once Jamil generated the list of possible suspects, they divvied it up and got started.

*

After half an hour of dead ends, Jessie pulled up the file for the eighth name on her list: Veronica Reyes. The girl in the accompanying photo was in her early twenties, attractive in an unfussy way, with long, dark, curly hair and big brown eyes. She had an open, trusting face and a cute, little button nose.

More importantly, she matched several of the criteria: she had gone to Pepperdine with Addison. She joined the Realm two years ago, around the same time that Addison unsuccessfully tried to recruit Miranda/Skyler. She'd been with the Realm for about a year before allegedly expressing doubts to her father.

But before she took any further action, she was sent on an M&M in an isolated part of the Pacific Crest Trail in the Sierra Nevada mountain range. When the Realm representative went to the designated pickup spot at the end of the M&M, Veronica didn't show up. A week-long search ensued, but she was never found. The search was called off for good eleven months ago.

But none of that was what drew Jessie's attention. Instead, she was focused on Veronica's father, Ricardo Reyes. He was everywhere during the search, organizing search parties, speaking to the media, pleading for help. When the search was called off, he turned his attention to the Eleventh Realm, both in interviews and on social media. He called them out, accusing them of being a cult that destroyed lives and specifically alleging that they intentionally "disappeared" his daughter when she wanted to get out.

The Realm sued him. The case was still pending but it was clear that it had drained his resources. They'd used their media contacts to discredit him, get him fired from his job with a defense contractor, and labeled as a conspiracy nut. Addison was quoted in several stories as being afraid of him because he supposedly verbally assaulted her when confronting her about her involvement in recruiting Veronica.

All that was compelling, but what got Jessie to stand up and hand the file to Karen was something else. She waited while her partner reviewed the file, with Jamil looking over her shoulder. When she came to the photo of Ricardo Reyes on the second page, Karen looked up.

"He's fifty-one years old," she said. "And his skin is—how did the bellboy describe it?"

"Leathery around the eyes," Jessie reminded her. "Plus his hair is salt and pepper. He looks like a Latino Logan Bauer."

She turned to Jamil to ask for the address but before she could say a word her phone pinged. She looked down to see that he'd already sent it.

CHAPTER THIRTY FOUR

Ricardo Reyes lived in the boonies.

His small house was on a dusty, deserted stretch of road near Acton in the Antelope Valley. It took almost an hour to get there from the station. When they arrived it was 10:04 p.m.

They pulled up on the street rather than alert him to their presence by driving down the gravel driveway. Two squad cars had parked a hundred yards farther down the road out of sight and the four officers had joined them behind a thicket of trees just off the property.

"We're hoping to gain entry peaceably," Karen told everyone. "Assuming he lets us in, then you can surround the house. Don't enter unless we call for you or you hear gunshots, got it?"

The officers nodded. Jessie and Karen walked up to the house on the grass at the edge of the driveway to keep quiet. There was a single light on in the window at the front of the house, which looked gnarled and rickety, like it belonged on a prairie hill circa 1875. They could hear the TV, which slightly mitigated the effect. Then again, it sounded like he was watching a documentary on the Civil War, which reinforced the old-timey vibe.

Both of them undid the holsters on their guns but neither removed them. They exchanged a look to make sure the other was all set. They both were. Karen knocked on the door.

"Mr. Reyes," she called out. "This is Karen Bray with the Los Angeles Police Department. We'd like to speak with you."

The TV was immediately muted and they heard movement inside. A few seconds later, the sound of a barrel bolt lock sliding open eased Jessie's concerns slightly. It didn't seem like he was trying to get away or intending to barricade himself inside.

The door opened to reveal a man who looked much like his photo. Ricardo Reyes was handsomely distinguished. His hair was more gray than black and he looked more worn-down than in his picture. But he had a wiry fit look to him and even late on a Friday night, he wore slacks and a button-down dress shirt. He didn't seem surprised to see them.

"You're way out of your jurisdiction, aren't you Detective?" he said mildly. "I thought this region was served by the Sheriff's Department."

"You don't know that for sure, Mr. Reyes?" Karen asked, wisely deciding to start with some small talk to break any tension.

"I only recently relocated," he said, "so I'm still learning the area. What can I do for you and your friend here?"

"This is Jessie Hunt," Karen said. "She's a criminal profiler who works with us from time to time. We were hoping to talk to you about some issues related to your daughter's disappearance, if you have a few minutes."

"Of course, please come in," he said, opening the door wide.

They entered and he indicated that they should sit on the loveseat near the easy chair, which he settled into. The house was small but tidy. At least on the inside, it looked like it at last belonged in the twentieth century, if not the twenty-first. Jessie could see several unopened packing boxes in the adjacent sitting room. A few more lined the short hallway that led to the back door, partially blocking the path.

"Still unpacking?" she asked.

"I guess I'm taking my time," he admitted. "I've been here almost three months now but just haven't had the oomph to get it all done yet. It's hard to see the point lately."

"We understand," Jessie said. "This must have been a very difficult last year."

"That, Ms. Hunt, is an understatement," he said, sitting up straight in his chair. "I lost my daughter once to the cult she joined. Then I thought I had a chance to get her back only to have all my hopes dashed as I lost her again, this time for good. Then the very people responsible for what happened to her made it their mission to destroy me, which they've pretty much done. So, opening those last few boxes hasn't seemed like such a priority. But enough about my challenges—you wanted to talk about Veronica. Has there been a break in the case? Do you have a suspect?"

"I'm afraid not," Karen said. "We're actually here about another matter that we think may be connected to her case."

"What's that?" he asked.

"We're investigating the death of Addison Rutherford," she said straightforwardly. "Were you aware that she died?"

"It's been on the news," he said, seemingly unperturbed by the question. "I saw that big-time actor was arrested and then the big kahuna himself, Sterling Shepherd."

"That's right," Karen said. "Are you familiar with Addison?"

"Of course," he said. "She was the one who initially seduced my daughter into joining up. And according to what Veronica told me when she said she wanted to leave, Addison Rutherford was central to the Realm's sex trafficking operation. Addison was the one who groomed girls to be Sterling Shepherd's human sex toys. Then when he got bored with a girl, Addison facilitated her "redeployment."

"What's that?" Jessie asked.

"It was just a fancy way of describing how a girl would be passed around to other powerful Adherents, and eventually to wealthy non-Realm guys, who would happily pay for a compliant partner. Veronica told me she'd been with about two dozen men at the behest of Shepherd, all coordinated by Rutherford and someone named Inara Reynolds. The last guy she was with before she called me for help choked her into unconsciousness, then raped her, and ended the evening by beating her up while she was out cold. She refused to tell me his name because she knew what I'd do if I found out."

Jessie tried to hide her surprise. Reyes had just admitted that if he had the name of his daughter's attacker, he would have taken matters into his own hands. It wasn't a leap to imagine that he might also seek out someone else who knew the man's identity. She looked over at Karen, who shook her head. She didn't want to go there just yet. Jessie deferred to her judgment as the detective asked her question.

"And you think that the Realm had Veronica killed while she was on her Meditation Mission to keep her from exposing their trafficking operation?"

"I'm sure of it," he said.

As he answered, Jessie noticed a small pouch on the coffee table in front of him, partially concealed under a magazine. It looked a lot like the Faraday bag that Huell Valchek had held up for her in his basement, which supposedly blocked signals to and from cell phones. She instantly recalled how Jamil had said that the signal from Addison's phone had simply disappeared soon after leaving the Buckingham Hotel.

Just as she was processing that information, she and Karen got simultaneous pings on their phones. Jessie glanced at it. The text was from Jamil and said simply: *city camera caught license plate for Reyes's car a block from Buckingham Hotel within widow of death.* She looked up to see Reyes eyeing her warily.

"Everything okay?" he asked.

"Getting there," she said. "We may have to go soon, Mr. Reyes. Can I get your cell phone number in case we have to reach out later?"

"Sure," he said and gave it to her. "Does that mean we're done?"

177

"Almost," she said. "Just a few more questions before we go. What's that, by the way?"

She pointed at the Faraday bag. Reyes looked nervous but when he answered, his voice was calm.

"Oh, it's a special pouch you can put your phone in to block signals. It makes it harder to trace. I learned about it once the Realm started doing their Rightful Targeting on me. I couldn't understand why they always knew where I'd be. But when I did some research, I learned that they'd probably hacked into my GPS. So I got a new phone and started using the bag as an extra precaution."

"I see," Jessie said. She knew where this was headed and felt her fingertips and toes prickle as adrenaline started to zip through her system. "And to be clear, you said earlier that you knew who Rutherford was and what she did for the Realm."

"Yes."

"So you also knew that she could tell you who brutalized Veronica?"

"Right," he confirmed without hesitation.

"I see," she said, holding off on the final question. "Do you mind if I call you, just to make sure that I got your phone number down right?"

She had already input the numbers and hit "send' before he could protest. A phone buzzed, but not in the bag on the table. The sound came from one lying on the kitchen counter. She hung up and looked at him. He met her gaze without shame.

"Mr. Reyes," she said slowly. "You're not making this very hard for us."

"How do you mean?" he asked without much curiosity.

"I'm wondering—if I were to pull the phone in that bag out and dial Addison Rutherford's number, would it ring?"

"I couldn't say." He seemed to be on the verge of either smiling or crying.

She did exactly what she'd suggested. After taking the phone out and laying it on the table, she called Addison's cell and, sure enough, the phone in front of her buzzed.

For one interminable second, no one moved. Then, faster than Jessie could have anticipated, Karen pulled out her gun. Reyes didn't react. Instead he sat placidly in his easy chair.

"Mr. Reyes," Jessie said quietly, "we want to hear your version of events, but before that can happen, Detective Bray is going to read you your rights and handcuff you. Do you understand?"

He nodded slowly.

"Should I come to you?" he asked, pushing himself up out of his easy chair.

As he did, and with lightning speed, he yanked a small pistol out of the space between the chair's cushion and arm. Jessie knew she didn't have time to get her gun. Karen raised hers, but before she could aim, Reyes had pressed the muzzle under his own chin. His eyes blazed as his finger started to squeeze the trigger.

CHAPTER THIRTY FIVE

"They win!" Jessie shouted.

She saw Reyes blink and took advantage of his moment of indecision.

"If you kill yourself, they win," she said forcefully but with more composure than before. "Mr. Reyes—Ricardo, Sterling Shepherd already destroyed your daughter. Now you're going to let him destroy you too, just when you have the means to stop him. If you pull that trigger, you're doing exactly what he's been trying to get you to do for that last year. If you pull that trigger, you lose, and not just your life. Your daughter's name will be forgotten and a monster walks free. Is that what you want?"

His finger was still pressed on the trigger, but it appeared to be trembling. To Jessie's right, Karen still had her weapon trained on him if he decided to point his at anything other than himself.

"What do you mean?" he whispered as tears rolled down his cheeks.

"I'm not going to lie to you, Mr. Reyes," she said. "You killed someone. You are going to prison. There's no way around that. But before it happens, there will be a trial. And at that trial, you'll be allowed to present a defense. That defense can include your allegations about what was done to your daughter, about the sexual trafficking. You might even be able to get Shepherd on the stand. The world will be listening to you and it won't be filtered through Realm-friendly propaganda outlets. People can watch the trial live and judge for themselves."

"How can you be sure?" he asked. His finger was no longer touching the trigger but it was close.

"Are you kidding me?" she said. "Not to be blunt, but with a story this salacious, you won't be able to keep them away. They'll eat up every word you say. But none of that happens unless you give me the gun. Do that; let Detective Bray cuff and Mirandize you. Then tell us your story. Isn't that what Veronica would want?"

He kept the gun at his chin and closed his eyes. Jessie feared that he was about to pull the trigger. But he didn't, instead staying in that position, seemingly frozen, as the seconds stretched out. Finally, he opened his eyes, pulled the gun down, and without a word, handed it over.

As Jessie took it, Karen moved in swiftly, setting her phone to record, then reading him his rights as she placed the cuffs on him, hands in front.

"With those rights in mind," she concluded, "are you willing to speak with us?"

"Yes," he said without reservation.

Karen nodded at Jessie, indicating she should ask the first question. She decided to keep it simple.

"What happened last night?" she asked.

He sighed and leaned back in the easy chair, where they'd let him stay for now.

"It was a fluke that I saw her at all," he said. "I was at the Book Soup bookstore near the hotel that afternoon. An author I like who writes books on grieving was doing a reading and book signing. I was just leaving after getting my book signed when I saw her on Sunset, about to turn left onto Larrabee Street. She'd been the cause of so much of my pain that I just followed her without thinking about it. She pulled into that hotel and checked in. I hung out in the lobby and got in the same elevator as her."

"She didn't recognize you?" Karen asked.

"No," he explained. "I was wearing a baseball cap pulled down over the top half of my face. We got out on her floor and I walked the other way, then doubled back to see which suite she was in. Then I left."

"You left?" Jessie repeated, surprised.

"For a while, yes," he said. "I went to a bar down the street and had more than a couple of drinks. I went to see a movie nearby. Then I had dinner and a few more drinks. I told myself that I was going come back here when the traffic settled down."

"But you didn't do that," Jessie prompted.

"No," he said, his tone suddenly hard. "Eventually I started stewing over everything that had happened. I was pretty drunk. I decided I had to confront her. So I went up to her suite. When I knocked, she opened right up. I was surprised, but looking back on it now, it makes sense."

"What do you mean?" Karen asked.

"I saw on the news that Logan Bauer was there that night, which I guess is why you arrested him. I've been told that I look a little like him. Maybe with the cap, she thought it was him coming back again.

Anyway, she didn't realize who it was until I came in the room and took off my cap."

"What happened then?" Jessie asked delicately.

"I reamed her out," he said flatly, making no attempt to hide his anger. "I told her that I knew about the sex trafficking and her part in it. I said that I knew that they'd eliminated Veronica on that M&M to keep her quiet. I told her that she had blood on her hands."

"How did she react?" Karen pressed.

"She was dismissive, even flip," he replied, his voice cracking slightly. "She said that she didn't know what I was talking about with the trafficking, that Veronica's disappearance was a tragedy, that she had sympathy for me but that my daughter had chosen her own path, that no one forced her to do anything, and that she wasn't responsible for Veronica's choices."

"She just denied everything?" Jessie asked.

"Yes," Reyes said, struggling to contain himself. His eyes were wet. "So I changed course. I told her that I would give her and the Realm a pass on their involvement if she just gave me the name of the man who choked my daughter unconscious before assaulting her. But she wouldn't even do that. She wouldn't even acknowledge it. But she did say that every female Adherent in the Realm knew her body and soul was in the service of the Creed, that anything that happened to Veronica was something that she had willed to happen. It was too much for me."

He stopped talking suddenly and bowed his head, as if in prayer. Jessie wasn't sure if it was just the emotion of the memory or if he was having second thoughts about coming clean. She worried that after all of this, he might shut down before admitting to the actual crime.

"What happened next, Ricardo?" she asked gently.

He sighed deeply, lifted his head, and then, with a quavering voice, continued.

"I asked if she was saying Veronica had asked for what happened to her. I remember she said 'in one way or another, we all ask for what happens to us.' I lost it, grabbed the lamp and smashed it into her head. She fell to the ground right away. I remember yelling 'did you ask for that?' to her. She looked up at me but I don't think she could really see me. She kept blinking over and over, even as the blood seeped out from underneath her head. I remember she opened her mouth and I thought she was going to finally apologize or ask for forgiveness. But all she said was 'the way is love.' Then she died."

They were all quiet for several seconds. Jessie wasn't sure how to proceed. The man had just confessed to murder. Rarely had she felt more sympathy for a killer than his victim. Part of her thought they should let him have a moment to regroup. It was Karen, always the detective, who moved to a more prosaic question.

"Why didn't we find any prints or DNA on the lamp?" she asked.

He looked at her with a rueful half-smile on his face.

"Probably because I was still wearing my gloves," he admitted. "It was really cold last night. I also wiped down the lamp with a disinfectant wipe from a package that I found on the bathroom counter. That might have made a difference. I took it with me when I left."

"Was it you who texted from her phone after she died?" Karen pressed.

He nodded, again lowering his head.

"Yes," he replied quietly, "Someone named Josh texted, asking her to call them off or something. I didn't know what that was about and I wasn't going to do anything. But then I realized that if I texted back, it might help give me an alibi if it seemed like she was alive later than she really was. So I used her facial recognition to open it and texted back something vague that I hoped wouldn't be suspicious. Then I thought that I could take her phone, that maybe there was something useful in it to help prove what happened to Veronica. So I left with it. I had just walked out of the hotel when I realized that after they found her body, they might try to track her phone, so I swapped mine out and put hers in the Faraday bag that I use to hide my location from the Realm. But the joke was on me."

"Why do you say that?" Jessie asked.

"Because I couldn't open her phone. Without the facial recognition, it required the password. I didn't know it and I didn't want to risk guessing and having everything erased if I got it wrong too many times. So I was stuck."

"And then what did you do?" Karen pushed.

"I came back here," he said simply. "I haven't left since it happened. To be honest, I was surprised when you hauled in Bauer and Shepherd, that it took this long to find me. I figured I'd be spotted on some hotel camera and wake up this morning to a SWAT team outside the house."

Jessie and Karen exchanged looks, though neither explained the reason for the delay.

"Is there anything more you want to tell us, Ricardo?" Jessie asked.

183

"No. I think that's everything. I just wish what I've done won't been in vain."

Jessie motioned for Karen to stop recording the conversation. Then she leaned in close to Reyes and spoke softly.

"You murdered someone, Mr. Reyes. You'll have to pay for that. But I give you my word—when this is all said and done, you won't be the only one to pay."

He looked like he was about to respond when they all heard a loud crunching sound behind the house. The man's eyes went wide. Jessie immediately knew something was wrong.

"What is it?" she asked.

"I set out dried leaves around the house every night to warn me in case those DRA thugs come after me," he whispered. "Please tell me that's just your officers out back securing the place."

"We told our people to stay back unless we said otherwise," Karen said, unholstering her gun.

There were several more loud crunches now, moving faster and coming closer.

"Then I think we have a problem," Reyes hissed.

"Quick, lie down on the ground," Jessie ordered.

Before she could say anything else, the lights cut out. A second later, a loud blast came from behind the house. In the moonlight, Jessie saw Reyes try to get out of the easy chair, but with the handcuffs on, he couldn't generate enough momentum.

Jessie yanked him by the arm, pulling him forward just as a shot was fired where he had been a second earlier. Feathers exploded everywhere, creating a white cloud that filled the living room.

Jessie shoved him to ground and pulled out her own gun. As she did, she heard something metal rolling down the short hallway from the back door. Within seconds, the room filled up with smoke. Between that and the feathers everywhere she couldn't see much of anything. She had no idea where Karen was.

"Stay down," she whispered to Reyes, before crawling behind the loveseat she'd been sitting on moments ago.

She heard a male voice near the back door yell "get ready!" and recognized it immediately. It was the big guy with the beard from Miranda Dessler's apartment, the same one she'd seen at Sterling Shepherd's Dolby Theater event. That meant the smaller guy was likely here too.

She tried to focus. She'd seen the little guy favoring his left leg at the theater, which meant he probably still wasn't at full strength. That made him vulnerable. But the big guy was another story. How was she supposed bring him down if she couldn't see where he was?

And then it occurred to her. She might not have to. The cops outside would have heard the explosion and gunshot. They had to be close now. All she had to do was throw the big guy off a little. And she thought she knew how to do it.

"Are you coming in or what, big fella?" she yelled brazenly in the direction of the back door, where the gunshot and the smoke canister had come from. "Or are you worried you'll get your ass kicked by a girl again?"

It only took a second to get her answer.

"Assault!" the big guy yelled, and she heard his heavy footsteps move in her direction. Then, as she had hoped, she heard a bumping sound, followed by a much louder thud, suggesting someone had fallen. If she was right, the man had run into the moving boxes that Ricardo Reyes had left in the hallway and tripped to the floor. She poked her head out from behind the loveseat to make sure but still couldn't see a thing. She'd have to chance it.

"Don't move a muscle," she shouted, going into full-on bluff mode. "I've got my weapon trained on you, big fella. If you so much as twitch, I will blow a hole straight through you. You got it?"

"Uh-huh," she heard him grunt from the floor.

"Good," she said forcefully, hoping her voice didn't betray that fact that she was lying through her teeth. "Now slide that gun toward the easy chair you just shot. And while you're at it, let's have your little limping buddy drop his gun and get down on his stomach. Otherwise, my partner over there might have to give him a few more reasons to limp, isn't that right Detective Bray?"

"That's correct," Karen shouted back from somewhere closer to the hallway. "Locked and loaded here."

Jessie had no idea if that was true but was happy that her partner was going with it. She was about to respond when a booming voice outside the front door interrupted them.

"This is Officer Littleton," he barked. "Detective Bray, are you and Ms. Hunt okay? Should we breach?"

"Hold, officer!" Karen shouted, before speaking loudly to the men inside the house. "Big fella, little limping buddy—there are four law enforcement officers outside this structure. Two are making their way to your position by the back door. Two more will be entering forcefully from the front. If you keep your hands visible and stay still, there's a chance you could survive the evening. If you don't comply, they are authorized to employ the deadly force that we've refrained from using so far. Do you understand?"

There was silence from the men.

"I need verbal confirmation," she instructed.

"I understand," the big fella said quickly.

"I understand," the little limping buddy repeated.

Officer Littleton smashed in the front door. A few seconds later, Jessie heard the sounds of the officers entering from the back and the reassuring words "suspects in custody."

She sighed and lowered her gun. She still couldn't see either of them, but through the haze, she could see Ricardo Reyes, still lying on his stomach on the floor. She moved over to him and helped roll him over onto his side.

"Are you okay?" she asked.

He looked at her with sad eyes.

"I'm not injured," he told her. "But am I okay? I'll never see my daughter again, Ms. Hunt, so the answer to that is 'no.'"

Jessie sat beside him as the last lingering feathers drifted down to the floor. She didn't try to offer him false comfort. She knew better than anyone that nothing she could say would ease his pain right now. His daughter was gone. He was going to prison. And there was the distinct possibility that Sterling Shepherd would walk free.

She couldn't do anything about the first two. But she was determined to stop that last one from happening.

CHAPTER THIRTY SIX

Hannah stared at the "send" button on her phone, as if it could make the decision for her.

She'd been sitting in the same chair at Tommy's Coffee for hours. And for the last fifteen minutes, she'd been debating whether to make the FaceTime call.

Finally, sick of the internal back and forth, she closed her eyes, adjusted her ear buds, and pushed the button. It rang twice before she heard it connect. She opened her eyes to see Dr. Janice Lemmon staring back at her. The woman was sitting on a couch, sipping tea. She didn't seem at all shocked by Hannah's late night call.

"Hello Hannah, how are you?" she asked, a question that could be innocuous or probing, depending on how it was interpreted.

"Not great," she admitted.

"What's wrong?" Lemmon asked, taking another causal sip from her mug, which read: *I charge by the lie.*

"I'm sorry to bother you so late—," Jessie began before Lemmon cut her off.

"Let's dispense with that, shall we?" Lemmon told her. "You reached out for a reason. I'm glad you did. Let's just cut to the chase, shall we?"

"Okay," Hannah said. The music in the coffeehouse was loud and she had her earbuds in, but she still spoke quietly. "Every time I think I've made progress in our sessions, I backslide. I worry that I'm getting worse. I worry that I'll never be able to feel emotions like other people, that I'll always need some sort of intense artificial stimulation to feel anything."

"What happened?" Lemmon asked.

Hannah looked around to make sure no one else in the coffeehouse was paying attention to her. Though there was no logical reason to, she leaned in closer to the screen on her phone and whispered.

"I was at a convenience store and saw a kid my age bullying a younger one, threatening to beat him up if he didn't steal some beer for him. I told him to leave the kid alone. Instead, he threatened me. I started screaming that he was assaulting me and the store clerk chased him out. But here's the thing: before I did that, I had visions of smashing a wine bottle and jamming the jagged end in his throat. I could picture every detail. It was only at the last second that I went with the assault thing."

After she was done, to her surprise, Dr. Lemmon smiled. And when she replied, it was in a gentle tone.

"While the most responsible response would probably have been to alert the store clerk to what was happening, and while lying about an assault isn't ideal, I consider your reaction preferable to the alternative option you were considering."

"But I still used the moment for an adrenaline high," Hannah insisted. "The little kid getting away was secondary to me. And I still felt no remorse about what I did. I wouldn't have cared if the clerk beat that guy up with his baseball bat."

"Acknowledging that is an important step," Dr. Lemmon said. "Listen, Hannah, for a long time I've known you've had sociopathic tendencies. And it's pretty clear that you knew that too. But until you admitted it out loud to another human being, instead of just to yourself, there wasn't much more progress we could make."

"What do you mean?"

"I'm saying that now that this is out in the open and you're willing to discuss the real reasons that you've been making these dangerous, self-destructive choices, we can finally start to do the hard work of finding techniques to help you navigate the treacherous minefields your mind sets up for you."

Hannah sat for a moment, pondering the doctor's words. And in that moment, she understood that she was still holding back. Unless she told Lemmon the whole truth, including what really happened when she shot the Night Hunter—that it wasn't self-defense, how thrilling it felt to take his life, and how she longed to recapture that feeling—then she would never really be able to get control of the monster inside her, clawing to get out.

As scary as it was to be completely honest, it was the only path to having the life she wanted, one with family, with friends, and with the person she had to look at in the mirror.

She glanced around the coffeehouse again. It was mostly empty. There was a couple at a faraway table and a guy playing a videogame on his laptop in the corner. Behind the counter, a barista was texting disinterestedly on her phone.

Still, Hannah wondered if she ought to go elsewhere for this— somewhere outside, somewhere private. She wondered if she should ask to call back in ten minutes. She wondered if there was still time to back out entirely or at least delay. Maybe this wasn't the right time.

"Dr. Lemmon," she said, feeling suddenly as if she was in a plane that had just dropped a thousand feet in a second. "There's something else I have to tell you."

CHAPTER THIRTY SEVEN

Jessie was amazed that they'd managed to keep it quiet.

None of the officers who'd accompanied them to Reyes's house knew exactly what he was being arrested for, or even that it involved the Rutherford case, which was by design.

So when they arrived back at the station that night just after 11 p.m., it was without fanfare. A small cohort of devoted Adherents was still out in front of the main entrance, but the media was gone. Before they put Reyes in a private cell, Jessie gave him an explicit warning.

"Don't tell anyone, including other cops, who you are or why you're here," she instructed. "You'll get your lawyer soon enough. But as soon as anyone outside our little circle knows why you're here, it will leak and Sterling Shepherd's attorneys will be clamoring for his release. Once he's gone, we may never get him back. So if you want justice for Veronica, you need to keep your mouth shut. Got it?"

He nodded without saying a word. It felt odd to be colluding with a confessed murderer but if the alternative was letting Shepherd leave before they had to, Jessie was more than willing. They walked into Research, where Jamil was still typing away like a machine. He glanced back briefly and spoke with just a bit of fatigue in his voice.

"I've been able to confirm most of Reyes' story," he said. "The reading at the bookstore, him on the street corner when Addison Rutherford's car is at the intersection, hotel footage from the afternoon showing him there, the receipts at the bars and movie theater he said he went to—it's all coming back legit."

"That's great," Jessie said, placing Addison's phone on the desk next to him. "I was hoping you could prioritize this now."

"Is that her phone?" he asked.

"Yes. I need you to crack her password so we can find out if there's anything useful on it."

"You just want me to break the code like I'm the NSA or something?" he replied, giving in to a rare moment of sarcasm.

"You're better than the NSA, Jamil," she told him, hoping to boost his confidence with her own. "Come on, you've got her entire life history: birth date, old addresses, the works. I bet you could uncover her old pets' names if you tried. Plus there's the whole 'twil' tattoo thing. According to Reyes, those were also her last words—'the way is love.' I wouldn't be surprised if that fits in somehow."

Jamil sighed heavily.

"How long do I have?" he asked.

"Technically, until Monday morning," Karen said. "But realistically, we're not going to be able to keep a lid on why Reyes is here much longer. Once word gets out that he's the real killer, Shepherd's release will be imminent. And if he leaves this building, it may not matter if we nail him for something. He's got the human and financial resources to relocate someplace where we can't touch him. He'll just move his entire operation abroad and do his damage from a country without an extradition treaty."

"So, until the morning, then?" Jamil pressed, hoping for something more clear-cut.

"If we're lucky," Karen told him.

Jessie was about to give him a few more specifics that they'd learned from Miranda/Skyler when a familiar face poked his head into the room.

"How's it going?" Ryan asked.

Jessie turned to Karen.

"Can you share all our notes from the loft interview with Jamil?" she requested. "Maybe something in there will help him. I've got to deal with this guy."

"Not a problem," Karen said, settling into the chair next to Jamil.

Jessie took Ryan's hand and they walked to the empty break room, where she got a granola bar. It occurred to her that she hadn't eaten lunch or dinner today.

"Congratulations," Ryan said. "Decker gave me the short version."

"Thanks," Jessie said. "Don't go spreading it around though. We're still trying to nail another bad guy and we need to keep him here to do it. How are you doing?"

"Okay," he said, though he didn't look it. "Forensics confirmed that the machete blade matches the injuries to Kaylee McNulty, so even without Livia Bucco, we can close the case."

"That's great," Jessie said. "So why do you look so down?"

"I just feel like I should have been able to talk her off that ledge," Ryan said. "What she did was brutal, but I got the sense that she wasn't in control of her choices. There was so much pain and confusion in her eyes before she killed herself. I would never say this to anyone but you, but in some ways, she was as much a victim of her mental illness as Kaylee."

"I get that," Jessie told him, squeezing his hand. "But remember, none of this is on you. You tried your best. Obviously she wasn't stable enough to leave the hospital. Someone really screwed up there."

"But that's the thing," Ryan said. "I reviewed her file. It appeared like she had made real progress. Looking at the notes of her therapy sessions, I might have released her too. It was like a switch was flicked inside her and she just had to do this thing that even she couldn't explain. I don't get it."

"Please don't beat yourself up, Ryan," she pleaded. "You've done enough of that lately."

"I know," he conceded, "but I also feel bad for involving you. I hate that you had to make that deal with Andrea Robinson."

"That's not on you," she reminded him. "You were just the messenger. It was going to come to a head at some point. It just happened to be today. Besides, if talking to Andy Robinson saved even one other person from Kaylee's McNulty's fate, then it was worth it."

Ryan seemed to accept that, but then thought of something else.

"And you're really going to write a letter with a full-throated endorsement for her transfer?"

"Maybe not full-throated," Jessie allowed, "but I made a commitment and I intend to honor it. Besides, if I want her to keep helping, she needs to believe I made a good faith effort to get her moved. And I think that she may actually be able to help us. She has access to so many unbalanced criminals in these prison hospitals and she has a way of making them feel comfortable enough to share things that could prove invaluable to us. It's like having an agent on the inside."

"But how do you know she's not a double agent?" Ryan asked.

"I don't," Jessie admitted. "That's why I won't be accepting any more mojitos from her."

They both laughed despite the darkness of the joke.

"So you're not coming home yet?" he asked as they exited the break room into the hallway.

"Soon, I hope," Jessie said. "I want one more crack at Shepherd. Will you text me when you get there and tell Hannah goodnight from me?"

"Of course," he said.

Jessie smiled and gave him a long kiss. He returned it enthusiastically before walking slowly down the hall. As he did, and for reasons she couldn't explain, Andy Robinson's words about Ryan being taken with Susannah Valentine popped into her head.

She knew it was a cheap dig by a manipulative killer intended to unsettle her, and yet, she still wanted to ask him how Valentine had been as a partner that day. She bit her tongue, deciding that would play into Andy's hands. Even if she didn't trust Valentine, she loved and trusted her fiancé and refused to let herself be played.

Luckily, her thoughts were interrupted by Karen, who shot into the hall. Her face was flushed and she was breathing heavily. It was clear that she'd been running.

"What is it?" Jessie asked.

"It's Jamil. He found something. Actually, he found everything."

*

Karen wasn't kidding.

As Jessie sat in the research office, looking at the data on the screen, her jaw dropped open.

"We gave you until morning and you cracked her password in minutes?" she said in disbelief. "How did you do it?"

"It was shockingly easy," Jamil said. "I started thinking about what you told me about the tattoo and her last words and what was important to her and it came to me. I got it on the fourth try: LITWTWIL11. Love is the way. The way is love, 11, as in the Eleventh Realm."

"She really did have a one track mind, huh?" Karen marveled.

"I suppose," Jamil said, pulling up a new screen with an Excel document, "but she managed to make time for this too."

"What is that?" Jessie asked.

But even before he answered, she understood. As he scrolled from screen to screen, her eyes kept getting wider.

"Let's get Shepherd into an interrogation room ASAP," she said suddenly. "And we should call his lawyers too. I want to do this by the book."

"Why?" Karen asked, surprised. "It's almost 11:30. And you know there's no way he's going to talk to us. Hell, his lawyers will probably put duct tape over his mouth."

"Let's just make it happen," Jessie replied. "We can worry about that once they're in the room."

Both Karen and Jamil looked at her skeptically.

"Trust me," she said.

CHAPTER THIRTY EIGHT

Considering the hour and where he'd spent the last several, Jessie thought that Sterling Shepherd looked unexpectedly alert.

Nor did he seem especially troubled as he sat in the interrogation room with his attorney, Walter Serra, who was whispering in his ear. The handcuffs had been removed and he was gingerly rubbing his wrists. Serra didn't seem all that concerned either. In the adjoining observation room, Jessie and Karen watched him.

"You ready?" Jessie asked.

"I'm not entirely sure what you're planning," Karen said, "So no. But I have to admit I'm curious. So I guess we should get started."

They left the observation room and stepped into the hall, where the other two lawyers from earlier today were standing with a man that Jessie didn't recognize. But Karen, who obviously did, stopped in her tracks. For a second Jessie thought she was going to faint, but as quickly as she'd lost control, she regained it.

"Hi Karen," said the unfamiliar man, who was good-looking in a washed-out, tired-eyed sort of way. He was wearing dress clothes but his blond hair was longish and unkempt and he wore loafers without socks.

"Hi," she replied before turning to Jessie, "Jessie Hunt, this is Derek Burke. You may recall that I mentioned him. He's the guy who runs Detoxibrate, the bogus rehab program the Realm operates."

Burke smiled.

"Is that the only way that you described me?" he asked playfully. "No other part I played in your past?"

Karen looked ready to deck him, but before she responded, Jessie leaned in close to Burke.

"You didn't play anywhere near the part in her past that she's going to play in your future," she muttered quietly so that only he and Karen could hear her.

The smile faded from his face as the look on Karen's brightened. The two women left him in the hall as they entered the interrogation room. They hadn't even spoken before Walter Serra stood up.

"Unless you're here to release my client, this is a waste of time," he announced. "He's not going to answer any of your questions."

194

"That's okay," Jessie said sunnily, taking a seat opposite them. Karen joined her. "We can do all the talking."

Serra sat back down, unsure what to make of the comment.

"Jamil, go ahead," she said, knowing the researcher could hear her through the room's audio system.

The lights dimmed slightly and an image appeared on the wall. Shepherd squinted slightly.

"You can put on your glasses, Mr. Shepherd," Jessie said. "No one here is going to blab about your declining vision."

Serra handed him a pair and he put them on. Now able to see the screen clearly, his relaxed demeanor stiffened noticeably.

"As you can see," Jessie said casually, "what appears before you is a comprehensive list of every girl who has sexually serviced Mr. Shepherd over the last four years, collected efficiently in an Excel spreadsheet. Next screen please, Jamil."

Before anyone could say a word, a new data set appeared on the wall.

"This page includes the names of other high-profile Adherents these women were with, including dates and times."

Even in the darkened room, Jessie could see that Sterling Shepherd had turned pale.

"This is outrageous," Serra bellowed.

"I agree," Jessie said, "and we're not even to the best part. Next screen please, Jamil."

A new image appeared. It was more involved than the first two.

"In case there's any confusion, this is a separate document that lists other men who aren't Eleventh Realm Adherents, many with names you'll recognize, next to girls' names, along with dollar amounts, dates, and locations. Next screen please, Jamil."

A screen showing what appeared to be an online bank ledger flashed in front of them. Shepherd looked like he wanted to speak but Jessie beat him to the punch.

"These are records from several bank accounts, with deposit totals and dates that conveniently enough, correspond exactly to the amounts on the preceding Excel sheet."

"What is all this?" Serra shouted. "Is the LAPD in the business of forging documents now?"

"No sir," Jessie said pleasantly. "All this information came from the cell phone of Addison Rutherford, who kept a comprehensive record of the Realm's sexual trafficking scheme on it."

"You expect us to take this seriously?" Serra demanded, making up for his client's silence with impressive bloviating.

"I know," Jessie agreed. "It's hard to believe that she would keep such sensitive, potentially cult-destroying information on her personal phone. But I guess when you've elevated so high in the organization, your head starts to get a little fuzzy."

"Ms. Hunt," Shepherd said, trying and failing to infuse his pinched voice with its typical honeyed warmth, "I think there's been some kind of misunderstanding here, just like the misunderstanding about Ms. Rutherford's death, which I had no part in. You see, Sonny had a long history of mental illness. We were actually trying to help her with that. She led a fantasy life, where she imagined that—."

"Stop, Sterling," Serra said under his breath. "It's better if you don't say anything."

"Walter," Shepherd insisted. "I'm confident that we can clear this up if—."

"You should listen to your lawyer, Shep," Jessie said standing up. "We don't actually need to hear from you. In fact, we don't have any questions. We just wanted to let you know that it's all over in person, right Detective Bray?"

"Right," Karen said, doing a decent job of hiding the fact that until two minutes ago, she had no idea what was planned. Normally Jessie wouldn't leave her partner blind like that, but in this case, she considered it a special gift for someone who'd suffered long enough.

Shepherd peered more closely at Karen. Jessie saw him trying to make the mental connection that her partner had feared he would just a few hours ago. And then, in an instant, he did.

"I know you," he said excitedly, a big grin on his face. "You're Karen Bartlet, that Disavowed girl from Occidental College. I figured that you eventually went back to Toledo to lick your wounds."

"Nope," Karen said, without any of the apprehension that had dogged her most of the day, "still here. Any the name's Bray now, as in Detective Karen Bray, as in the cop who will be escorting you back to your metal cot in a minute."

Shepherd's grin faded away.

"I'll be going now, Shep" Jessie said pointedly. "I guess you didn't really need to be here for this. I just wanted to see the look in your eyes when you realized that your whole corrupt scheme is about to fall apart, that everyone will know what you really are. The alphabet soup of acronyms that you use to hide your illegal acts— TEROTH, DRA, M&Ms, COHP, TS and TC, FIC—it won't protect you now. Thank

God, because I can't keep track of all of them. Now I won't have to. Get ready for a lot of prison time, Shep, along with a lot of lawsuits, and hearing the names of lots of your victims too, names like Veronica Reyes."

She started for the door, but then turned back.

"Oh that reminds me—speaking of the Reyes family, I suppose you should know that you're no longer being held for the murder of Addison Rutherford. We found the real killer and he's in custody right now. His name is Ricardo Reyes, Veronica's father. But I have a feeling you already knew that, considering that you sent your goons to follow us and take him out earlier tonight. It didn't work, by the way. Maybe you can learn the details when you're sharing a cell with them. Speaking of that, I think Detective Bray has a few new charges to levy against you."

She winked at Karen, who had a smile so big, it looked like it might hurt.

"Please stand up, Mr. Shepherd," she said, pulling out her cuffs. "You are under arrest for violating California Penal Code 236.1, banning human trafficking. That charge should suffice for now until we can come up with a more comprehensive list."

He did as he was told, slowly getting to his feet. For the first time since Jessie had seen him, he didn't have that self-satisfied smile plastered across his face. Instead, his expression was one of desperation. Beside him, his lawyer looked positively forlorn.

Karen snapped the cuffs on him and looked over at Jessie, who was about to leave.

"Hey, Ms. Hunt," she called out from across the room, "love is the way."

Without a moment's hesitation, Jessie replied enthusiastically.

"The way is love."

*

"I'm tired, Captain," Jessie pleaded. "It's almost midnight. Can't we talk about it tomorrow?"

She'd just finished her paperwork and was getting ready to leave for the night when Decker called her into his office. He closed the door. Instead of sitting at his desk, he leaned against the front of it, in what she suspected was a clumsy attempt to appear casual.

197

"It can't wait," he said. "I know that if we don't lock this down now, it might be weeks before I can corral you again. I need a decision."

Jessie shook her head with a mix of frustration and exhaustion.

"We just closed a murder case and arrested a cult leader for sex trafficking. Don't I get a little break?"

"That's why I want you to come on permanently, Hunt. You did an amazing job. I have to admit that when you were pulling in movie stars and it looked like a litigious, multi-million dollar organization—."

"You can safely call it a cult now, Captain," Jessie reminded him.

"In any case," he said, refusing to be baited, "I was concerned how this might all play out for a while there. But as usual, you came through. That's why we need you. And it's why I'm willing to add 25% to your already exorbitant rate as part of your annual salary. You have to admit, that's pretty good for a city employee."

"Captain, that is very generous, but as I told you before, I went into teaching because this job was so emotionally taxing on me, not to mention the fact that I'm my sister's guardian and she doesn't need to deal with another dead relative. And I really meant what I said this morning: once I started the seminars, it turned out that I actually love working with those students, helping them hone their skills so that maybe one of them can be the next Garland Moses."

"There was only one Garland Moses," Decker said, "and the closest thing to him is in this room right now."

"Thanks, Captain," Jessie said standing up. "That means a lot to me, but—."

"I'll remove the prohibition on you partnering with Detective Hernandez," he interrupted.

"I thought that had to go some human resources review board," she said.

"I have sway," he replied.

"What about public perception and the jealous people looking for HSS to fail?" she said, reminding him of his objections from this morning.

"That should tell you how much I want you back," he said. "The fact that I'm willing to take that crap means I'm serious about this."

Jessie could feel her resolve wavering. It was a good offer, probably the best she'd ever get. She looked at Roy Decker, who was doing his best to hide the desperation he obviously felt.

His expression reminded her slightly of Shepherd's when he knew he was beaten. The memory was sweet. Even more satisfying than his defeat that was the realization of just how many lives she'd changed today, almost all for the better. Maybe the high of the moment was affecting her judgment, but part of her wondered if the classroom wasn't necessarily the best place for her to make a difference after all.

She sighed.

"I can't make this decision without talking to Ryan and Hannah," she said. "But I promise, I'll have an answer for you by next week."

He stood up and walked over to the office door, which he held open for her.

"I'm holding you to that," he said.

"When have I ever not followed through on a commitment?" she asked.

He allowed himself a slight smile before answering.

"That's what I'm counting on."

EPILOGUE

It was well past lights out, but Andy couldn't fall asleep.

She lay awake in her cell, on her metal-framed bed with its thin mattress, looking up at the ceiling. Her mind was racing with thoughts, so many that it was hard not to speak them aloud. But she knew how that would be received in a place like this, so she kept quiet.

Of course if all went well, her time in the Female Forensic In-Patient Psychiatric Unit of the Twin Towers Correctional Facility wouldn't last much longer. If she knew Jessie Hunt—and she did—the profiler would have that letter to the CDHCS's Mental Health Services Division by Monday morning. The woman would consider it a moral imperative, despite her apprehensions about Andy's motives.

And while there would certainly be delays, once that letter was delivered, the outcome was inevitable. If the brilliant, illustrious Jessie Hunt, a near-victim of the inmate, was recommending a transfer, it would invariably happen. That meant Andy had to get to work.

She might only have a matter of weeks, maybe even days, to touch base with her disciples. She needed to remind them of the Principles, ensure their devotion, and work each of them up into a nice, bloodthirsty lather before their impending releases from the facility.

How was she supposed to help Jessie catch these people if she hadn't properly instructed them on the details and the appropriate order of the crimes they were to commit? She needed a steady stream of mayhem-makers to offer up to her once and future friend if she was going to earn back Jessie Hunt's trust.

And then there was the new facility, wherever that might be. She'd need to win over a whole new collection of pathetic psychos there. Even with the most weak-minded among them, it would take time to make them her bitches.

It was a lot of work but she was up to the task. Eventually her efforts to make amends, along with her seeming rehabilitation, would wear Jessie down, and she'd open the door to some kind of reconciliation.

And when she did, Andy would be ready to take her rightful place next to her dear friend, even if that meant pushing aside the usurpers who were currently there, even if it meant eliminating them.

THE PERFECT INDISCRETION
(A Jessie Hunt Psychological Suspense Thriller—Book Eighteen)

"A masterpiece of thriller and mystery. Blake Pierce did a magnificent job developing characters with a psychological side so well described that we feel inside their minds, follow their fears and cheer for their success. Full of twists, this book will keep you awake until the turn of the last page."
--Books and Movie Reviews, Roberto Mattos (re *Once Gone*)

THE PERFECT INDISCRETION is book #18 in a new psychological suspense series by bestselling author Blake Pierce, which begins with *The Perfect Wife*, a #1 bestseller (and free download) with over 5,000 five-star ratings and 900 five-star reviews.

A wealthy husband is found murdered in the wake of his 50th birthday bash, a lavish affair that included a dozen couples, a private jet and a debaucherous night. Jessie is in over her head as she enters the world of ultra-wealth and peels back the sordid relationships between couples and friends. So many people, it seemed, wanted their host dead.

But the truth, Jessie finds, is far more complex—and far more sinister.

A fast-paced psychological suspense thriller with unforgettable characters and heart-pounding suspense, THE JESSIE HUNT series is a riveting new series that will leave you turning pages late into the night.

Books #19-#21 are also available!

Blake Pierce

Blake Pierce is the USA Today bestselling author of the RILEY PAGE mystery series, which includes seventeen books. Blake Pierce is also the author of the MACKENZIE WHITE mystery series, comprising fourteen books; of the AVERY BLACK mystery series, comprising six books; of the KERI LOCKE mystery series, comprising five books; of the MAKING OF RILEY PAIGE mystery series, comprising six books; of the KATE WISE mystery series, comprising seven books; of the CHLOE FINE psychological suspense mystery, comprising six books; of the JESSE HUNT psychological suspense thriller series, comprising nineteen books; of the AU PAIR psychological suspense thriller series, comprising three books; of the ZOE PRIME mystery series, comprising six books; of the ADELE SHARP mystery series, comprising thirteen books, of the EUROPEAN VOYAGE cozy mystery series, comprising four books; of the new LAURA FROST FBI suspense thriller, comprising six books (and counting); of the new ELLA DARK FBI suspense thriller, comprising nine books (and counting); of the A YEAR IN EUROPE cozy mystery series, comprising nine books, of the AVA GOLD mystery series, comprising six books (and counting); and of the RACHEL GIFT mystery series, comprising six books (and counting).

An avid reader and lifelong fan of the mystery and thriller genres, Blake loves to hear from you, so please feel free to visit www.blakepierceauthor.com to learn more and stay in touch.

.

BOOKS BY BLAKE PIERCE

RACHEL GIFT MYSTERY SERIES
HER LAST WISH (Book #1)
HER LAST CHANCE (Book #2)
HER LAST HOPE (Book #3)
HER LAST FEAR (Book #4)
HER LAST CHOICE (Book #5)
HER LAST BREATH (Book #6)

AVA GOLD MYSTERY SERIES
CITY OF PREY (Book #1)
CITY OF FEAR (Book #2)
CITY OF BONES (Book #3)
CITY OF GHOSTS (Book #4)
CITY OF DEATH (Book #5)
CITY OF VICE (Book #6)

A YEAR IN EUROPE
A MURDER IN PARIS (Book #1)
DEATH IN FLORENCE (Book #2)
VENGEANCE IN VIENNA (Book #3)
A FATALITY IN SPAIN (Book #4)

ELLA DARK FBI SUSPENSE THRILLER
GIRL, ALONE (Book #1)
GIRL, TAKEN (Book #2)
GIRL, HUNTED (Book #3)
GIRL, SILENCED (Book #4)
GIRL, VANISHED (Book 5)
GIRL ERASED (Book #6)
GIRL, FORSAKEN (Book #7)
GIRL, TRAPPED (Book #8)
GIRL, EXPENDABLE (Book #9)

LAURA FROST FBI SUSPENSE THRILLER
ALREADY GONE (Book #1)
ALREADY SEEN (Book #2)
ALREADY TRAPPED (Book #3)
ALREADY MISSING (Book #4)

ALREADY DEAD (Book #5)
ALREADY TAKEN (Book #6)

EUROPEAN VOYAGE COZY MYSTERY SERIES
MURDER (AND BAKLAVA) (Book #1)
DEATH (AND APPLE STRUDEL) (Book #2)
CRIME (AND LAGER) (Book #3)
MISFORTUNE (AND GOUDA) (Book #4)
CALAMITY (AND A DANISH) (Book #5)
MAYHEM (AND HERRING) (Book #6)

ADELE SHARP MYSTERY SERIES
LEFT TO DIE (Book #1)
LEFT TO RUN (Book #2)
LEFT TO HIDE (Book #3)
LEFT TO KILL (Book #4)
LEFT TO MURDER (Book #5)
LEFT TO ENVY (Book #6)
LEFT TO LAPSE (Book #7)
LEFT TO VANISH (Book #8)
LEFT TO HUNT (Book #9)
LEFT TO FEAR (Book #10)
LEFT TO PREY (Book #11)
LEFT TO LURE (Book #12)
LEFT TO CRAVE (Book #13)

THE AU PAIR SERIES
ALMOST GONE (Book#1)
ALMOST LOST (Book #2)
ALMOST DEAD (Book #3)

ZOE PRIME MYSTERY SERIES
FACE OF DEATH (Book#1)
FACE OF MURDER (Book #2)
FACE OF FEAR (Book #3)
FACE OF MADNESS (Book #4)
FACE OF FURY (Book #5)
FACE OF DARKNESS (Book #6)

A JESSIE HUNT PSYCHOLOGICAL SUSPENSE SERIES

THE PERFECT WIFE (Book #1)
THE PERFECT BLOCK (Book #2)
THE PERFECT HOUSE (Book #3)
THE PERFECT SMILE (Book #4)
THE PERFECT LIE (Book #5)
THE PERFECT LOOK (Book #6)
THE PERFECT AFFAIR (Book #7)
THE PERFECT ALIBI (Book #8)
THE PERFECT NEIGHBOR (Book #9)
THE PERFECT DISGUISE (Book #10)
THE PERFECT SECRET (Book #11)
THE PERFECT FAÇADE (Book #12)
THE PERFECT IMPRESSION (Book #13)
THE PERFECT DECEIT (Book #14)
THE PERFECT MISTRESS (Book #15)
THE PERFECT IMAGE (Book #16)
THE PERFECT VEIL (Book #17)
THE PERFECT INDISCRETION (Book #18)
THE PERFECT RUMOR (Book #19)

CHLOE FINE PSYCHOLOGICAL SUSPENSE SERIES
NEXT DOOR (Book #1)
A NEIGHBOR'S LIE (Book #2)
CUL DE SAC (Book #3)
SILENT NEIGHBOR (Book #4)
HOMECOMING (Book #5)
TINTED WINDOWS (Book #6)

KATE WISE MYSTERY SERIES
IF SHE KNEW (Book #1)
IF SHE SAW (Book #2)
IF SHE RAN (Book #3)
IF SHE HID (Book #4)
IF SHE FLED (Book #5)
IF SHE FEARED (Book #6)
IF SHE HEARD (Book #7)

THE MAKING OF RILEY PAIGE SERIES
WATCHING (Book #1)
WAITING (Book #2)

LURING (Book #3)
TAKING (Book #4)
STALKING (Book #5)
KILLING (Book #6)

RILEY PAIGE MYSTERY SERIES
ONCE GONE (Book #1)
ONCE TAKEN (Book #2)
ONCE CRAVED (Book #3)
ONCE LURED (Book #4)
ONCE HUNTED (Book #5)
ONCE PINED (Book #6)
ONCE FORSAKEN (Book #7)
ONCE COLD (Book #8)
ONCE STALKED (Book #9)
ONCE LOST (Book #10)
ONCE BURIED (Book #11)
ONCE BOUND (Book #12)
ONCE TRAPPED (Book #13)
ONCE DORMANT (Book #14)
ONCE SHUNNED (Book #15)
ONCE MISSED (Book #16)
ONCE CHOSEN (Book #17)

MACKENZIE WHITE MYSTERY SERIES
BEFORE HE KILLS (Book #1)
BEFORE HE SEES (Book #2)
BEFORE HE COVETS (Book #3)
BEFORE HE TAKES (Book #4)
BEFORE HE NEEDS (Book #5)
BEFORE HE FEELS (Book #6)
BEFORE HE SINS (Book #7)
BEFORE HE HUNTS (Book #8)
BEFORE HE PREYS (Book #9)
BEFORE HE LONGS (Book #10)
BEFORE HE LAPSES (Book #11)
BEFORE HE ENVIES (Book #12)
BEFORE HE STALKS (Book #13)
BEFORE HE HARMS (Book #14)

Made in the USA
Middletown, DE
20 December 2023

46614585R00119